A Curse on the Wind

by

Joni Sensel

A Curse on the Wind

Cover Art by *Jennifer Greeff*

The Wild Rose Press, Inc.
PO Box 708
Adams Basin, NY 14410-0708
Visit us at www.thewildrosepress.com

Publishing History
First Edition, 2022
Trade Paperback ISBN 978-1-5092-4282-5
Digital ISBN 978-1-5092-4283-2

Published in the United States of America

Some trick of the wind brought the fire's roar to her ears, a deep whoom she'd not heard before. She could only hope the smoke rose from smoldering bricks and not flames raging hopelessly out of control. The column of dark clouds towered above her.

Her breath caught—there it was. Her hunch had been right. The billows of smoke took a shape, a long forehead, hollowed eyes over high, angled cheekbones. The features shifted and blurred but never vanished for long. A strong nose peaked, subsided, and grew sharper again. A black jaw cracked open to reveal glimpses of fire—a grin from a demon in Hell.

No. Geth spun to leap the stairs two at a time. Smoke didn't form faces. Not real ones, at least. None with voices that called her by name. No monster leered at her back as she ran. The fire started by accident. Nothing more. Nothing caused by a ritual under a tree.

Still…if her performance could wield such power? Her gestures and voice, her emotions laid bare, with a roar from the world in response—the idea fluttered in her, exhilarating.

Dedication

For my own unexpected Ohio love

Author's Note:

This book draws on the history and features of Springfield, Ohio, where I lived for a spell and which inspired Geth's story. These include a company that patented a burglar-proof casket, early photoplay (movie) production, and notable stops on the Underground Railroad. I've taken liberties with neighborhoods for convenience, making Amity more compact than Springfield during its heydays in 1909 and swapping out its water tower with another in Ohio at the time. But I want to credit the town as my source because it and the Ferncliff Cemetery upon which Fernlawn is patterned hold a special place in my heart.

SOCIETY NOTICES for MARCH 4, 1909
Cogglesmith Nuptials

Mr. Bertram Jones, known to many as Amity's station master, announces the marriage of his only daughter, Gethsemane, to Mr. William Cogglesmith of this city at 4:00 p.m. two Mondays hence. The groom elect, an heir to the Champion Ironworks, is currently pursuing a career in patent law. Private vows will be taken at First Lutheran Church of Christ the Redeemer.

SOCIETY NOTICES for MARCH 12, 1909
Nuptials Cancelled

The wedding of Mr. William Cogglesmith and Miss Gethsemane Jones will not take place as previously announced in these pages. Both families request privacy, please.

Chapter One

The day Gethsemane Jones was supposed to be married, she rose before dawn to sneak out of the house. A cat yowled outside as she slipped off her nightcap.

Perfect. The opening lines of a play sprang to mind, one with witches and spirits and vengeance. "Thrice the brinded cat hath mewed," she recited in a whisper. "Well, once. That's enough mewing, thank you. Don't rouse anyone else."

She shoved off her quilts, careful not to dislodge the warming pan in her bed. The terrible din if it fell would put a quick end to her mischief. The wood floor was cold, so she pulled on thick stockings, but she didn't touch the dress that had once been her mother's. She also ignored her corset, simply pulling on the gray house dress her fingers recognized in the dark. Finally, Geth shoved her feet in her shoes, which she'd left halfway laced for such haste. Poppa's clock in the parlor tick-ticked in the hush. She placed her steps in its rhythm to hide any creak as she eased down the stairs from her attic bedchamber.

The muted pop of a coal greeted her in the kitchen. She passed the stove's warmth to go straight to the kitchen cabinet. Her fingertips slid across tins. Rounded, tall, square—that one, the salt box. She thrust her fingertips in. The salt crystals scratched at her skin.

It should've been rice in her grip today. She'd tied handfuls of it into lace for guests to throw over her head at the church doors to wish the new couple good luck. That rice had gone in the waste bin two days ago. Like the rosemary sprigs she'd dried for her bouquet. Like the money Poppa had paid for the matrimonial service at First Lutheran Church of Christ the Redeemer.

Maybe Christ would redeem her former fiancé, Will. God knew nothing else could.

"Gethsemane?" Her stepmother's voice made her jump. Geth hid the salt in her fist as Mamie's feet thumped in the hall. "Is that you?"

"No, it's not me, so it must be a thief." Geth's voice covered the clatter of the salt box's lid. "One who's…stirring the coals. This room's too cold for crime." She whirled and grabbed the poker so her lie might look true. She didn't have long before sunrise.

"Careful. Thieves get slop-buckets dumped on their heads." Mamie appeared with her chamber pot sloshing between her hands. "Your father's not up yet, but I'm glad you are. Pastor Duncan promised to be at church early for us. I know your heart's broken, but you've moped long enough, pet. Prayer will be the best way to get past this day."

Geth bent to awaken the banked coals in the stove. "For an evil stepmother, Mamie, you have a good soul."

But I don't, she thought. *So please hurry up.*

She had no intention of spending an hour on her knees. If prayer worked, the fever wouldn't have taken her mother. But even if prayer worked some of the time, Geth would not pray for Will. She wasn't turning a cheek for him, either. She had other plans for the morning.

"Good soul, my foot," Mamie replied. "It's entirely selfish. I'm sick of the scowl on your face."

Geth replaced the fire poker on its hook with a clank. "That's not a scowl. It's just not a coy smile. You're always warning me not to be vain."

"You've minded all at once, and too well. If I had your hair, I'd never hide it in plaits. A pompadour would show it off better." Mamie peered through the fire's shadows. "And you're not wearing that dress to church, are you?"

"I didn't expect you this early." Geth ground the salt tighter into her palm and summoned a smile. "While you're in the privy, I'll put something more suitable on." She opened the back door so the March cold coming in would keep her stepmother moving.

"Good girl." With an alarming tip of the chamber pot, Mamie nudged Geth's arm before passing outside. "Your doting poppa hasn't spoiled you yet."

Geth shut the door. Fourteen steps to the outhouse. She counted six to be sure Mamie was well on her way. After grabbing her coat from a peg, she ran through the parlor, unlatched the front door, and slipped out.

Chapter Two

The wind came to help Geth flap into her coat sleeves. Its icy blast hit the back of her throat. She turned away from it there on the porch, ducking her head while it flipped up her collar before swirling around and retreating. Downtown, the electric streetlights cast a yellow glow upward, turning the world into black silhouettes. In just a few years, Amity had grown from the kind of Ohio town where everyone knew everyone else—by reputation or relations, at least—to a small city with roaring factories, newcomers looking for work, and startling modern conveniences. Though Geth enjoyed the electric streetcar as much as anyone else, the unnatural glow of electric lights made the darkness around them more threatening. She looked away so her eyes wouldn't be dazzled. She had to make her way in the gloom.

After a moment of juggling the salt she carried—she should've knotted it into a napkin—she balanced it in a mound on the porch rail. Her hands freed, she fastened her coat and swept the salt back into one palm.

Shadows loomed from her things on the porch—the things Poppa had trussed in canvas for delivery to the rowhouse which Will had told them he'd rented. All of these things were meant to make her new home feel cozy from the first moment he carried her over the threshold. Except no hired wagon ever arrived.

That's how she first learned her wedding was off. Since then, these belongings had huddled here, waiting—jilted, like her. Her trunk, now a coffin for her gray wedding slippers. Linens embroidered with Will's name and hers. The knotty pine chest where she'd packed them, along with her keepsakes and hopes. The reed rocker, a gift from Mamie, where Geth might have someday nursed a child. The whole of her dowry sat there, abandoned. She wouldn't touch them again until she'd found some revenge. She'd promised herself. And Geth didn't make such vows lightly—unlike Will, who apparently didn't respect vows at all.

The wind nudged the rocker, making it nod in its canvas. Poppa had wheedled and tried to bring it inside, but Geth wouldn't have it. She'd put it back out. She wanted it seen, all that broken dowry, like a stage for a play about falsehood and shame. Geth refused to withdraw like Ophelia, drowning her pain and her life in a stream. Will's faithlessness shouldn't be so quickly forgotten.

Unfortunately, his departure had made him shame-proof. He'd abandoned his patent clerk's office, too, and left town in the night, leaving only a note. It implored his family not to fret about him while he sought new adventures. Not even a mention of her. The gossips decided he'd murdered someone, or caught a train east to see President Taft, or fled to a sweetheart in Cincinnati. Only the last rumor might've been true. Geth's broken engagement was already fading, replaced in the gossip by the latest invention, Champion Ironwork's new Burglar-Proof Casket.

The rocking chair nodded and creaked in the wind. Waiting for her—a seventeen-year-old spinster, an unruly wretch her own mother had struggled to love. The chair's runners rasped on the porch, muttering, "unworthy, unworthy." A voice inside Geth or deeper yet, in the earth, whispered about mistakes saved by hasty escapes.

Geth jumped off the porch like a ten-year-old boy. She would not be Will's cast-off. She'd become someone else, not unloved and helpless but powerful. Fierce. The star of her show, not a discarded prop. She had to start now, without further delay. Men would be rushing to fields and factories soon, and she wanted to reach the end of Plum Road unseen.

She scurried down the street past the streetcar platform to the scrolled iron gate of Fernlawn, the town's oldest cemetery. No fence circled the graveyard; the dark gate stood alone. But no one went around. They passed beneath its black arch. It formed a more subtle boundary between the world of machines and a world where other forces held weight.

Frozen leaves crackled as she crossed through on the path.

The wind tugged at her coat, murmuring, "*Shh.*"

It had comforted her here after Mother died, and though that had been nearly six years ago, it seemed to have kept up the habit. Geth yanked her coat tighter and moved on, past the newest graves and the tiny, heartbreaking ones in the Lamb's Garden. The pillars and columns of stone were taking on shape in the colorless dawn.

She didn't glance toward her mother's grave as she passed. "Don't look, Momma," she muttered. "I'm about to do something wicked." Not that Mother would have been too surprised.

"*Ahhh*," sighed the wind, which knew more than one secret.

She left the graveled path, skirted slabs in the grass, and headed beyond the rows left by the 1890 flu toward the oldest stones in the graveyard's rear corner. A gray fringe of trees hid the railway beyond. Engine steam billowed through their skeletal branches. Geth hurried faster. She couldn't be late. If that steam rose from the 6:28 Ohio Southern, the sun must be near the horizon.

Then, through the wisps, a man's shape emerged. Geth froze in the shadow of a tall marble plinth. Some worker cutting through on his way to Mill Road? He wore working clothes, dungarees and a sweater. But instead of a lunch pail he carried a rifle, a threatening line against the brightening East.

A tremor went through her. A rifle—for what?

He raised the gun. Pointed it at her, almost. His boots crunched on gravel as he crossed a path toward her. Now she could see he also held a large sack.

Grave robbers. It had happened last week, as soon as the frozen earth started to thaw. Somebody awful had desecrated the dead. Jewelry, watches, gold teeth, a whole rash of dark thefts that put her in fear of Mother's safe rest. Was the thief here again? Had she interrupted his work?

Too aware of the thin fabric covering her ribs, with not even her corset stays to protect her, Geth whirled to face the trees and beyond them, the trains—platforms, electric lights, friendly conductors. Could she run?

No. Too far. She clasped her salt with both hands to keep from hugging herself. She hadn't even pulled on a thick petticoat. There weren't enough layers between her and him, and the breeze flapped and worried what armor she had.

She'd fling salt in his eyes. Or a broken headstone. She scanned for a chunk she could lift.

He called out. The wind stole his words until her ears caught a question. "...here all alone?"

"*Ohh*," moaned the wind. "*Ohhh*."

The gun's muzzle dropped. "Geth? I mean, Miss Jones, is that you?"

That rough voice—someone she knew? He still had that gun and his strides lengthened, but his posture didn't look furtive.

"Yes," Geth managed, breathless. She stayed ready to scream.

He drew closer, revealing corn-tassel hair and square cheeks. Oh—Aaron Holmes, the gravedigger's son. They'd shot marbles and worked figures in school together, until he'd stopped coming a few years ago. He'd finally grown into his nose.

Her spark of panic now seemed foolish. The wind spoke for her. "*Whewww*."

Sturdy again, she stepped up to meet him. Aaron peered into the shadows behind her. "Your pa isn't with you this morning?"

Feeling guilty, she bristled. Young ladies ought not to wander alone, and nobody proper would go half-dressed and without a hat. Still, did she need a keeper? "Is yours?"

He grinned. "No. I've been hunting." He juggled his sack whose dark stains matched the sharp scent of blood. "Boneyard rabbits have the luckiest feet."

Geth averted her eyes. "Not for the rabbit. But don't let me interrupt. I'll try not to look like a hare."

The sky had paled enough to show the gap in his teeth. She would soon miss the dawn. She sidled around him.

He turned to keep pace. "I heard about…well. The engagement. I'm sorry."

Her jaw clenched. The pity. That was the worst. Will's betrayal would sting her again and again until she reclaimed some strength. And maybe some justice. If Aaron would leave her so she could get to it.

He drew a white rabbit's paw from his pocket, a crown of ribbon knotted over the bone. "Can I give you a token for better luck next time?"

"There won't be a next time."

"Aw, surely there will."

No. Will had come to his senses, and nobody else would make his error again. Nor would she risk a repeat disappointment. When she didn't take the charm, he put it back in his pocket.

"But thank you," she said. "It was nice to see you again." Aaron did not take the hint. When she sped up, he remained alongside her.

Geth stopped at Old Freedom, the town's controversial oak. The tree, a hundred years older than Amity itself, bore an X-shaped scar in its bark marking it as a way station of the Amity U.G.R.R—the underground railroad. Not so long ago, conductors met "passengers" here in the night to hide them in a boxcar until a wagon arrived to carry them north to Troy or Urbana. U.S. Marshals once tried to burn the tree down, more in frustration than to any effect, since it wasn't the only secret station in town.

The tree, although blackened, had refused to burn. Its base had been bitten by the teeth of saws, too, as plenty in town resented its name and would just as soon return certain people to bondage.

But Poppa and Mamie and Geth weren't among them, and the tree resisted all efforts to harm it. The lumpy roots at its base, grown over with weeds, stood for the graves of old lives that gave birth to free ones. Geth's troubles couldn't touch the sorrows of slavery, but this felt like the right place for casting her salt and freeing herself forever from Will. Not to mention the mortification he'd caused her.

She stepped up on the rise formed by one massive root. Aaron glanced at the tree before scuffing his boot through dead leaves. "It's too soon for fiddleheads, if that's what you're here for?"

Oh, would he hound her until daylight spilled over? Twilight or dawn, that's when she had to do it. She could come back tomorrow or even tonight, but then today would be over and she'd have survived. Then hating Will Cogglesmith would become childish. Petty. And she wanted her moment of pettiness now—now, while she could. While she'd let herself have it. Before gritting her teeth to make plans and move on.

She lifted her fist. "You want to know why I'm here?" Her fingers splayed to flash the salt in her palm.

Aaron held back a smile. "You don't believe in that, do you?"

"Me? You've got rabbits in a sack for their feet."

"Might as well sell the parts we can't eat. I might have bad news, though. Most all of that's lies."

He began spouting all the graveyard lore she'd ever heard, from the rabbits to protecting your thumbs when you passed and finished by saying, "None of it's true. Living here showed me that." He looked up into the tree. "Though I admit there's something about this old oak. It's eerie. The strangest things get caught up there or appear at its base. But I suppose anyone else would say that's nonsense, too."

She pressed one palm to the ragged bark of Old Freedom. It was hard not to feel the tree was canny. And watching. "If it's nonsense, then what I do here doesn't matter. You might as well leave me to it."

He shuffled his feet and adjusted his load. "I could, but Miss Jones? Instead of staying here in the cold, would you like to come in and get warm by our stove?"

He gestured toward a roof at the south side of the graveyard. His family lived in one half of the clapboard building. In the other, the workshop, his father made coffins for paupers who couldn't afford a more fancy final rest.

"*Oooh*," said the wind, as if scandalized. "*Oooh*."

"My mother's inside," he hurried to add. "She'll brew tea, if you like. We've got hazelnut biscuits."

Tea. With biscuits and buttoned-on smiles.

Her disinclination must've shown on her face. "I guess not."

His eyes dropped. "Good luck then, I suppose."

He trudged toward his house. The wind *tsked* and scolded, flinging torn leaves.

"Some other time?" Geth called weakly. She hadn't meant to dismiss an old friend the way Will had brushed off her—without second thoughts.

Aaron's stride never broke. She had spoken too late. She could see clearly, too. Dawn was breaking on a day that couldn't end fast enough. The only thing to make her feel better would be to christen it with a curse.

Chapter Three

Geth's favorite plays were full of poxes and plagues, but she didn't want to start an epidemic. Plus she was determined to make her curse fair. No untimely grave, no bloody misfortune—she didn't want Will dead, not in her deepest heart. She only wanted him to be punished, to hear from the gossips that he'd suffered, too. Maybe then he'd crawl back to his family for help so she could snub him as they passed on the street.

Gusts curled around Old Freedom to tug at Geth's hair. The breeze was ready. It seemed to confirm the ditty she'd learned as a child.

Cast a curse in a graveyard—
Once, twice, then once more.
Seal it with the salt of dried tears.
If the curse is deserved,
Fair play will be served.
The wind will even the score.

If anyone deserved a small curse, Will did. Geth wasn't sure salt from the kitchen would work, but she'd cried herself out. She was all out of tears. Salt from the sea had to do.

She cried, "Hear me, oh wind!"

Why not? Aaron had already passed out of sight, and nobody else ever listened to her. Even Will mostly smiled and sweetly patted her hand. Then he silenced their wedding vows before they could speak them and left town to stop her from voicing her hurt. Now Geth recognized the condescension behind his smiles.

But her shout to the wind felt so wild, so playful and freeing, she decided to do it again with more art. She faced the distant gate, a proscenium for this still, quiet stage of the dead. Spreading her arms, she raised her chest toward the sky, which began to glow as the sun breached the horizon.

"Hear my plea, wind—hear my curse and obey! May the unfaithful wretch who sullied this day find disaster before the week's out. Make his bed crawl with bugs, bring shame to his name, and, and…let his underwear itch."

She turned toward the North Wind and faltered. Facing the four winds didn't make sense if she was only meant to say it three times. Which wind got left out— the mild south? And which should hear first? Most likely the north. She'd probably ruined her curse.

Not that a curse was a thing that came true. Certainly Aaron was right. But the wicked idea had forced her from her bed, and now it brought spiteful joy to her heart, so welcome after days of humiliation. In fact, it was like losing herself in a role—forgetting her troubles, and sometimes her chores, in a witch's enchantment or Lady Macbeth's bloody spots.

Or Titania's delusions, whispered her conscience. Certainly Geth, like Shakespeare's willful fairy queen, had been ready to marry an ass.

Brushing thoughts of fairies aside, she repeated her curse, once facing Old Freedom and again toward the train tracks. As she did, she clenched her fist tighter, crushing her frustration into the salt. When it couldn't bear more, she drew her arm back and flung it. The grains sailed high and rattled into the grass, more like hail than anyone's tears.

A train whistle blew—fitting punctuation, like a chime at the end of a sermon. After Will's disappearance, every blast of a train had struck her as a taunt, a rude reminder that a train had whisked him beyond shame. This time, that screech was her fury. She reclaimed the sound, and the wind carried it farther. Her spirits high, Geth dropped a curtsey to no one and brushed clinging salt from her palm.

As she headed back toward the gate, the wind rose and tugged, working to catch her attention. It tumbled a withered nosegay past her feet. It tried to unwind her coat, lift her hair, lick her nape.

She yanked back strands of hair. "Stop that," she said. "Haven't you got a curse to deliver?"

The breeze fell off. If only Poppa so readily met Geth's every request.

The calm only lasted until she reached the gate. "*Done-ne-ne*," said the wind, making the iron bars thrum. "*Done, done, done-ne-ne*."

The low tones struck an ominous chord. At once Geth remembered what she'd tried to ignore. The verse she'd recited in casting her curse did include another few lines. She murmured them softly under her breath, ashamed of a twinge of superstition but afraid to speak them any louder.

"No escape will suffice
From a curse spoken thrice.
Your intent will be done by the wind—
For a price."

What sort of price might the wind ask—a kite? A hat of its own it would not have to steal? Once she

14

arrived home—and calmed Mamie's annoyance— maybe she'd spritz perfume out the window to sweeten the breeze for its work.

That was silly. There'd be no curse.

Not one enforced by the wind, anyhow. Instead of turning toward home as the day blossomed, she wandered farther down the street, musing. Spewing her anger had given her power, and the mark carved on Old Freedom sparked an idea.

Geth need not depend on fairy tales and the wind. She could deliver at least some of her curse by herself.

Chapter Four

The fine house where Will grew up lay halfway down Fountain Street. She'd enjoyed a dinner there once. His parents and older brother were kind enough, but his sister had been rude, dismissive of Geth—a trait Will apparently shared. If only she'd realized it sooner. Geth averted her eyes from the home's stately columns and hurried past toward a small park and the fountain that supplied the street's name.

Gossips watched her from behind parlor windows. She could feel their eyes. And well they should stare, now the sun had come up and she went about in a day dress without petticoats. But the fire of her curse buoyed her, and she wanted to act while it did. Then she'd return home, placate Mamie, and perhaps even unwrap her rocker. She could sit on the porch as a spinster and read Mr. Dickens' *Great Expectations*. Or maybe the Greek play *Medea*.

She'd wanted to believe Will loved her. His sudden departure from town blared the truth. He didn't love anyone but himself. He obviously didn't mind bringing shame to his family. She'd simply been fooled when he encouraged her dreams, though he'd asked her to be content with homemaking first.

"Later, perhaps," he'd advised. "I'm not sure about vaudeville, for all the same reasons your father's laid out. My family will also object. But a part in a photoplay made here in town? I heard Cyrus Ray has begun to produce them."

Charmed, she'd agreed. Then he ran off, when a man of his means could do what he wanted—although nothing his father might disown him for. Will often muttered about family money. He'd never jeopardize that. Maybe he simply found a wealthier girl, sweeter and more of a lapdog than Geth, and couldn't bear to face her reaction. If so, the new couple deserved one another. Geth almost felt sorry for whoever she was.

It wasn't even that Will quit caring for her. Honestly, she enjoyed having a beau more than the soap smell of him. "Betrothed" was a role she could play. And she had to admit Gethsemane Cogglesmith would've been a ridiculous name.

No. The error Geth made when she trusted his words, when she took his soft hand and agreed to his suit, only proved she could not trust herself. She lost track of the line between acting and life and forgot how much the real thing could hurt.

No betrayal went deeper than that.

Geth puffed an angry breath through slipped wisps of hair. A theater life sounded better than ever—spend her days on the stage and leave her real self behind. But Poppa refused to hear mention of it. The Nesbit scandal a few years ago in New York, where one man shot another over the same young actress, convinced him everyone in the theatrical world was a murderer, a scoundrel, or a fallen woman. Geth had to admit he might have a point. Not because she'd become the harlot he feared, but so many operas and plays spoke of love. Clearly theater people were liars.

There it was—the sycamore that bore Will's carved

name. He'd so proudly shown her the letters in the bark, put there when he was a boy. This was hardly the only tree near the fountain scarred by a penknife. Just the most prominent. That's why Will picked it.

What Geth needed now lay near her feet. Horseless carriages were a hazard in town, but the farmers and merchants still drove wagons and drays, leaving manure in their wake.

A handkerchief, though—she'd dashed off without one. The sycamore's leaves would've been large enough, but they wouldn't unfold for another few weeks. Of course, those fallen last autumn moldered on the ground. How badly did she want Will's name here besmirched?

She swiped up a handful of wet, floppy leaves and muttered, "Horse apples are too good for you, Will." Before the leaves' slimy feel could dissuade her, she folded them around two balls of manure, which she scooped up and ground into the name carved before her.

She flung her handful away and wiped her palm clean, first on tree bark and then the hem of her dress. Mud already marred it; a bit more wouldn't hurt. Then she straightened to admire her work. Horse dirt caked in the grooves on the tree.

"Your name is now dung, sir," she said.

"*Heh-heh*," said the wind among the sycamore's branches, puffing as if it approved.

The rain would eventually wash the tree clean, but perhaps she'd return with a knife. If she added an S, he'd be "swill." True enough.

Satisfied, Geth turned to leave.

She wasn't alone.

Chapter Five

The egg girl, Pris, stood a few paces away with her wagon. Geth had helped her with reading in school, reciting in silly voices to make it more fun. This morning the girl's ears, cupped like a monkey's, looked red from too long in the breeze.

Pris gave a shy wave. "Hiya, Miss Geth." Her wagon was loaded with soiled laundry, which she collected for her mother as she sold their hens' eggs.

Geth gaped, feeling the more childish of the two. First Aaron and now his sister had caught her being spiteful. As if the Holmes family conspired to shame her back into line. Or some heavenly force had begun to work through them.

Despite obvious efforts, the girl's eyes strayed to the tree. "You trying to make that tree grow?"

Geth laughed, her embarrassment bubbling out. "Priscilla, I'm no farmer, but I know how dirt works." She cast a guilty look toward the sycamore. "No. I…I'm sorry you saw that. A slip of my temper. But never mind. I have a better idea."

She turned her back squarely to "swill" and took the tongue of the wagon from Pris. "Have you any eggs left? Come home with me and I'll buy two. On the way you can tell me what's happened in school since I left."

The child's hand on the handle was cold. Pris wore only a thin gingham dress and a flannel shirtwaist that must once have belonged to her brother. At nine, she could still get away with that, barely. But boys' clothes or no, she needed a coat.

Geth shrugged out of hers. "You could help me out. I'm too warm. Will you hold this for me?"

She draped it high around the girl's neck and ears like a cape, fastening the top button to secure it.

"That's not holding," said Pris, sounding wise to Geth's ruse.

"Keeps your hands free this way." Geth pulled the handle of the wagon to forestall further protest and hoped Pris would fall in beside her. "And it's dashing— you're a Russian princess." Not that she knew what Russian royalty wore.

"Priscilla the Great." Pris hopped to catch up, clutching the coat lapels to her chest.

From a sidelong glance, Geth saw her grin. "I do believe you'd better keep that," she said, defying the chill that pinched her without it. "It's too small on me anyhow."

Pris looked down and reluctantly fingered the button. "Mama doesn't like us to take charity."

"Nothing wrong with a trade, though, and you cheered me up. That's a fair trade, don't you think?"

Pris squinted and dug beneath the coat. "No, miss, I can't figure how. But do you want a bite?" She drew a dusty licorice pipe from some pocket. Brightening, she added, "We can break it from the end that doesn't have my spit yet." She snapped off a thumb's length.

Geth smiled. "Oh Pris, you're so kind. I'm pleased to accept. But do you think someone so old she's called 'miss' should eat penny sweets before breakfast?"

"Don't see why not, miss." As Geth nipped off a

bite, Pris added, "Granny Ableman gives 'em to me with her washing, and she's a far sight older 'n you."

Geth shifted her bite of licorice into her cheek and tried to forget she'd just been compared with town's oldest spinster. Not to mention a possible witch.

The girl's eyes strayed to the Cogglesmith house down the block. "You live on Fountain Street now?"

Geth yanked at the wagon, caught on a cobblestone. "Priscilla. Surely you hear more gossip than that?"

Pris picked invisible lint from her candy. "You coming back to school, then? We miss your help with our reading. And those stories you used to tell about girls named Pris—or somebody else in my class."

"Aw, you remember? Those were fun to make up. But no, I've graduated. I took the test early." At least she'd accomplished that much. Not that it mattered, since Poppa couldn't afford to send her to college.

"Then what will you do? Just help out at home?"

Step, step, step…One of the wagon wheels squeaked. Geth chewed her licorice, which finally grew soft. Sugary comfort flooded her tongue. She swallowed when she couldn't delay the truth any longer. "I don't know." If she never said what she wanted aloud, she wouldn't have to admit how impossible it was. "How's your momma these days?"

Pris cast her a curious look, probably wondering how this question bore on the one she'd asked Geth. "Right fine. A strange hen blew in on the windstorm last week. Aaron can't figure out where she lives, so we've got extra eggs. That means cake."

Geth picked up her pace. "So the wind brought a gift." At least the blustery weather did good for someone. "Better enjoy it before the hen flies back home."

As the words left her lips, she stuck more licorice in. Too late. She needed a cork. Everyone learned soon enough about loss. Why crush this child's good cheer? The warning sounded too much like things Mother once said. The lump of licorice threatened to gag her. And more of her mother's words echoed now—"Who'll love a girl who cannot hold her tongue?"

Pris's bright face didn't dim. "Yep, we—"

A church bell clanged and kept on. Another chimed across town. Too many, too fast—eight, nine, ten. Eleven? As the ringing went on, Pris and Geth shared a look. "That's not clock bells," said Pris.

Geth scanned the horizon. There it was—smoke. Downtown near the market, or the post office, maybe. A factory whistle blew three sharp blasts to confirm it. Soon after, the firehouse bell rang out too. "Fire. It's fire, Pris! You better run home. Just save me some eggs for tomorrow."

"I'd best get my brother."

"He probably already heard."

Men and boys were emerging onto the street, buckets in hand. The shadows of more darted toward the smoke. Geth craned her neck, trying to account for the roofs she could see. St. Andrews' steeple, the market's clock tower, the Warder Library's red slate, the Arcade Hotel—the smoke rose from somewhere between. She squinted, as if that could help. Which chimney or roof was ablaze?

The wind shifted, coming to hiss past her ears. "*Sseee?*" A gust fluttered the curtain of smoke. Orange blades speared through the gray.

"I think it might be the courthouse," Geth said. "Or next door? I can't tell." It dawned on her slowly—Will's office, in flames. All the books they had shared. Even one she bought him as a gift.

The breeze in her ears shaped and sharpened somehow, not merely a hiss but a whisper. "*Heh-heh-heh. Missssery. Dissss-as-ter. Cursssse.*"

Geth whirled, but nobody stood at her shoulder. "Did you say something, Pris?"

Not breaking her stare at the smoke, Pris shook her head.

The wind swirled in Geth's ears. "*Yesss. S-s-cur-r-rsse.*"

Her thin dress felt heavy and warm. Much too warm. She thrust the wagon handle at Pris and gave the girl a nudge. "Here. Go home now. Stay safe."

As she hurried downtown, her thoughts raced ahead. Maybe it wasn't the courthouse at all but F. W. Woolworth's or the YMCA. She had to find out and help if she could. How best to learn if anyone had been hurt?

But her mind kept returning to a scarier question—did the fire have anything to do with her curse? Sparks flew from every hearth, every chimney in town. Uncontrolled fires were accidents, that's all. This one couldn't have caught in the graveyard.

The sly voice in her ears wouldn't stop, though. Her running feet couldn't drown it.

"*Scurrsse, Geth-eth'ss Currsse.*"

Chapter Six

The smoke only told Geth which way to run until the buildings rose higher. Then its dark clouds wafted all around her. Her feet growing sore from so much hurrying today, she followed late additions to the bucket brigade who ran past. As she turned, first east and then south, the rushing tones of the wind in her ears moaned in an accent she couldn't pin down. Gaps broke some words. Syllables ran together.

"*Misserrrree…dissaster, yess. Miz-miz-miserry, mmisery ssoooon…*"

She tilted her head to alter the rushing tones, but they neither grew clearer nor stopped. Broken, sibilant words teased her.

A curl of black smoke squirmed from an alley ahead. It crooked a finger at her and curled back on itself as if beckoning for her to follow. "*Seeeee?*"

She stopped, unnerved by that sinister twist. Where was everyone? She stood alone on the block, apparently still far from the flames, and yet here twisted smoke, so shaped and distinct.

A blast of wind pushed at the small of her back. "*Ssee-yess seeee.*"

Geth stumbled forward, barely breaking a fall. The finger of smoke receded before her until the fire's roar and heat made its beckoning unnecessary. Perspiration sprang to her skin. The next block was ablaze, people shouting ahead. The old Reed building, full of clerks and law offices—the fire almost certainly burned there, alongside the courthouse. Smoke billowed down the block.

With her chest heaving to draw in the hot, dirty air, she didn't get much farther. Just outside Dillard's furniture store, a man in duck-canvas coveralls stepped into her path. He splayed his arms wide. "Stop. Not a step farther, miss. It's not safe."

She tried to dart around him.

He caught her sleeve. "No you don't." His fist worked its way to a grip on her shoulder. "It's the sheriff who says so. He conscripted our crew to keep onlookers safe and I won't be the man who disappoints him."

"I just need to know what's on fire. The Reed Building?"

The man pivoted her. "I reckon." He marched her back up Limestone Avenue. "The three-horse pumper is on the job now, and the mayor's new ladder truck will arrive any minute. Ladies can help most by getting on home. And making up bandages, maybe."

Geth bit back an impulse to call him a name that would dispel any notion she was a lady. "Was anyone inside?" Will might have sneaked back during the night for his books. The gossip that he'd abandoned those, too, shocked her nearly as much as his betrayal. He intended to send for them later, no doubt, but what if he'd returned instead? Caring was a difficult habit to break. She wanted him sorry, not dead.

"Judge Kunkle, Mayor Todd, a few others from the courthouse are safe, that I know, but I don't know about anyone else. They're still working so all of downtown doesn't burn." He shoved her gently away. "Make the job easier now and go on."

"Wait. How did it start?"

"There'll be rumors enough once we stop it."

What did she expect him to say? That the flames came with a label, like a fine tailored suit—"Made to order for you by Gethsemane's curse"?

She could circle around from another direction, but a glance at the sky stopped her. Smoke churned upward, mesmerizing, pulsing like some beastly heart. A hot breath stroked Geth's forehead. It seared inside her nose.

Abruptly aware of her skin, that tender barrier between her and embers, she spun away from the smoke and ran back as she'd come. Her neck wouldn't stop prickling. She couldn't resist the urge to look back, a crazy suspicion that if she turned quickly enough, she'd glimpse a face in the smoke. Dirty clouds boiled up like dark fleece; no glaring eyes returned her stare.

She decided to stop by the railroad station. Surely her father hadn't joined the brigade. As round as he was, he became too easily winded to do much but get in the way. But even if she didn't find him in his office, the porters and clerks might have news.

Drifting ash from the fire landed on her dress and hair as she went. Geth flicked off the gray petals with frantic fingers. She didn't just fear they might burn her. The ashes made her think of blown dandelion seeds, reminding her of a wish she might not still want. They connected her to the fire as if calling her back.

On the staircase that led up from Fountain to North Street, she turned to make sure the flames themselves weren't leaping across buildings toward her. Some trick of the wind brought the fire's roar to her ears, a deep *whoom* she'd not heard before. She only hoped the smoke rose from smoldering bricks and not flames raging hopelessly out of control. The column of dark clouds towered above her.

Her breath caught—there it was. Her hunch had been right. The billows of smoke took a shape, a long forehead, hollowed eyes over high, angled cheekbones. The features shifted and blurred but never vanished for long. A strong nose peaked, subsided, and grew sharper again. A black jaw cracked open to reveal glimpses of fire—a grin from a demon in Hell.

No. Geth spun to leap the stairs two at a time. Smoke didn't form faces. Not real ones, at least. None with voices that called her by name. No monster leered at her back as she ran. The fire started by accident. Nothing more. Nothing caused by a ritual under a tree.

Still…if her performance could wield such power? Her gestures and voice, her emotions laid bare, with a roar from the world in response—the idea fluttered in her, exhilarating.

She told herself that thrill came from fear. And she couldn't help thinking, as the station appeared in her sights, that the smoke wafting past smelled not of woodsmoke or coal, not of factory fumes or burnt corn stubble or Poppa's sweet pipe tobacco. No. It stank of baked soil.

Boneyard dirt.

Chapter Seven

Poppa was not in his railroad office. The ticket agents and waiting passengers knew less than Geth did. The midmorning local to Akron wailed and thundered into the station, but it couldn't help. She had little choice but to go home and wait.

The abandoned furniture on the front porch accused her more than it had ever blamed Will. She had promised herself she'd flirt with revenge before she put it away. That resolve now seemed childish. She'd soiled his name where it was carved on the tree, a silly spite no one was even likely to notice—but had her ill will ended there?

Or become a force of its own?

She passed the canvas lumps quickly, her gaze on the wooden planks of the porch.

Mamie swept sense back into the world. She stood at the board mixing bread as Geth slipped through the parlor to the rear of the house. "Thank goodness you're back here and safe," Mamie said. "I heard the alarm and had a terrible moment. Forgive me, I know you'd never do such a thing, but for an instant I feared you'd set fire to a certain Fountain Street mansion."

Geth nearly choked. Mamie's confidence in her was so wrong it burned. To cover her wince, she said, "The fire's downtown. I think in the courthouse."

But when she fretted about how the blaze started,

Mamie's hand flapped. It left a shimmer of flour in the air behind it. "You've seen Mayor Todd's cigars," Mamie said. "An ash probably fell in the pile of money some factory owner brought in to bribe him."

Geth had to admit that sounded more likely than a blaze sparked by a curse. Still, as she shuddered, she thrust her hands in the washbasin to rinse off the ash and the guilt.

Mamie noticed. "Where's your coat? No wonder you're chilled."

"Oh. I gave it to Pris Holmes. You know, the egg girl? I went out to catch her before her eggs were all gone. I've been longing for cake and—" She stopped her tongue from embroidering further. "She looked to be freezing, so I put it on her. Then the fire bells rang. Never mind. If we don't have an old shawl, I'll wrap up in a curtain."

"You'll do no such thing," Mamie said. She scolded Geth for her deception that morning but didn't drag her to the church to atone. She simply turned out her dough.

Geth swept up the loose, floured shreds and began kneading. She enjoyed the rhythm, the cushiony softness. As she leaned into the work, the hot stove ticked behind her and the dough sighed and sagged under her hands. Should she confess? "Do you believe in curses?"

Mamie smoothed a loaf pan with lard. "Curses? I suppose it depends how you mean. Christ himself damned a fig tree, I seem to recall."

That wasn't the response Geth hoped for.

"But you're not a fig tree," Mamie added. "And certainly not under a curse." She poked Geth with her work-hardened thumb. "Don't be kneading self-pity into my loaves. Your poppa prefers your baking to mine as it is."

Geth's hand spun the dough. "He only says that so you'll put in more sugar."

"You both need less bread and more Good Book, my girl. Now tell me why eggs were so secret this morning that you had to sneak out—and took over an hour at that?"

The board creaked under Geth's pressure. "I visited the cemetery."

"Hmm. What for? Not to speak with your mama. She had less patience for sneaking than I do."

Geth didn't want to admit what she'd done, but not because it was childish. No, until she knew what the fire had damaged, it didn't sound childish enough.

Mamie pinched the dough like she'd rather pinch Geth. "I hope you weren't picturing an addition to the Cogglesmith plot. You have more imagination than a healthy girl should."

"Don't I have an old skirt we could cut down to make Pris a cape?" It wasn't a lie but a sharp change of subject. "My coat's too big, and her mother won't let her keep it. But Mamie, her poor ears were raw."

Mamie eyed her suspiciously before softening. "Let's see what we can find while this rises." She took the dough and set it to proof.

Geth caught Mamie's fingers and pressed them to her cheek. They smelled gently of sugar and yeast. "Thank you."

Mamie pulled her hand loose. She wasn't one for affection, except toward Geth's father. "Make yourself useful. Bring in more wood for the stove." She opened the firebox to shove a piece in. The coals winked and glowed in the draft.

Geth snatched the wood basket and hurried out the doorway before any tendril of smoke formed and beckoned. As she stacked lengths of wood into the basket, something bumped against the heel of her boot—a green, bumpy pod from a hedge-apple tree. She nudged it out of her way. As she watched, it rolled back, though the ground appeared flat.

Frowning, Geth glanced around the yard. There wasn't a hedge-apple tree for three blocks, and last autumn's fruits should be rotten by now. This one glowed as green as if it had just fallen. Some boy must've thrown it, but not any she saw.

She bent to chuck it over the fence and paused with the fruit in her hand. A split in its skin curved too much like a smile. It whispered. "*Gethsssem*—"

Convulsing, she flung it away. Seed husks didn't whisper! The thing was unnatural. Only after it thudded against the woodshed did her stunned ears inform her that the hiss kept on sounding.

"*Haff I done well? Are you pleasszed with me, Geth?*"

The husk rolled straight back to stop short of her toes. Its split curled and widened, a mouth. Too much like the maw she'd seen in the smoke. The voice grew louder and into a buzz, words flying around her like invisible bees.

"*Pleazzed with your currrse? Izzz it done well? You owe me.*" The breeze dandled her skirts and twined in her hair. "*Will you sspeak to me now? There'zz a price to discuss.*"

Geth whisked her hands through the air at her ears,

batting at nothing, at noises, at wind. That voice—like hornets burrowing into her head.

She clapped her hands to her ears and bolted into the house.

Chapter Eight

When a knock sounded at the door, Geth lay reclined on the horsehair settee, a cool cloth on her face, but she wasn't resting. The wind whined in the eaves. She jumped every time a loose shutter banged.

She startled at this latest noise, too, and huddled into the settee, but Mamie made a soothing motion and went to the door. "It's a visitor, that's all. I hope she brought news of the fire. If it's not out yet, in this wind it could destroy half the—"

Geth leapt to her feet. "Wait! It might be a trick."

Too late. The door swung open and cold air rushed in, but so did a young woman, Geth's friend Sarah, who squealed and flung her arms around her.

"Why haven't you come to see me? Are you feeling that poorly?" She took Geth by the shoulders and peered up at her face. Alongside Sarah—as delicate as a wren—Geth felt like a horse with six legs. But Sarah's exuberance always made her seem taller.

"Not crying, at least," Sarah answered herself. "But not sleeping well, either? And I saw that you haven't yet cleared off your porch." She shook Geth a little. "Don't you think it's time to relent? Here, I'll help you." She grabbed Geth's hand and pulled her toward the door. "If you don't, I'll come steal that divine wooden trunk. And maybe the rocking chair, too."

Geth planted her heels. "I can't go out now. Why

aren't you at work?"

Sarah's pixie lips curled into a smile. "Well, there's a 'thank you for coming.' It's luncheon time, silly. I worked through yesterday to take forty minutes today. Your stepmother kindly invited me over." She and Mamie shared a look. They'd been plotting. "You might be relieved to hear the fire is out. The men came back to the shop not long ago. I don't have more news than that, though."

Mamie clapped her hands. "We'll take it. I have baked beans and dried apples to lay out. I'll get them." She disappeared toward the icebox.

Sarah tugged again at Geth's hand. "Truly. We should bring in your things, and I'm happy to help. Let's catch up while we do. The wind's making a mess with the canvas."

Geth tugged back with more strength. She pulled Sarah to the settee and hissed, "Never mind that. I have so much to tell you."

Smelling faintly of sewing machine oil from her shop, Sarah took Geth's hands. "I can't wait to hear."

Geth licked her lips. Now that she had a confidant who, unlike Mamie, would not call her imagination overwrought, she struggled to find the right words. Would saying it aloud make it too real?

"Do you think the devil can take shape in smoke?" she said slowly. "With a man's face, I mean, so we can see him? And talk? Like we're talking now, in sounds, not bad ideas forming."

Sarah poked Geth's knee. "If you'd read the Bible like you pore over plays, you might know." She softened her chiding with a smile. "You can do both, you know."

Geth nodded. "I think I may have accidentally…summoned the devil."

Sarah leaned closer. "Will's a lout, but 'devil' might be a bit much. He's more like a wart on Lucifer's arse."

Despite her mood, Geth laughed. "Sarah Brannon, you have the tongue of a one-legged pirate."

"You're a fine one to talk, calling up devils. But I'm sorry to tease you. What do you mean? Are you tempted to do something wicked?"

"I think I already have." She told Sarah what she'd done in the graveyard.

To her surprise, Sarah giggled. "Oh, you've been spending too long with Macbeth."

"Shh." Geth threw a glance over her shoulder. "Poppa doesn't approve of dramatic recitals. And Mamie thinks it's a vanity. She'll tell him."

"There's your evil, then, disobedient girl. The devil works through our faults, not through nursery-rhyme curses. Stop play-acting dramas and your spirits might lift. Try a farce or a romance—well, maybe not that."

"Sarah, listen. I've been…hearing this voice."

"An angel, I expect. Or your conscience, trying to be heard over your stubborn heart."

Geth pulled Sarah to her feet and marched her to the door. "I'll show you. Come out to the porch."

When they stepped out, however, the wind stopped howling. Geth scanned for anything out of place. Like hedge-apples with Cheshire cat grins. "Listen."

After a moment of silence, Sarah asked, "To what?" The only sound came from the distant strike of horseshoes on cobbles.

"The wind. It's been blowing a tantrum all day,

and…" Geth trailed off. *The Tempest* was full of aerial spirits that spoke. But Prospero was a magician in a play, no one real. Could a guilty conscience drive someone mad?

Her rocker had blown over sideways. Sarah turned it upright. "All I hear is time passing. I'll soon have to get back to the shop. Take that side; let's go in to eat."

Alert for any sinister voice in her ear, Geth helped maneuver the rocker inside.

Their luncheon awaited in the parlor. Mamie had laid out only two plates, not three. "I'll eat mine in the kitchen so you girls can talk," she explained. She took Geth's rocker to unwrap the canvas and wrestle it upstairs by herself.

While Sarah attacked her baked beans, Geth picked at a slice of dried apple.

Sarah put her spoon down. "Geth, I have to say…I don't understand why you're taking this so hard."

Geth wrinkled her nose. "Should I be dancing a waltz? I think I'm holding up rather well." If she didn't count hearing words in the wind.

She dropped her gaze to the tiny emerald gracing Sarah's left hand. "How would you feel if Alfred did the same thing?" Sarah, engaged for ages already, waited patiently while her beau studied architecture at college.

"That's different, I think," Sarah said slowly. "I know it hurt, the way he did it. But—forgive me for saying this—we both know you didn't love him."

Shocked to silence, Geth gaped.

"You were playing a part, trying it out. Isn't that true? Is there a play called *The Too-Eager Bride*? You did a good job of convincing yourself, but you can drop the act now. The role of pining dove doesn't suit you."

Heat rose into Geth's cheeks. "I was only doing what Poppa advised. What any girl would do in—"

"But you're not any girl. It seemed like a lucky match, yes. And the usual hens are nattering that you won't get another offer like that. But aren't you a wee bit relieved?"

Relieved? Geth thought. *No. Yes? That isn't the point.*

Sarah put her chapped hand on Geth's arm. "It's not a rejection if you don't want what he offered. A predictable life in polite company and a few invitations from the Ladies' Society to put on the pageant at Christmas. And otherwise hiding the thing you love most."

Geth shook off her grip. "Easy for you to say, Sarah. Nobody frowns when you quote too vividly from the Bible or says you're in danger if you read aloud in the evening. Everyone likes you just as you are. Including a man who wants you for his wife."

"Others like you as you are! Or they would, if you'd let them. You ought to allow people to see the real you. People who aren't your father and Mamie."

"You've just called me a fake and a liar," grumbled Geth. She'd been trying so hard to be someone to love. So much for her skill as an actress. "Are those the real me? Should I show them?"

Sarah grinned. "Maybe. That feisty Geth, though— she's the one I expected to cheer up today. Not the imposter swooning on the settee. The rebel is the one some hardy fellow will marry."

Geth gave her a speculative look. Maybe she *had* slipped too far toward Ophelia. The strange whispers that morning, the fire, the wind—they'd thrown off her vow to be strong.

"You may be right." Guilt might be playing tricks on her mind. "I should have started the day toasting a narrow escape. Or at least gone to church like Mamie wanted." If nothing else, the pews should be safe from unholy whispers.

A distant mill whistle blew, and a second from another direction. "It's never too late." Sarah scooped up a last mouthful of beans. "But I will be, if I don't go quickly."

Geth knotted sliced apple into her napkin. "Eat these on the way. Better yet, I'll walk you back. I have sewing of my own to do before the light's gone, but first I may stop by the church."

"For confession? It may be best to be vague," Sarah teased. "Pastor Duncan might choke if the sin he absolves sounds anything like consorting with demons. Let's go."

The air in the streets smelled of smoke, the sun lost in haze. No morning wind blew to clear the air. Geth and Sarah hurried the few blocks to the factory district.

Sarah spoke around a bite of apple. "There's something else I meant to tell you. I checked with our matron at the shop, Mrs. Cheatham. She'll give you a job if you want. We just got a large order we need help with. And more likely to come. Sewing seams till your eyes pop is boring, but it's nice to have your own money to spend."

The idea filled Geth with dread. Sarah worked for what she called an "industrial drapist." Geth didn't really understand what that meant except that instead of sewing curtains for windows, Sarah made theater curtains and trim or linings for countless other goods, from trumpet cases to automobile carriages. Men did most of the installation, but Sarah worked with the cutting and piecing, stitching corners and shirring and decorative seams.

She found an answer that didn't sound like an insult. "You know I'm not a great seamstress."

"Believe me, Mrs. Cheatham will make you one inside a week. And the taffeta and velvet are lovely to touch."

Was that the nearest Geth would ever get to theater curtains? "You're a dear to suggest it. I'll think about it. Though I rather doubt Poppa will let me."

"Yes, I wondered. He's so set against suffrage. He might find a job just as bad."

Geth kicked at refuse in the street. "Maybe worse. Though he keeps hinting about lady clerks at F. W. Woolworth's. I think he hopes I'd bring candy home."

When they reached the shop door. Sarah embraced her. "You're more suited to be a nanny or tutor—but you won't find a husband in a nursery. Or at a candy counter crowded with children. Tell him that." She giggled. "It would be lovely to work near each other. We could eat luncheon together every day."

Geth focused on her best friend's embrace, the hard stays of her corset, her breath on Geth's neck. Heartbeats and giggles and laughter and life. Before they parted, the thought of a job twisted to become an idea. She had to consider—and plot carefully. She turned toward High Street and her church. The steeple gleamed a threatening red through the haze.

Despite her intentions, her feet led her on a detour.

Chapter Nine

The breeze felt unnaturally warm and carried remnants of ashes. Their grit somehow coated Geth's teeth. When she inhaled, the charred smell scraped down her throat. She forced herself onward, down Spring Street, to see the burned building and what was left of Will's office.

There it was—not the neat lines of clapboards but charred, jagged timbers, stark and unnaturally black, like gouges scratched out of the world by huge claws. Surrounding buildings bore witness with walls of scorched brick. Geth searched for a doorway, a corner, a lintel, trying to see the office this ruin had been. A chimney, now leaning, stood as the only touchstone. Ash shimmered in the air all around—demon magic.

The street's bustling horse teams faded behind her. People were avoiding this block.

She approached slowly, as if a devil might leap from the soot. Water stood in scummy puddles. The charred spines of books lay strewn in black mud with a warped file basket, the pendulum from a clock, and a snarl of wires from electric lights. The breeze whined and sputtered across flakes of char.

Geth didn't know what to do with her hands. Had spite done this? Could she possibly be so powerful? Talking to Sarah had straightened this day, knocked askew before it began with a fire bell ringing in place of wedding chimes. But the coincidence of this fire kept her mind out of kilter. Could it be divine justice? Or a diabolical spark?

A skitter of motion disturbed the debris. Probably a rat, already scavenging the ruin. Whatever it was darted toward her. A flutter the size of a fist spun the ashes. Waiting for a tail or twitching nose to aim at, Geth reached for a heat-cracked cobblestone to chuck. Its gritty weight felt warm.

A wisp like smoke rose from the flurry. Was the fire catching again? She glanced both ways for help, but the nearest workers kicked around the far side of the ruin without casting the slightest attention her way.

Faster the ash spun, a small whirlwind. An ash sprite. It hissed in the char, "*See-see-see-see?*" A whisper to no one, the sound filled the air until it swirled around Geth. "*Ssseee? You see?*"

She threw the stone.

The sprite shimmied left to avoid being hit. It *chuckled*. The wind rose behind Geth to moan, "*Oooh.*"

Or maybe not *ooh*. Perhaps it was "*Yoou.*" Accusing. Revealing who was to blame for the fire's destruction. "*Yesss. For you.*"

She hurried down the brick walk, whisking ash off her fingers like Lady Macbeth. *Out, damned spot.* She'd never seen it performed, but she'd spoken the lines. And imagined bloodstains on her hands.

The sprite moved, too, tracking beside her. It grew taller and blacker as it picked up more ash. Broadening on top, it unfurled short wings. Or shoulders.

"*For youuu,*" said the wind. Its pitch changed, or her ears did, so the sounds came more clearly. "*Youu, Gethh. For you. As you wishhed.*"

No. She shook her head to clear her ears and her conscience. Nothing could be speaking to her.

"*Yess. Yourr currsse. Pleassed?*" This time the whisper came right at her collar. Behind her then, circling. "*Why do you sseem sssscared?*"

A workman passed by with a handcart. "Do you see that?" she gasped. She flailed one hand toward the sprite.

He bumped his handcart over a melted lump of tin ceiling and through the ash cloud without flinching. "It'll smolder awhile. We'll be at it a week." He glanced her way. "There's enough smoke and ash to be Hades. Stay out of the mess."

A chuckle and a whisper sounded in her right ear. "*A mess,*" it repeated. "*Misery. Yes.*"

"No." Geth clutched her shawl tighter and spun toward the dervish like she'd back down a menacing dog. Better to meet it directly than let it threaten from her peripheral vision.

Seen squarely, the dervish's shape was now clear. Long, thin legs, a head, and definite shoulders. "*Gethhssemane.*"

"Stop," she begged, without force. Was it magic? A trick? Had the men who'd invented nickelodeon shows turned their talents to monsters and let one escape?

The sprite skipped from the burnt lot to the walk. "*Sstop so soon? But your curse was so well-deserved, and there's something I sseek. Your rrespect.*"

It came at her, pebbles skittering onto her boots. Ash and dirt whirled about it like a fluttering cloak. Her shawl and hem snapped toward the dervish. Flying grit hit Geth's cheeks. She squinted against it.

Squinting gave the eerie presence more weight. She could see a human shape there, its face far too mobile.

"*Ah yess. Your full attention. At last.*" This close, the voice had a hollow, rough warmth. It thrummed in her sternum as much as her ears and drew a whimper from her throat. "*At last, Gethsemane,*" it said. "*The pleasure is mine.*"

Choking on ash, Geth whirled and ran. Businessmen along the street turned to stare.

A tumbling laugh followed her, right at her ear. "*Once you listen and hear, you can't unhear,*" it said. "*Once you've noticed my touch, you can't numb your skin. You can't silence the sense of me, sweet. My mistress of a salt-cast curse.*"

She clapped her hands to her ears, but that slowed her too much. Clenching her fists, she sprinted away.

Chapter Ten

By the time her mind worked again, Geth was closer to home than the church. Her heaving breaths drowned any sound of the wind. Tiring, she slowed, but the breeze left her alone, and nothing could have turned her around toward the steeple, since retracing her steps might have taken her back toward that monster of ashes and wind. Instead she returned to the cemetery, where angels on the stones offered peace.

Geth had never felt so brittle. Not even during her mother's funeral. She fell on her knees before Mother's headstone. She'd once taken such comfort from the kiss of the grass, the sense of crawling into a lap. But many months had passed now since she last rested here. She'd wandered past, listless, after Will jilted her, too embarrassed to stop and visit. Too afraid she'd hear Mother murmur she wasn't surprised, that a girl who caused as much trouble as she did would never find someone to love her.

Moments passed, assaulted by no wind or whispers, only the call of a cardinal somewhere in the trees. The cold of the earth soaked in through her knees. Geth traced her mother's given name with her finger. Frost on the stone melted under her touch, the sudden wetness as slippery as tears.

"Poppa is fine," she murmured. "Mamie takes good care of him, and me, too."

She let a few breaths pass through a familiar twinge of guilt. Truth be told, she maybe loved Mamie more. Mamie was kinder than her mother had been, or at least more reliably warm. Even if she didn't display much affection, Mamie was steady. She didn't run hot and cold. She didn't coddle and rage. But those were the thoughts of an ungrateful daughter.

Geth tried to amend them. "But we miss you. Ferociously and from the heart." She tipped her face to the sky, torn, as always, between addressing her mother's name on her gravestone and the angel she hoped watched from above.

"As for me…I'm not well. As you've probably seen. Are my failings coming back to me, Momma? My sins? Or am I losing my wits? I didn't mean to be evil this morning. I was…thoughtless, I guess. As you always said. And spiteful. Is God punishing me?"

No answers came, not even a memory, though her mother had scolded her often enough.

"I wish you were here to tell me what to do next." Should she beg help from Mamie? Their pastor? The doctor? She'd retire to her bed, but Mamie would roust her. Even Sarah blamed Geth's imagination. No one would believe she'd seen a creature made of ash.

Perhaps they were right. Here among the peace of the headstones, it was easier to blame her own guilt. Confession, a Bible reading, a cape sewn for Pris— ideas for penance flashed through her mind as though from her mother above. Maybe the whole day's misadventures sprang from skipping the church visit planned by Mamie. Geth had to fix that.

What then, though? She shifted to relieve the pressure on her kneecaps. Her future lay blank before her. Clearly, she needed to keep her mind busy with something other than Will and the fire. Scowling, she brushed a crumble of moss from her mother's stone. The drapist's shop didn't hold much appeal, even if Poppa agreed. He'd probably prefer she stay home and garden while he sniffed out some eligible man, but she wasn't about to do that. And selling candy and dry goods all day would be worse. Like admitting she'd be a spinster.

She swept a curled leaf from the grave. New shoots of green barely poked through beneath, velvety under her fingertip. Velvet. Miles of theater curtains. They rippled in her imagination, along with the stories Sarah told about needles and scissors and sewing machines. The drapist's could be a stepping-stone, maybe. She still had a theater program tucked away from the night Poppa escorted her for her birthday. She thought she remembered a notice in it that might hold her key to a secret stage door.

A train whistle wailed, the sound stretching as it departed. Geth closed her eyes and imagined the steam billowing behind it like a flag. If she were bolder, she could be on that train. Buy a ticket to New York or at least Cincinnati. But she had no idea how to join a stage troupe or audition for a vaudeville role. She suspected you had to know someone important or stun the right men with your looks. Or perhaps, as Poppa maintained, be willing to take off your clothes. A train ticket wasn't enough.

"Spooky sound, isn't it?" The voice, coming so close, made her eyelids fly open.

Aaron Holmes stood with a shovel over one shoulder and a big burlap sheet gathered under his arm.

Both the shovel and he were streaked with fresh dirt.

"No," Geth retorted. "I like it."

How had she let someone sneak up on her like that? Rising quickly, she looked past him. The great hole he'd been digging and the pile of dirt alongside it lay not the throw of a baseball away. When she spied it, she resisted a shiver of dread. She hadn't noticed him there, up to his neck in the earth, and the breeze hadn't carried the sound of his shovel. Not like it did the wail of the train.

Mindful of her rudeness that morning, she softened her voice to add, "Though I see how it seems spooky if you work in a graveyard."

He scowled and twisted the shovel handle on his shoulder. "It's honest labor. I like it. It's quiet."

"Except for mourners who wail, I suppose."

His gaze dropped to her mother's headstone. "Aw, hog spit. I didn't mean to interrupt any grieving. I just saw you, and…this morning I…" He shook his head with a final mutter. "Sorry. My condolences for your loss. I imagine even old ones still hurt." He turned on his heel to stride off.

Geth dodged the blade of the shovel as it swung. "Aaron wait. Please wait this time."

He halted, still facing the new grave he'd dug. It couldn't be for a victim of the fire? Heaven forbid. But she had to stop taking her unease out on him.

"I didn't mean to bite. Or to…to sound proud about your work. That's twice now I've been rude today." She moved into his field of view, though he wouldn't look her in the eye. "Please forgive me. It's been a very strange day."

He nodded curtly. "Mmm. The fire and—and all."

He shifted his feet, perhaps unsure whether to leave or remain.

She fussed with one end of her shawl and glanced toward the train station, unable to bear how he avoided looking at her. "I like the train's cry. To me it sounds like a hawk. Or—" She swallowed and pressed on. She had to get past her delusion, to make the wind normal again. "Or the wind. They all sing of far-off things I'll never see."

He turned his face up as if listening to the breeze. "Everything sings, I think. Different songs. Not just the train and the birds. The trees, too. The creek. The grass, when you're still enough to hear it. But if you ask me, the wind plays a devious tune. I reckon it whispers secrets."

She flushed. Was Aaron mocking her—or raving, as lost as she was? Maybe the boneyard had driven him mad. Then again, with the breeze moaning past her ears now, she could almost believe he heard words in it, too.

Perhaps even words about curses and fire.

He returned her gaze at last. She resisted an urge to hide her face with her hands and said, "I hope not. I don't like secrets much. But I suppose we all have some."

A smile tugged at his lips. His dark eyes seemed wiser than she remembered. And piercing. Had he heard her curse somehow? His gaze felt too knowing. Every inch of her buzzed under that close attention.

Just as she thought about running away, he juggled his armload of burlap and looked down at his boots. "Well. Gravediggers know something about keeping secrets. Even those told by the wind." Glancing up, he let his smile bloom. "I'd best be covering that dirt mound, I suppose. Been nice speaking to you again though, Miss Jones."

Before she could stop it, her hand flashed out to stop him from leaving.

"Aaron—does the wind really whisper to you?"

He kicked a tuft of grass, suddenly shy. "Seems like it sometimes. It's hard to explain. But…it's told me a thing or two about you."

Geth hugged herself, drawing back. "What?"

Her motion wafted the scent of ash from her shawl. Aaron must know she deserved blame for the fire. What else could it be? Her mind, already skittish, darted. Had she ever behaved indelicately here at Mother's grave? She probably had, wiping her nose on her sleeve or letting her skirts bare her leg. Oh—or had Will bragged about her affections, starting a crude rumor about her?

She braced herself for the answer. And wondered if Aaron only brought up the subject to use it against her.

Chapter Eleven

As Geth chastised herself for crimes yet unknown, Aaron peeked up at her through his bangs. His sly smile faded. Did her distress show on her face?

Quickly he said, "It's nothing to be bothered about. I've just heard you reciting on Beech Hill. Performing your plays."

So far from what she feared he might say, his words took the span of a breath to sink in.

He gestured toward the wooded rise west of the cemetery. "The wind carries the sound down from there. Especially when I hack at the brambles in that corner."

Her hand flew to her mouth. It was even worse than she'd thought. Beech Hill wasn't much of a hill, not like the mountains on Poppa's stereoscope views, but it was the highest rise in Amity still growing wild. A flat boulder near its crest had served as her stage many times. Surrounded by brambles and bracken, it seemed private. Nobody went there. It sported no berries or mushrooms, no good soil to plow, no water for a house, no romantic view. It mostly looked over the cemetery and the shanties along the levee and railroad tracks. Alone on its summit, she acted her favorites, even the roles meant for men—Caliban's rages, Juliet's sighs, Mercutio's death, again and again. Also wooing and fights and tales she invented, stories straight out of her head, confident she was masked by the noise of steam engines and the switching yard not far away. She felt undressed before Aaron now.

Watching her reaction, he blurted, "No one else knows. I won't tell anyone. I remember from school that your pa doesn't approve. I like hearing you, though." His gaze dropped. "I wish I could hear more."

Geth stared, unable to drop the hand from her mouth, let alone reply to this news.

"You all right?" he asked softly. He set down his burlap and shovel as if he thought she might swoon, and he needed to catch her. "You don't have to stop. No one's ever in that corner but me. Sometimes Pa."

She turned away, preparing to bolt. "I didn't think anyone could hear me up there!"

He touched her elbow and held it to keep her from fleeing. "They can't. The wind brought your voice, that's all. I told you it whispers secrets. Don't be upset, Miss Jones. Please?"

She inhaled. "I—I should go. I need to get home. But…" She risked a glance at him. His brow furrowed in concern, nothing more. "Thank you for telling me, Aaron. I hope you don't think me a fool. But I am. Poppa would bust a vein if he heard."

He smiled. "He doesn't know what he's missing," he said. "To me it felt like a gift, nothing foolish about it. Better than a nickelodeon ticket. It reminds me of stories we read in school. And hearing your voice helps me feel less lonely. Less like I'm stuck here with only the dead."

"Oh, I—you're awfully kind not to laugh. But it must stop. Immediately." The words were out before she heard an implication beneath them, condemning him to be lonely.

His face fell. "Then I'm sorry I told you. Don't you believe I can judge what I hear? Or only that I can't keep the secret? We're not all as fickle as Will. Even if we don't all have families so fine."

Geth's shoulders sagged. "I didn't say any of that. But thanks for pointing out all my foolish choices at once."

"That's not what I—" With a huff of exasperation, he picked up the shovel and thrust its blade into the earth. "You twist my words."

"You eavesdrop on mine."

"I couldn't help it." He snatched at his burlap. "I thought an actress might like some applause. Forgive me if I figured wrong."

That was Geth's cue to storm off. She didn't. He tussled with his burlap, suggesting he too was loath to leave on sharp words.

"Oh, Aaron." She sighed, unsure what to say next. Had he actually liked what he heard? He wasn't the type to flatter her, though.

He glanced up, both anger and misery in his face.

"I'm sorry your work is so lonely. I…" She couldn't promise to keep using the hill as her stage. She had nothing to match his honesty with her, nothing to offer that wouldn't come freighted with layers of meaning she couldn't sort out. Her mind whirled as if the wind had invaded her head—which it had—and now nothing could hold her thoughts straight and grounded.

He looked at her dubiously, waiting for her to finish her sentence.

She blurted the first thought that blew into her

mouth. "Maybe you'll invite me to tea again sometime?"

Without waiting to see how her question landed, she spun and raced for the gate. Her shoulder blades felt the weight of every eye in the graveyard, the gazes of stone angels and spirits and his. But the wind held its tongue, and her pulse filled her ears, and Geth arrived on her porch with no one the wiser.

Holy Mother of God, someone had heard her. She could never recite on her stone stage again. The next one to eavesdrop might know her father and carelessly mention it to him.

Aaron hadn't mocked, though. Or scolded, like Poppa. Aaron liked it. He called it a gift.

Tea with a gravedigger still sounded odd, but she found herself hoping to try it.

Chapter Twelve

Once back home, Geth gritted her teeth and removed the evidence of her humiliation from the porch. She pretended to be clearing away props from a stage, props for a play she'd never seen. Meaningless. But before she started stitching a cape to give Pris, she slid a souvenir from the box that held keepsakes as well as her marred wedding linens.

A program from the Rose City Theater, it marked a departure from Poppa's objections to theatrical shows. He'd enjoyed their evening there, too. She could tell. In addition to the bill of acts, the printing inside included a thanks to the company who provided the pianos, a reminder of the ladies' retiring room on the second floor, and smaller notices for shops and restaurants soliciting the theater trade.

Geth turned one page, then the next—yes. She'd remembered it right.

From Exotic to Stylish
The opulent attire and historical costume of the
STARS
in this week's performances owe to the skills of
* Mrs. Augusta Morton, seamstress *
Commissions taken for private gowns.
Due to growing demand, apprentices may inquire.

Apprentice herself to a costume maker? Geth didn't think she sewed well enough—yet. But what better way to meet the men who put on the shows, who made sure their kings wore robes and not seersucker coats? If Sarah was right, a job at the drapist's might teach her enough about sumptuous fabrics and stitching for her to approach Mrs. Morton. Or use her earnings to find a similar chance in Cincinnati. Now that her mind had slipped loose and she'd begun to encounter unlikely things, nothing seemed impossible. Not even a career on the stage. Maybe a madwoman could start making costumes and step in as an actress once her father was gone.

She eagerly took up the fabric she found for Pris. Snipping and shaping and sewing new seams, she imagined a play starring Red Riding Hood. Blue Riding Hood in this case, since the skirt she'd outgrown had been navy. The work also felt like a penance. The morning's events made it hard to sit still, but her task helped pass time until Poppa came home.

Only once did she take a break, heading outside for air and the outhouse. As she banged out its door to return to her work, a puff of breeze sprinkled a flurry of pale bits over her.

She exclaimed. Ash from the fire, still fluttering down? She plucked whatever it was from her shirtwaist. Ah—pink petals, tear-shaped and satiny soft. Spring was so late snowflakes seemed more likely than blossoms. Smiling, she glanced at the plum tree alongside the house.

Its buds were still sealed tight. The tree in the neighbor's yard looked equally dormant. Not even the redbud showed color yet. Strange, since she caught a whiff of more blossoms somewhere. How far could they drift?

"*A present*," whispered a voice. "*See how I try to please you?*"

She whirled. The yard was empty, the breeze suddenly still. "Where are you?" Her voice trembled. "Or what?"

The whisper did not come again. She flicked off the blossoms still clinging and hurried back to safety indoors.

Bedtime loomed before Geth's father walked through the door. "Finally!" she cried, as she rose to embrace him. "We were starting to think you got caught in the fire."

Her father shook off his coat. "You might say I did. I got caught in the talk about it." His unbuttoned waistcoat suggested he'd stopped at his club. Every tankard of Red Head he drank seemed to pop more buttons loose.

He gingerly gave Geth a hug. Then a sniff. "You've got smoke in your hair. Did you venture downtown?"

A bowl of stew poised to hand him, Mamie asked, "Was anyone hurt?"

Poppa sank into his high-backed chair. "No, no. Oh, a few rats in the char, but we expect those in law offices, don't we?" He held out his hand for his bowl.

Mamie withheld it. "Keep talking, my dear. Before your mouth gets too full."

Geth, who'd finished her own supper an hour ago, sank into the chair nearest his to cover any quaver in her voice. "What started the blaze, do they know?"

He gave her a tight smile. "It's curious. I wasn't

sure you'd want to hear mention of him, but it sounds like it sparked in Will's office. Hard to imagine brazier coals smoldering for quite so long, eh? If he were still here, I'd suspect arson. A villain by one stroke, a cad by another—"

"Mr. Jones," scolded Mamie. "Were any city papers destroyed?"

He shrugged. "The courthouse was spared, with most of the irreplaceable papers, the charter and property records and so forth. Others are probably ash. But town has recovered from fires before." His eyes pleaded. "Supper?"

Mamie gave in.

He took two bites and swallowed. "Makes the city hall tax sound like a good idea, though. Stone, that's the only way to build a city these days. Some say the mayor got it started on purpose, just to promote his tax, but it was probably a spark on the wind."

Poppa kept speaking about steam engines and factory boilers. Geth's thoughts echoed louder. *A spark on the wind.*

She came back to his words when she heard Mamie say, "Enough politics. You'll spoil your digestion. What other gossip today, Mr. Jones?" She coaxed him by stroking the back of his head.

He licked his spoon. "Mostly rumors about your cruelty to me." He carefully set the spoon down, darting a glance toward Geth. "But…somebody tampered in Fernlawn again. This morning. Broad daylight—"

Geth whirled toward the window. "Tampered?" She stared as though to watch Mother's grave, behind the curtain and far down the street.

Poppa patted her hand. "Rest your fears, GoGo.

Your mother's place wasn't touched."

The pet name caught her off guard. He hadn't called her that since they buried her mother. Her girlish nickname had been laid to rest that day, too.

"They're getting bolder, these thieves," he continued. "It's sacrilegious. Fernlawn needs a fence all the way around. Since the caretaker doesn't seem to be doing his job."

Geth smothered a weak protest. Aaron wasn't his father. He only helped dig. Why did she need to defend either of them?

Mamie refilled Poppa's bowl. "You said this morning? Then a fence wouldn't help. They can't keep a cemetery locked night and day."

Poppa nodded. "They didn't even wait until nightfall. Several new graves were opened this week, with the ground finally thawed out to dig them, and the fire gave the thieves a distraction. Every man Jack was downtown, hauling hoses or trying to keep back the crowd."

Geth shifted her unseeing gaze a degree. "Not *every* man Jack, obviously." Aaron might not have run downtown, for instance. He hadn't even mentioned the fire or the crimes when she saw him.

Poppa slurped broth. "Whoever it was may have set the fire first, though I don't know how, without being seen."

Geth tried to remember how dim the morning had been when Aaron finally left her at dawn. If he ran downtown while she cast her curse, he had time for mischief between the streetlamps going out and full sunlight. Were rabbits all that hid in his sack?

Her father interrupted her suspicions. "But that's

what delayed me this evening, my dears. The sheriff came asking about unsavory figures who might've come and gone on the train. But the blame may fall on the unfortunates in the camp down the rails. We can't seem to keep them chased off."

"A better sheriff would help," Mamie muttered. "Obviously it's someone in town."

Geth turned in time to catch Mamie's glance and roll her eyes in agreement. No strangers would know which graves held treasure and which the bones of a pauper or widow buried with charity funds. And only the dentist or someone near a smile could guess who'd died with gold teeth.

Geth rubbed her lips. Mother had all her own teeth, but they'd sent her off with a few favorite baubles.

Aaron would know all that, too. And no one would question his work with a shovel.

"Who was it this time?" Mamie asked. "Did you say more than one?"

"The only name I recognized was old Mrs. Garner," Poppa said.

"Gretchen?" exclaimed Mamie. "She didn't have jewelry, poor thing."

Poppa shrugged. "It's too crude to discuss, but I understand the medical school in Columbus isn't always particular about, er…the source of its teaching materials."

Geth closed her eyes against the image that rose. Where had Aaron dug that day, exactly? In the new grave she'd seen, or one not yet settled? *Was* it a new grave, in fact, or had her view blocked a burst coffin inside? Had jewelry—or, heaven forbid it, a skull?—been hidden in the burlap under his arm? Or his bloody sack that morning?

A sudden need filled her—to again pet the winter-brown grass on her mother's grave, to smooth it like a blanket tucked under a chin. She tugged Poppa's arm. "Poppa, come with me to Mother's grave for a minute. I want to make sure."

Mamie's gaze moved between them. "Shall I get out the lantern?"

"No, dear," Poppa said. "I told you, Geth. Your mother wasn't disturbed. We're not tramping out there this late. We might find ourselves fingered for grave robbing ourselves. The sheriff promised to post a man."

hGeth stalked to the window, flicked the curtain aside, and leaned her forehead on the sweating glass.

Poppa heaved himself up from the table. "If you're going to fret every time something happens, Gethsemane, perhaps we should move Mother's rest to Greenmount, the new cemetery. It's fenced, with the gate locked at sunset each night."

"That's all the way across town." Geth crossed her arms. "And I'll not have her treated like seed potatoes, dug up and mounded over again."

"My dear Geth—"

Mamie laid a hand on Poppa's arm, one that silently said, "Let it go."

Geth, who would rather argue, scowled. But he'd checked her impulse to go long enough. Now she imagined a brute with a shovel—no one she'd want to interrupt in the dark. Anyone willing to dig up the dead might add an extra corpse to the grave.

Or obtain a fresh one for the medical school. If that villain was Aaron, she may have already made a narrow escape.

Poppa stepped toward the parlor. "Time for something more pleasant. Come read to me a while, my dear."

Geth shoved down a surge of resentment. She used to love reading for him and complied frequently. Then one evening she made the mistake of mentioning the audition for bit parts in a play being mounted downtown. The argument that ensued soured the habit.

"Play-acting is fine for the classroom, Gethsemane," he'd insisted. "For a young woman otherwise? No. Oh, read for your husband and children, of course, once you have them. And until then for me, to be sure. I do enjoy the voices and gestures you add—so amusing. But no, not appropriate outside the home."

The way he'd patted his vest as he said it made her feel he wanted to keep her voice all to himself—his to turn on and off, and not hers. But she wasn't a faucet. Her voice would not flow into his ears tonight.

"You'll have to ask Mamie or read for yourself," she replied. "I'm going to bed." She stomped up the narrow staircase without a lamp, undressed in the dark, and lay sleepless.

The wind hooting in the bare trees outside came to tap a branch against the wall near her head. *Tap-tap, scritchity tap.* She'd heard it for years, the hickory in the yard, but now it seemed to speak more. Like a train whistle's code, the taps and scritches held meaning. She just didn't know how to crack it.

In the end, all the blasts from the train meant *Beware.* These noises seemed to say the same thing.

She imagined long fingers, black in the dark, sliding into the house through a crack between boards. They might twist the curtain or twine in her hair. Or ruffle her blankets enough to slip underneath, sinister air creeping in alongside her, cold fingers against her bare skin.

Geth pulled her quilt tighter. No one got hurt in the fire that day. The harm only hit papers and wood desks and walls. She'd finished a cape that would help Pris stay warm and read Bible verses to Mamie for nearly an hour. Plum blossoms, from somewhere, hinted of spring, of nature behaving as it should.

So why was she so scared to let her eyes close?

Sleep seemed too much like smoke, filled with too many voices. She couldn't risk meeting certain faces there, too.

Chapter Thirteen

Geth didn't even eat breakfast before bustling out of the house the next morning. With a knitted shawl thrown over her shirtwaist and skirt, she grabbed the cape she made Pris and set out for the Holmes' modest house. Perhaps a good deed would start the day right and prevent her from imagining a voice in the wind.

She wished she'd delayed just a bit when she spied Lynelle Cogglesmith scurrying along one of the cemetery's graveled paths. Geth detoured sharply and steadfastly looked elsewhere, making it easy for Will's sister to avoid her.

Two figures worked on the north side of the graveyard. The breeze brought the scrape of shovels on dirt. Aaron and his father, most likely. Perhaps fixing the damage for poor Mrs. Garner. They didn't work where Aaron had dug yesterday.

She should've paid more attention to the action close by. Lynelle, two years younger than Geth, caught up with her a few paces from Mother's grave. "Gethsemane Jones—hmm. Fancy meeting you here."

Geth studied the girl, wondering what she could want. She and Lynelle had never even been schoolmates. Will's sister attended a fancy girls' school, and on the few occasions they'd met, Lynelle behaved as though Geth were a rival, not a future sister-in-law. Now the youngest Cogglesmith child struggled to keep up her disdain, since her arms were clasped around a tangle of muddy clothing.

Geth wondered at that. Usually Pris collected and delivered the laundry her mother took in—and Lynelle had been leaving the cemetery. Shouldn't the linens and shirtwaists she left with be folded and clean?

But what did Geth care? She forced a brittle smile. "My mother lies here, as you probably know." Turning away, she added, "Thank you for leaving me to pay my respects."

No grave robber's boot prints marred Mother's resting place. The earth beneath Geth felt abruptly more solid.

Lynelle hissed at her ear, "I saw you go past our house yesterday morning. I suppose you know nothing about this." She shook the fabric piled in her arms.

Geth spared barely a glance. "I don't even know what you're talking about." Had Aaron's mother refused the Cogglesmiths' laundry in some show of support for Geth? The idea warmed her but didn't make sense. Laundrymaids couldn't afford scruples.

Lynelle laughed a high giggle that was nearly a squeak. "Like the fire, I suppose. I wondered why you were downtown so early."

Gasping, Geth spun on her. "Are you accusing me of setting the fire?"

Lynelle balled her fists. "You enjoyed it, at least. I'm sure he planned to send for his books. Now he can't."

Sitting in Will's office, reading aloud to him over luncheon—the memory stung. "There's a reason your brother left town. He can't show his face."

Lynelle's lip trembled but she thrust her chest

forward. "He had more cause for shame when he made your engagement than in breaking it off. A station-clerk's daughter?" Tears clogged her voice. Lynelle took two rapid breaths and regained self-control. "I knew you were common. I didn't realize you were a thief. Until our housekeeper discovered our wash had been stolen not a quarter-hour after I watched you skulk by. I knew it had to be you who sneaked into our yard. Honestly, I'm embarrassed for you." Tears tumbled from the girl's blazing eyes.

A laugh of disbelief escaped Geth, then a tendril of pity uncurled inside. "Me? What would I want with your laundry? You're not making sense. Perhaps you should go home." *And leave me alone* stayed unsaid.

Heavy footsteps approached. Aaron's.

He stopped a considerable distance away as though scared either young woman might light into him. "Anything I can help with here, ladies?"

Lynelle shot him a poisonous glance before flouncing off.

Aaron watched her go, then stepped nearer to Geth. "We heard the raised voices." He jerked his head toward his father, still digging. "I wanted to make sure you weren't being bothered."

Geth swept locks of her hair from her face where the breeze toyed with them. "She's very upset, but I couldn't tell why."

He bit off a grin. "Knocked off her high horse, I reckon. A whole bushel of Cogglesmith laundry showed up tangled in Old Freedom this morning."

Geth looked to the distant tree, whose juddering limbs seemed to laugh. Something white still fluttered in the highest branches.

"Couldn't reach that one," Aaron explained. "Pa made me climb up with a rake to free 'em. The bespoke shirts had her father's name stitched in. It seems the wind stole them off their line yesterday."

"The wind?" A thread of hysteria twined in Geth's voice. She took a deep breath. "Well, it has been a blustery spring…?"

"I'd think it would take a tornado to keep that laundry flying all night. It wasn't in the tree yesterday."

She couldn't meet his eyes. Was he too busy robbing corpses yesterday to notice? But her own guilt made his easy manner seem guileless. The grass on Mother's grave looked oddly inviting—soothing and low, away from the wind, away from misgivings and Aaron's attention.

He shrugged. "Ma offered to wash it and let Pris deliver, but they wouldn't wait."

"I didn't do it," she blurted.

His face remained carefully blank. "I wouldn't suppose you did, Miss Jones."

She didn't believe him. "Well. I'm sorry you had to climb the tree for it. But speaking of yesterday—when I saw you after the fire, why didn't you mention the grave robbers were back? And apparently right under your nose?"

He winced. "You heard. I…didn't want you to fret about your mother's grave. And it's painful to know folks are thinking like you are, that Pa and I are incompetent somehow. This graveyard is full of trees and large vaults. You played hide-and-seek here when we were small, didn't you?"

"Yes."

"Then you know it's easy to slip between shadows.

And now the ground's thawing. We're digging as fast as we can to bury the people who died this winter and got stuck in the receiving vault—months, some of them." He swung one arm wide to encompass Fernlawn. "We can't be waist-deep in a grave and still pay attention to thirty acres of headstones. It's not hard for someone to get up to no good."

She stepped back from his righteous anger—if that's what it was. Could his words be an act? Nothing but a show of innocence?

Abruptly his arm dropped and, cramming both fists into his pockets, he looked at his boots. "Sorry. I don't mean to give you a sermon. It's frustrating, that's all. The town council could pay for a watch or a fence. Without either, we're doing our best."

If that was an act, he'd be better onstage than she would. She shifted the cape for Pris in her arms. "You need a little help from Old Freedom. Maybe it's making sure they escape."

"No. Freedom Tree knows what true justice is." He turned to look at the tree and the X blazed into its bark. "Someone told me that blaze is what makes it so canny. Like an eye. It's always watching. It knows who the grave robbers are, I warrant. If it'll only mutter their names to the wind, sooner or later, the wind will tell me." He did not wink or smile.

Geth shivered as she eyed the shirt still in the branches.

He added, "I wish it would hurry up, though." A wry grin crept to his face. "Maybe now it's done catching runaway laundry, it can."

That jibe seemed directed at her. Airily, she replied, "Perhaps you haven't asked it correctly." She took a few steps toward his house, wanting to leave certain subjects behind.

He came with her. "Are you saying I need to use salt, Miss Jones?"

"I wouldn't know. But please, call me Geth. It hasn't been that long since we worked algebra problems together." Being called "miss" made her feel like a spinster.

He nodded. "Gethsemane. I remember." He plucked a fallen maple leaf, still red but silvered with frost, from the grass and twirled its stem in his fingers. "Like a garden. God's refuge."

She laughed to cover a sob. "Refuge? Gethsemane is where Christ was betrayed." She couldn't imagine why her parents had chosen her name. For years she suspected her father felt betrayed by the baby who wasn't a son.

Then her mother, in a fit over some broken dish, revealed the truth. "I named you just right!" Momma shouted. "Looks pretty but causes nothing but grief."

Later, Mother relented and kissed away Geth's tears. Geth didn't remember what she'd broken that day. But her mother's slip didn't fade from her memory. Not ever. Nor would it—not after being stabbed now by betrayal herself.

Aaron didn't flinch at her outburst. "Well, it's a name for both refuge and torment. Both can be true. This place is like that." At her confused look, he added, "To the families, death feels like a crime. But for sick ones and old ones, it's peace. And it's pretty here, if you notice." He twisted to look over his shoulder and gaze pointedly after Lynelle. "And what seems at the time like a burden, we might later see as a gift." He handed the maple leaf to her.

"Goodness. I didn't know you were such a philosopher."

He shrugged. "Lots of time alone with hard work. And the wind."

His face was so open, so easy to read. How could she suspect he might be the thief?

Geth ran the rimed leaf along her lips to feel the ice dissolve between. "About that wind…" There might be no way to ask without sounding insane. "I wonder…"

The deep weight of his gaze was too much. She thrust the cape at him. "I brought this for Pris. To help her stay warmer in this terrible spring."

He stiffened. "We don't need charity, Geth. She was told to return yours during her egg rounds this morning." He eyed her shawl. "Didn't she do it?"

"She may. I just missed her. But she's a little girl, Aaron. Not so hardy as you. Her poor ears and nose looked chapped last time I saw her."

"She's got things she can wear. She's too stubborn."

Geth had used up her best self-control on Lynelle. "And her brother's too proud. For heaven's sake, why can't I give her a gift? You're not her father."

His Adam's apple twitched. Finally he said, "S'pose I can't stop you, then. Ma's at home." He jerked his head toward their house. "I need to get back to work." He trudged off.

Geth groaned. How did she keep insulting him? He was so sensitive. She hurried after him. "Aaron, please. Don't leave in anger. I'm sorry. I was thinking fondly of the days when I helped Pris in school. It took my mind off my troubles to sew it for her. That's all."

Though he didn't glance at her, his strides slowed. "I can see that, I s'pose."

She kept pace alongside him, not sure what else to say or do.

The silence worked in her favor. "Probably getting grumpy myself," he admitted. "Staying awake half the night to no end, and still burying the same coffins twice. I keep telling Pa we need a big, barking dog. But you can't have one lifting his leg on the headstones." He shook his head. "At least the ground's always softer the second time around."

She stared, but he gave no indication he meant her to laugh. "Heavens, Aaron. Are you always so forthright?"

He stopped to face her. "I live on the edge of a graveyard, Miss Jones. It reminds me not to waste time with airs."

Oh—was he suggesting she did? He was gone before she found a retort.

Geth sighed. He'd called her Miss again, too. So much for the idea of tea. She might as well deliver her gift and go home.

Her shoulders sagged. She turned toward his house, choking back the sharp flavor of tears without knowing why they were there.

Chapter Fourteen

Geth picked her way through the thawing grass toward the caretaker's home, tucked discreetly behind a row of cypress. A puff of wind skirled dead leaves ahead of her feet. Her eyes narrowed. The curled leaves of the pin oaks stood on their points as they tumbled. They looked like dead spiders.

A flash of white to her left stalled her. A length of cloth sailed toward her on the breeze. Geth's first horrified thought was that it must be a winding sheet ripped off a corpse. She recoiled.

It landed on the grass several paces away. Then the breeze yanked and tumbled it like another big leaf. Geth caught sight of sleeve cuffs and a collar. *Oh.* She glanced back at Old Freedom. The last laundry in its top had flown loose.

After hesitating, she moved to catch it. She needn't take it to the Cogglesmiths' house. She could leave it with Aaron's mother to handle.

The shirt lay limp until she bent to retrieve it. Then it leapt out of her reach. It rose up before her, a shift or nightshirt, and hung there as though on a hanger.

A squeak escaped her.

The wind filled her ears. "*Greetingss, ssweet Geth. Does a familiar shape for me help? You've seen only a sstart of my work. I've been busy with the one who hurt you.*"

The longer the voice hissed, the more clearly its words came. She saw a face, too, hovering over the collar, not in smoke or ash this time but a twist of the air, a ripple like a heatwave over a road. A high brow and cheekbones, thin lips, deep-set eyes. She could still see cypress branches behind them, but the unnatural features were plain.

Life stopped. The land around her disappeared, leaving her alone in a void with this demon. Too frozen to scream, too sure no one would hear, she closed her eyes. *Help me.* Few sounds broke the silence—only her breath, which came in catches and gulps.

She opened her eyes. The ghostly shirt, and the windy figure inside it, had blown slightly farther away.

"*I do not wish to ssscare you,*" murmured the voice in her ear. "*I mean you no harm. Far from it, ssweet Geth. Please, let us be friends.*"

A Bible verse rose from memory. She mumbled it under her breath. "Resist the devil, and he will flee from you."

The words made a flimsy defense. After a shaky moment, she broke her stare and dragged her attention away from the shirt. She glued her gaze on the caretaker's cabin and tottered a few steps with little strength in her legs. But the motion made her feel sturdier on her feet.

To her horror, the empty shirt fell in beside her. "*You've mistaken me for ssomebody else. But you'll become used to me ssoon, yes yes yes. You're already less scared, cor-r-rect?*"

She shot a look toward where Aaron and his father were working. Could they see the billowing shirt, too? From this angle, though, the monuments hid them.

Her jaw clenched. She quickened her pace.

One sleeve of the shirt rose as if in appeal. "*We must talk, my lass. Without you running away. I know where you might like to comfortably meet.*"

Geth spun and lashed out at the demon. "Leave me alone." She stumbled when her arm met no resistance and the possessed shirt flopped to the ground.

A gust of wind blasted. Geth fell to one knee. Her hair flew wildly into her face, blinding. The strands smelled like lightning.

Through the rush at her ears, Geth heard not the hissing voice but her own, repeating a line of her curse yesterday, like an echo only now returning to earth. "*Your intent will be done by the wind—for a price.*"

"I didn't mean it," she moaned. "It was mostly an act." She clapped her palms to her temples in a vain attempt to tame her whipping hair. And her fear.

The wind roared through her hair and the bare branches nearby. "*For what audience? Pfft. I thought you had honor.*" The rushing dropped to a growl. "*But even those without it cannot cheat me. Meet me on Beech Hill before day's end—or be sorry.*"

With an audible sucking, the gusting air whisked away. Limp, tangled hair fell back to Geth's shoulders. She held her breath, icy dew soaking her knee.

After a moment, a bird chirped a sound of surprise.

She rose unsteadily and trampled the shirt to prevent it from floating again. When it didn't leap up or trip her, she stood on it while she adjusted her shawl and smoothed her unruly hair. Her elastic ribbon was gone. She made do with tucking a twist beneath the collar of her blouse.

Her heart pounding, she retrieved the dropped cape

and gathered the dirty shirt in the other fist, keeping one boot on it to the last. She didn't want to touch it or let it brush the cape but turning her back on it would be worse. She hoped Mrs. Holmes would take it.

Aaron's mother answered at her knock. "Oh—Miss Jones." The woman glowed, her cheeks ruddy and damp from bending over her laundry, but her eyes narrowed quickly from surprise to concern. "Your coat. Was it dirty or torn? Or did my daughter lie about returning it?" She threw a sharp look back into the house.

"Aw, never did," said Pris from within. "Left it and two eggs with the missus before coming straight home."

"No, no. I—No," Geth said. "I mean, I wasn't there when she left it. I assume. I was…here. But I'm sure it's fine."

Mrs. Holmes raised her eyebrows at Geth's incoherence. "You look windblown, my dear. Would you like to step in?"

Longing to burst into tears and fall into her arms, Geth bit her lip. "I am windblown. Er—may I?"

Mrs. Holmes stepped back from the door. "We've no parlor, you'll see, but you're welcome."

"No parlor" was an understatement, since there seemed to be only one room of any kind, other than one closed door that hinted at a bedchamber or two. But that main room was warm and spacious and clean—with no wind whistling in cracks or around windowpanes. Steam and the scent of hot muslin infused it. A folding ironing board stood alongside the stove, a second iron heating within reach. Pris sat nearby cracking walnuts into a bowl. The work-a-day scene made Geth feel safe.

"I hope you'll excuse my work," said Mrs. Holmes. "Would you like to sit here by Pris?" Anxiously she offered a wing-backed chair behind the stove.

"Oh, no, I don't mean to stay long," Geth said. "I just have an errand. Well, two." She thrust out her fistful of white shirt, now muddied. "I…found this on my way. Maybe it dropped from your daughter's wagon? Accidentally, I mean," she hastened to add. What an idiot she was—she should've planned what to say. Now she'd probably gotten Pris in trouble. Unjustly.

The face of her hostess darkened. "I certainly hope not." She shook out the shirt and held it up for study as if she'd recognize it. Perhaps she would. Her expression cleared as she peered at the collar. "Ah, but no. This wasn't the first odd delivery this morning. You'd think the grave robbers left their laundry for me." She glanced up. "Oh, pardon me, Miss Jones. I oughtn't make light of that. But I know where this belongs. We'll set it right. Thank you." She tossed the shirt into a washtub and turned back to Geth. "That, too?"

Geth unfolded the cape. "No. This is something I hope you'll let me give Pris. A spring cape."

Pris scrambled to touch the blue velvet. "For me?" The nap was crushed from many hours of sitting, but the former skirt didn't look worn. Merely rippled, like water.

"We can't accept something so fine," Mrs. Holmes said.

"Please, it's only in exchange for a gift she made me recently. It's very simple, looser than a coat so she can grow." Geth thought fast—how to persuade this proud woman? "And…I made it as a penance for

75

something I shouldn't have done, so you'd do me a favor to accept it. Help me feel I can move on."

"Please, Mama?" added Pris.

"Well…as long as you'll let me work it off with laundry," said Mrs. Holmes.

"My father always has coal soot on his shirts from the trains," Geth replied. "I'm sure you'd earn it, and then some, scrubbing those."

Pris accepted the cape gingerly and drew it over her shoulders. "It's so soft."

Her mother gave her a loving smile. "You'll be the most stylish laundrymaid's daughter in town. You care for that right, you hear me?"

Before Pris could answer with more than sparkling eyes, the door opened and Aaron ducked in. He stopped short. The blue cape on his sister clearly made him unhappy.

Pris didn't seem to notice. She twirled to fan the cape around her and pulled the hood over her head. "Look, Aaron, what Miss Jones made for me."

He took a deep breath, but his face softened as Pris beamed. At last he replied, "That was kind of her, wasn't it? Now you won't have to wear my old oilcloth. Except maybe in rain. You wouldn't want such a grand cloak getting wet."

Horror flashed on the girl's face. While she clutched the cape to her ribs, Aaron turned to Geth. "I won't be a sore loser," he said. "But only if you'll stay long enough to have tea. I came in for a hat but could do with a warm drink, too. If you'll join us." His eyes flicked to his mother. "And it's all right with you?"

Mrs. Holmes reached for her teapot. "Certainly."

Geth returned Aaron's gaze but couldn't read it. He

must've known she'd still be there, but she saw no trace of his earlier irritation. If anything, he offered a challenge.

Well, let him. She could run hot and cold, too.

She stepped toward the door. "Thank you. But I can't."

Looking confused, he shifted as though to block her—then sagged. "I suppose not." He took the door handle to open it for her.

Mrs. Holmes scooped tea into her pot so fast it flew. "Please, Miss Jones. It won't take but a minute. The kettle's already hot. It's the least we can do."

"I'm expected back home." *Not to mention Beech Hill*. Her heart tripped at the terrible thought.

When Pris added her plea, Geth hesitated. It was harder to disappoint a child. "I'm afraid—"

A second thought rose—an excuse Pris might give her. Yesterday, while she worked on the cape, a question flitted more than once through her thoughts. A chat over tea might be a good chance to ask it.

And also keep her safely inside a bit longer. Maybe postpone another devilish sight, another wind-borne command to speak to thin air.

"You've convinced me," she added, just as Aaron opened the door.

Pris crowed. Aaron shut it again without so much as a click. Or a smile or a glance her direction.

"We've a nettle peppermint tea you won't taste anywhere else." Cups clattered in Mrs. Holmes's hands as she gushed. "Aaron harvests and blends it himself."

"Mother."

"Well, don't you?"

Looking embarrassed, he hurried to the closed

interior door. "I'll wash up."

Geth watched his stiff back as he vanished behind the door. Nettle peppermint, indeed. A pairing worthy of the prickling between them. The only questions were which of them did the stinging and which had the peppery bite.

And perhaps whether warm herbal tea could dispel the demon that now hounded her.

Geth allowed Mrs. Holmes to take her shawl. Given the unsettled state of her innards, it was a good thing herb tea would be soothing.

Chapter Fifteen

Her excuse for having tea failed. As the delicious brew softened her self-consciousness, Geth tried to steer the conversation to the cemetery. Mrs. Holmes resisted, urging teacakes on Geth. She talked of little but ingredients and recipes. Aaron remained remarkably quiet, watching over the rim of his cup as he sipped. Geth couldn't figure out how to ask her question without trampling a delicate subject—or once more summoning Aaron's disdain.

Pris chattered to hold up the conversation. "I sure miss you leading recitation at school," she said. "Maybe you could read with some of us in Snyder Park when it's warmer?"

"Oh, I couldn't," Geth said. "My poppa doesn't approve of public performance."

"Shame," Aaron murmured. He set down his cup, not quite empty. "I'd better go. Pa must wonder what's kept me."

Mrs. Holmes grabbed the kettle. "Here, let me pour a jar of tea you can take him."

Aaron rose. "It's been a pleasure, Miss Jones?" He sounded uncertain but added more quietly, "Geth."

Geth wished his mother were not within earshot. "Mine, thank you. Nettle peppermint might be my new favorite."

A corner of his lips curled, and he opened his

mouth. Then he noticed his sister's sharp attention. The smile faded.

"I'm glad it met your approval." He shrugged on his coat and slipped out.

Mrs. Holmes rushed after him, still fastening the lid on a canning jar filled with tea. "Aaron—"

Geth met Pris's expectant look. "Yes?"

Pris only grinned.

With Mrs. Holmes past the door, Geth took a quick chance. Her voice low, she said, "Pris, you must know all the strange things they say about cemeteries?"

The girl shot a glance toward her mother. "Plenty."

"Do they include a good way to cancel a curse?"

Pris's eyes widened. "Who put you under a curse?"

"Shh. No, no. I'm just curious."

Pris pulled at her lip, but Mrs. Holmes returned through the doorway. Seeing her, Pris gave a subtle shake of her head.

"Maybe later," Geth murmured.

"What's later?" asked Mrs. Holmes.

"The day—later than I realized," Geth said. "So bright outside when you stood at the door. I must be on my way, too." She finished her last drops of tea and rested the cup on its saucer.

Mrs. Holmes took the china. "You're very welcome again. I didn't want to mention it in front of my son, but you have my sympathies. About your young man, I mean. I hope you didn't take it too hard."

Geth looked away. "Thank you." The unexpected sympathy pricked the wound, nearly forgotten amid bigger problems. Like the threatening shirt. What on earth would she do about the summons to Beech Hill?

She said her goodbyes in a chill at the thought.

Geth only took a few steps from the yard before Pris came tumbling after.

"I told Mama I had to thank you again," the breathless girl said. "I figured out what you meant about curses—all the stories about graves and gravestones. I know what to do so you don't have bad luck or get stuck before Heaven. How to put spooks to rest. How to find out who murdered an innocent man, and a bunch more about whistling and dancing and moonlight. Aaron used to whisper all them legends at night. But I don't know any about curses."

Geth forced a smile. "Of course you don't. It was silly. Forget I said anything."

Pris squinted at her. "If anyone does, Granny Ableman might. Don't you think?"

Granny Ableman. Geth gazed toward town. Years ago, she'd stopped paying attention to rumors about the town witch. Once spinsterhood became a possibility for Geth, too—a remote one, maybe, but real—she'd realized how unfair such stories were.

That didn't mean nothing lay behind them.

Her smile for Pris, now more genuine, widened. "Forget about it. I was playing." She patted the girl's shoulder before turning away. "Enjoy your cape."

The only decision was which dread to face first—a jaunt up the hill or to Granny Ableman's house. A witch or a demon? The frying pan or the fire?

Geth chose the errand that invited less gossip. If she got lucky, she might skip the witch altogether—but she couldn't ignore the command to appear on the hill. She didn't dare. Maybe choosing the timing gave her some control.

But it certainly didn't muffle her fear.

Chapter Sixteen

Geth stood at the base of Beech Hill, steeling herself. At least this time the voice couldn't surprise her. She tried to step into the role of Macbeth, frightened at first by his prophetic witches and then later seeking them out. As she did now.

Not that Macbeth's story ended in smiles. Geth trudged up the slope.

She looked over her shoulder. Now that she knew Aaron heard her recite on this lonely hilltop, she wondered if anyone watched her now. She'd stood on the hill gazing out many times, spying on workmen on the roofs of town buildings and those who erected the new water tower. She'd tested the distance, shrieking a heroine's line or simply expressing her feelings. Nobody ever glanced her direction. Not once. Nor had passengers on the trains that ran closer below, even those with their noses pressed to the windows.

No one seemed to notice her now, either.

As she crested the hill, the long grass stood still. It rippled sometimes under the touch of the breeze in a way she always found lovely. Until now. She scanned the cloudy sky and the hilltop. "Is anyone here?" She waited for a rude puff of air or a voice. Every leaf's shiver below drew her eye, but the ground where she stood seemed to hold its breath. "Hello? Will you speak to me now?"

Apparently not. How strange she must look, speaking to no one. It was like performing a play while imagining the other players, which she did all the time. But today she didn't know what came next in the script.

"I've come as you asked. Are you here, or not?"

Her ear caught a hiss that grew louder, approaching like a distant train. "*Heeere.*"

Geth spun but saw nothing and felt no movement. "Where?"

From behind her came, "*Here.*" From her left. From above. "*Here*" seemed to settle on her like a breath.

She'd come unhinged. That was it. Will had driven her mad. Something certain at last, which came as a relief. He'd eventually hear Geth had started to rant, talking to thin air wherever she went. Maybe then he'd feel shame. Her father might put her in a sanitorium. A bright clean one, she hoped. Poppa couldn't afford one too fancy—

Last autumn's chicory stems rattled at the edge of the field. The disturbance approached as though a barn cat moved through them toward her.

"*Here.*" It was more than a whisper this time.

The idea she'd gone mad—and its comfort—evaporated. Fear brought her too alert for her mind to be lost. Indeed, her thoughts flew faster and sharper than ever. They told her running in panic would tip her into madness more quickly than waiting to see what happened next. She couldn't run forever.

She held her breath for whatever moved sinuously toward her.

The waving stems nearest her parted. "*Yess,*" murmured the stir. "*I am here.*" A breeze leapt up, too fresh, tugging her shawl, sliding cool fingers down the back of her neck.

She recoiled and clutched her shawl tighter. "Don't touch me."

"*No? But we know each other so well.*" The voice on the breeze sounded amused, but its invasion retreated. The long grass before her stirred in a twist. "*Perhaps you are right, though. Our connection is changing. Apologies...*" The word trailed into a hiss.

Geth swallowed hard but counted a victory. "What is your name?"

"*A pleasant question, at last. I have many. Bise, Mistral, Khamseen. Ghibli, Chinook. Xlokk. Shamal. Zonda. Is there one you prefer?*"

None of those words were familiar to Geth, but they sounded in line with Beelzebub. "You're a demon, then?"

"*No. Is that still what you think? I'm more natural on this world than you are, my dear. I was here before your kind. I'll be here when you're gone. But I admit you have caught my attention for now.*"

For now. Perhaps that attention might wane.

"Let me see you," she said. "If you want me to take you seriously."

"*You've already seen my effect, have you not?*" said the wind. "*Heard my whispers and sighs. Caught my breath in your hair. Felt my touch on your skin and responded, with shivers and goosebumps and smiles.*" The breeze tickling the grass leapt forward again, idly flipping her skirt hem.

"*Still, I'd like to please you,*" added the voice. "*I know humans are partial to things they can see.*" A thin stream of dust spiraled up from a bare patch of earth near her feet. *"When I took shape before, you were frightened. But I can't see for myself. Perhaps I've been clumsy. Will this do?"*

Geth slowly reached toward the dust. The color of yellow clay, the whirlwind held steady, though her hand parted it like a bird through a sunbeam. No grit pelted her fingers. They felt only a slight, silky stroke. Did the dust exist outside her mind?

An invisible touch caught her knuckles and raised them to an invisible kiss.

Geth snatched her hand back. Some power animated that dust.

"Why won't you say your name plainly? One name, not a riddle."

The dervish rippled with a sound like a chuckle. *"You think if you know it, you can tame me? Amusing. You have less musical names, I admit. Call me the Wind, if you like. Though my friends call me Breeze."*

Geth folded her arms. "The Wind. Nothing more?"

"You called me by name when you cast your curse, didn't you?"

Geth turned to stare over town. Where life went on, normal. She wished to be there. "What is it you want? You said I owed you. What?"

The Wind fell silent briefly. Considering its options, perhaps? Geth tried to imagine what it could possibly want. Chimes to rattle? A secret to share? A favor only human hands could accomplish?

At last the Wind spoke. *"You were about to be married. Become my bride instead."*

Geth choked. "Not likely. What would that even mean?"

"What does it ever mean? Be my companion, my

inspiration. I'll shower you with affection. Go about your life while my work keeps me busy, and I'll blow kindly to bear gifts to you and to others you choose."

"You've heard too many fairy tales around campfires at night."

The dust dervish grew larger. "*You owe me a price of my choice. I did your bidding and now I have chosen. You cannot say no.*"

"I just did. Name something else, and we'll talk." She turned and took two steps down the hill. "A weathercock to spin I could manage."

A shove in the back knocked her flat. Only instinct prevented her from banging her chin. Grass prickled her cheeks. Strands of loosened hair tossed about her face, blocking her view, but the grass nearest her swirled wildly.

"*You cannot defy me,*" the Wind huffed. "*Nothing can. I am trying to be gentle and kind. I will be, if you only agree. But I can do harm if I'm angered. Don't test me.*"

With a *whoosh*, the Wind ripped her shawl over her head. Geth gasped in the sudden tangle and curled against anything worse. Could it tear the clothes from her skin?

She knew the answer—how the Wind ripped sometimes. A funnel cloud that lit down in Waynesville last year tossed a cow the length of its pasture and left three chickens naked in their pebbly skin. Chickens were not easy to pluck.

The voice rose to a roar as her shawl flapped around her cheeks. "*We'll discuss the details tomorrow.*"

Sudden silence. Gasping, Geth pushed herself up

from the ground and fought free of her twisted shawl. The air around her felt sucked away, thin. But at least the hilltop lay quiet and still.

Other than the sound of her moan.

Chapter Seventeen

Geth had never visited Granny Ableman's house, but she knew it the same way she knew which homes in town might be haunted and which served as stops on the Underground Railroad—someone once pointed it out. She set out that direction before her courage failed. Though no wind hissed at her or tumbled trash in her path, Geth's skin rippled as though beneath watchful eyes. She caught the streetcar for part of the way to avoid feeling alone, but by the time she drew close, a blister still stung her left heel.

She found the old woman in her yard, knocking cobwebs from the eaves with a broom. Geth paused by the gate until Granny Ableman noticed her there.

"Nothing for charity today," she grumbled. "Most times, I need it myself."

"I'm not collecting," said Geth. "I came to see you—if I may."

The woman took a tighter grip on her broom and peered closer. "You're a mite old to be playing a prank. If you're here for my help, it won't be free."

"I wouldn't expect it to be." Geth withdrew a packet from under her shawl. She'd stopped along the way at the bakery. "I brought egg sandwiches. In addition, I mean. I thought maybe you'd be willing to talk over luncheon."

Granny rested her broom on one foot. "Cucumber's

better, but I suppose you can't help it's not summer. Come in." She went through her front door without looking back.

Geth opened the gate and followed, childhood rumors rushing back over her. Would there be a cat or a rat? An iron pot on the hearth? She once attended a ladies' Halloween party, but Granny Ableman wasn't pretty enough to be a Halloween witch, even if she could make love potions.

She wasn't much like Macbeth's *wyrd* sisters either, thank goodness. Her gray hair hung in a neat braid—a defiant choice for a woman her age, but Geth preferred a braid herself, when Mamie let her get away with it. The odd seaming of Granny's worn dress suggested it once included a bustle, but at least the old woman kept up with the times by cutting it off.

Her small home felt warm, its dim air smelling of sardines. Herbs and medicinals hung from a rafter. The mantel displayed the spookiest contents—a bird's nest, a dark pelt, and a ribbon of skin shed by an enormous snake. With relief, Geth confirmed the snake wasn't inside it.

Granny Ableman cleared a pile of tatting off a side table before easing herself into the nearest chair. "Let's see those sandwiches, then."

She made no mention of plates, so Geth unwrapped the paper to display the food on top of it, picnic-style, on the table. Granny peered over the bread critically before choosing a neatly cut triangle and daintily taking a bite.

Still standing, Geth shuffled her feet. Granny flapped a wrinkled hand toward a parlor stool. Geth perched there like a child at an elder's knee. The positioning was surely intentional.

As the woman chewed and swallowed, her eyes picked over Geth, lingering on her hands, her face, and her ankles. Abruptly she asked, "You in a family way? That's the main reason young women come see me. That, the fear of it, or the longing for it."

Shocked, Geth took a moment to find her voice. "Goodness, no."

"Hmm. I don't suppose you're here for a love potion, then. Too late for that. I know who you are. Though a little advice never hurts. What do you want, then? I'm sure we've never spoken, unless maybe at church. I enjoy the pageants you lead for the children at Advent."

"You attend at Redeemer?"

Granny smirked and took another bite. "Why wouldn't I?"

Geth couldn't stop it from turning into a question. "Oh, um…so many churches in town?"

Granny raised her eyebrows and picked up another quarter of sandwich.

Geth took her courage in hand. "Actually, you mentioned advice. That's what I'm here for, I guess. Not about love, though. More like…a curse." She grabbed a slice of sandwich to avoid Granny's gaze. Turning it between her fingers, she added, "I wonder if you know how to reverse one. Take a curse back, I mean. Stop it from working. One cast on somebody else, not on me."

"What good would I be in this town if I didn't?"

Geth looked up, hope surging despite how foolish she felt. "Truly?"

"No one knows I'm alive until they have questions

like yours. But what makes you think there's a curse working near you?"

Geth's face burned. "I'm the one who cast it."

"Hmmph. You'll need to show me more proof."

Geth toyed with the sandwich, wishing she hadn't touched it. She could no longer imagine taking a bite. "I think I...accidentally..." The other words stuck. If she admitted causing the fire, would Granny Ableman tell the sheriff? Would anyone believe her if she did?

"The fire," Geth said. "I might have...encouraged it. Without meaning to. In the ashes and smoke, I keep seeing a man. Or some monster. In leaves and dirt, too. It talks out of the air, on the breeze, tormenting me. It says it's not a demon, but—what else could it be?"

Granny's eyes narrowed. Too much skin drooped around them, but their stare remained sharp. "There's plenty in this world we don't understand. I once knew a boy whose own bedding burst into flames around him, and not even tying him up could stop it. Uncanny. But what have you summoned, and with what curse? Speak plainly."

Geth explained as best she could. Granny tapped her fingertips against her withered lips.

Her silence lay heavy in the room. "Can you help me?" Geth asked. "Or am I losing my wits?"

"I thought noisy machines had drowned all the wild voices. Maybe not." Granny rose to rummage in a trunk at the base of a narrow staircase. When she returned with her hands full, she didn't sit down.

"I'll make a suggestion to try. These things are not common, so you'll owe me a debt—"

"Of course. I'm sure I can pay it somehow."

"I'll tell you how, don't you fret about that. Heed

me now. You're in enough of a fix. You don't want to make it worse using these wrong."

After giving detailed instructions, the woman tucked the sandwich wrapper around what Geth needed and tied it with a string she removed from a yo-yo. "The better to call something back," she explained.

The package still in her hand, she walked Geth to the door and onto the porch, pausing in the open doorway. "Your mother came to me too, you know."

Geth nearly fell off the porch. "My—How—?"

While she stammered, the old woman added, "Oh, not herself. She sent some errand girl. But it didn't take long to figure who that girl came for. Town then was small enough to know everyone's business." She patted suggestively low on her belly.

Choking on the implication, Geth asked, "Did— was it when she was expecting me?"

"Yes, but not why you think. I won't help a married woman with that." The old woman surveyed the street, enjoying Geth's anxious attention. A garbage wagon drove by, followed by a two-horse buggy.

Abruptly aware how visible they were, Geth looked away from the road and sidled into the shadow of a post. She couldn't think of rushing away, though. Even if Granny's wrinkled hand didn't still grip what Geth came for.

"She wanted her baby," said Granny at last. "You were rough on her, though. Some babies just don't agree with their mothers. I sold her some brews to ease her stomach and sleep. They must've worked, because once you were here, she sent again for help to spark more babies."

"She did?"

Granny nodded and flicked a twig from the threshold with her shoe. "I didn't notice more came, though."

Geth shook her head. A clock indoors ticked as if counting lost children.

"Hard for you that way." Granny finally handed the package to Geth. "All those longings and hopes pinned on one little girl."

Geth snorted. "One disappointment, you mean."

"Don't be so sure. Few people try so hard to repeat disappointment."

Geth studied the lines on the old woman's face—lines from smiling and frowning and squinting to see. It wasn't easy to tell one kind of line from another. Had she gotten her mother's frustrations so wrong?

Granny Ableman shrugged. "Nothing's guaranteed. Including what I just sold you. Good luck with it, though." She cackled as she shut her door. "I hope to still be here for your daughter, too."

When Geth stepped out through the gate, anyone watching might have noticed the package she carried. But she didn't want to hide the bundle under her shawl. There, its unsettling contents would rest too close to her heart.

Chapter Eighteen

Geth's plan to steal quietly into her room was foiled when she found her father home and ensconced in his reading chair, either dawdling scandalously after luncheon or knocking off early. She whisked her package behind her back before he looked up from his newspaper.

"Oh, what's happened now?" she asked him. She wasn't sure she could bear another ounce of burden.

He dropped his newspaper into his lap. "Nothing so dramatic as that. But I want to discuss something with you." His serious tone alarmed her. Had someone spotted her talking to air earlier that day and reported the strange sight to her father? Shrugging out of her shawl, she hid the bundle in its folds before setting both down on the sofa.

Poppa added, "Where have you been?"

"Luncheon with a friend." On the way home, her feet carried her past the church. She'd almost stepped in to balance her time with the witch but kept going instead, terrified her package might burst into flames. Besides, she didn't have time to spare. She had to get started carrying out Granny Ableman's instructions.

Poppa wasn't helping, moving slowly as usual. He shook his newspaper, turned a page, and folded it in half several times. "Hmm, I can't fault that, can I?"

"I hope not."

He handed her the paper, an advertisement on top.

LOSE SLEEP NO MORE
Lying awake nights over the peace of lost loved
ones? Rest easy with the NEW Champion
Ironworks Burglar-Proof Casket (patent
pending). The permanent seal protects
memories forever and two choices of luxury
fabric provide a soft bed—while the modern,
steel outer shell delivers absolute security unto
the Hereafter. Don't settle for the insecure rot
of wood.

THE ANGELS' CHOICE
Standard and custom sizes, adult to infant.
You'll rest easier.
They'll rest safely in peace.
Guaranteed.
Call at Champion Ironworks
42 Leroy Street, Amity

Geth looked up from the notice with distaste. Poppa habitually thrust news pieces at her before asking her opinion and then lecturing her about how she was wrong, but he'd never presented a commercial message before.

"I knew they'd applied for a patent." She handed the newspaper back. "Will handled the paperwork."

Too restless to sit, she moved to the hearth and toyed with the miniatures on the mantel, turning their faces toward Poppa and away from herself. Her mind spun around Granny Ableman's packet.

"That's not my point." Poppa waved at the settee.

"Don't you want to sit down? It's not a frivolous subject."

"I'll stand, if you permit it," she said. "I sat a long while as we ate."

He settled himself deeper into his chair. "Very well. I have a decision to make, and I wanted to see how you'd feel about it. Ahem. How to begin? I've been thinking about our conversation last night. The security of your mother's resting place."

The newspaper advertisement took on greater dread. He couldn't possibly—No. Geth refused to think it. "I still don't want her moved, if that's what you're going to say."

"No, not that, exactly. Today I spoke with a man at Champion Ironworks."

"Poppa, no. It's a bit late for selecting a casket."

"I know this is a difficult subject, my dear. But you see, it isn't too late. They've also begun making a sort of sleeve to secure more old-fashioned coffins. It locks securely around without disturbing the original. It's an option, if it would put your mind to rest. Whether the sheriff catches these villains or not."

Geth frowned, trying to imagine what he described. "But…they'd still have to…to disturb her, wouldn't they?" This was so fearfully hard to discuss.

Mamie, who heard their voices or perhaps timed her entry, peeked in from the kitchen. Geth's father saw her and motioned her in.

Mamie hesitated. "It isn't my place."

"Come now," her father urged. "The decision involves money, so you might as well help us make it."

"It's fine, Mamie. Really it is," Geth said. "Answer my question, Poppa. Is…digging involved?"

He delayed until Mamie had perched in her chair near his. "Somewhat but done with respect. You'd hardly notice. Her casket would never be reopened. Simply enclosed and quickly replaced. Then you could feel her peace is assured. They guarantee the 'sleeves' are impermeable. Forever, not just for the current crime spree."

Geth paced the tapestry carpet. Was a little certain disturbance better than the unknown threat of worse? She caught Mamie's eye.

"Don't ask me," Mamie said. "But—and I don't mean to be crass—how much cost are you talking about, Mr. Jones? I wasn't aware we had a windfall to spare."

Her word—windfall—registered grimly in the back of Geth's mind as Poppa avoided Geth's gaze. "That's the thing," he admitted. "A guarantee against thieves is dear. I'm afraid I'd dip into Geth's dowry for it—"

She barked a laugh. "Dowry? Wasn't that already ill-spent?"

"For your invitations, of course, and a few other things. But I received refunds for some of the fees. People felt badly about what happened."

Geth scowled, torn between resenting their pity and gratitude that at least Will hadn't cost Poppa too much.

"It would mean little left for another—a real wedding, I mean. Any new engagement would need to be long."

Geth laughed again bitterly. "What makes you think a new engagement will happen at all?" Certainly the Wind hadn't asked for a dowry, and no wedding would take place in a church.

"You don't know," Mamie said gently. "A new

beau could be just around the corner."

Geth rubbed her face to hide her expression. Her "new beau" might be eavesdropping now while it tugged smoke from the chimney or slates from the roof.

"Moreover, there'd be no money for anything else," Poppa said. "You already know I can't afford teachers' college. But if we took this step. I might need you to work a few hours at the candy counter, or as governess for one of the finer families, for your gowns and purse money."

"I'd like to earn my own money," Geth said, careful not to look too eager.

Her father often railed about women who worked, certain they all secretly joined the Ohio Temperance League. Better to not bring up the drapist's until that job was secure. It'd be harder for him to object if she'd already committed herself.

Mamie eyed him. "I have some thoughts about that, Mr. Jones." She did not elaborate in front of Geth.

He took her hint. "We needn't decide this minute. It's getting late to place an order today, since I should return to the station." Poppa rose to take Geth's hands in his. "I want you to think about it. It might soothe your heart to know your mother is safe, but I can't do it without the funds I've held back for you. If that's disagreeable, we'd better squash the idea."

"You're a sweet man for having it," Mamie said.

She was right. Geth lifted his hands to her cheek. "Thank you for trying, dear Poppa. I'll sleep on the idea, I promise."

If she got any sleep that night at all, given the list of Granny Ableman's tasks and the hours it might take to do them.

Chapter Nineteen

Geth took her knitting basket upstairs to dig through it. It held several skeins of yarn, but none that was white. A cream-colored wool had to do. She cast stitches onto one of her knitting pins as if starting a mitten. Her ears remained cocked for noises downstairs lest Mamie appear in her room with Granny Ableman's talismans spread on the bed.

When the clatter of pots announced Mamie was busy cooking, Geth unwrapped the package. It held little enough—a long, thin spear of bone, smoothed into a rough knitting pin. An oak apple. A bent nail from a thrown horseshoe—unlucky. A crumbling handful of rue leaves, also called herb of grace, from a branch Granny Ableman claimed had been dipped in holy water and used to bless parishioners at St. Andrew's. They still held their odor. The string from the yo-yo, of course. And what Geth needed now, the thing she felt most reluctant to touch—a curling strip of dried, almost translucent skin. Unable to make herself ask about it, Geth told herself it was sausage casing, but she suspected a darker truth—it might've once linked a mother and baby.

The strip was stiff, but Geth managed to knit around it, using the bone pin as well as her pair, to work it into her now misshapen mitten. The yo-yo string was knitted in, too. She fashioned each stitch carefully, keeping her stitch counter close. Granny Ableman had warned her not to knit even a single stitch over or under her count. Though her instructions included nothing of the sort, Geth found herself reciting the first phrase of the Lord's Prayer in time with her needles, over and over again.

The knitting was nearly complete when her father's voice came up the stairwell. "May I have a private moment with you, GoGo?"

Geth jumped, nearly losing stitches off the bone. "Oh—oh. A moment, please, Poppa. I'll lose track of my count—" At his tread on the staircase, she scrambled to cover the strangest parts of her project with yarn.

Poppa appeared with a lamp. "I should think so, in this gloom." Daylight had leaked away without her notice. He placed the lamp on a shelf. With him there, she could do nothing about the oak gall or rue leaves, still spread on the used sandwich paper. She gulped and readied a lie as he sat alongside it on her bed.

He peered at the oak gall, the lamp giving it ominous shadows. "Dying some yarn the old way?"

Geth exhaled. His explanation sounded better than any she would've found. "Maybe. If I don't ruin it." She dragged the paper aside and curled on one hip beside him, spotting the folded letter in one of his hands. "What is it, Poppa? I'm sorry I didn't hear you come home again."

Setting down the letter, he tucked his fingers into a slim vest pocket. "Supper is ready, but there's something else." His words smelled gently of beer.

When he withdrew his fingers from his pocket, he placed a small miniature into her hands. The inner lid of a silver snuff box served as both canvas and frame.

"I probably should give this to you, but I can't part with it yet," he told her. "You have her brooch, which means more. But this is yours when I'm gone if you want."

She turned the tiny painting this way and that in the lamplight, not sure which direction was up. "But what is it?" It looked like a cherub with only one blurry wing and a misshapen ribbon falling over its face.

"It's you. Do you remember when your mother painted?"

Geth held her breath. Poppa almost never reminisced about Mother. He more readily talked about gravesites and bones.

"Not really," she murmured. "She did the portraits of you and her on the mantel, I know, but I thought those were from before I was born."

Those two miniatures, painted on ivory, weren't extraordinary. No one outside the family would've said they were good. But that wasn't why they enjoyed pride of place. Much like the moonstone brooch Geth wore to church and had expected to wear to her wedding. She glanced at her dresser to assure herself it still sat there.

Poppa took back the miniature and dabbed its surface tenderly. "I think of this as your first painting—and your mother's last. That little smear's from your curious finger. It upset her no end. She was hotheaded, your momma. You're like her in that way. I rescued this out of the dust bin, along with her paints. She couldn't do both—be a mother and paint. I encouraged her simply to wait until your naps, but she swore off her brushes until you were grown. She wanted so badly to be a good mother. And then, of course..." He pressed the painting to his heart.

"I'm sorry," Geth murmured. "I didn't mean it." Granny Ableman's story rang in her ears.

"No, no, let me finish." Poppa slipped the miniature back in his pocket and patted his stubby hand on her knee. "I don't tell you to make you feel badly, my dear. Far from it. You were a tot. You couldn't be blamed. I wondered if you remembered, however. I've noticed a—a tendency in you."

Geth's breath came more quickly, her heart raw. What was wrong with her now? "What tendency?"

"Like you're trying to make something up to your mother, to pay for some long-forgotten offense, even though you're a good girl and she's no longer with us. This worry you have for her grave, for instance."

He shifted on her bed to take one of her hands. "It's bones, darling, that's all. Your mother's in heaven. We can't truly protect what's left of her here, certainly not more than God could, if He chose. And you don't owe her anything but love and remembrance."

Tears flooded Geth's eyes. She wished she could believe him. And that the fretting she'd done over grave robbers didn't now feel like one more item in her catalogue of failings. She wasn't sure she deserved Poppa's kindness.

Her father offered his handkerchief to her. "Mamie thinks you spend too much time in the graveyard. I have to agree."

Sniffling, Geth saw no point in explaining she hadn't gone for Mother. Drained, she tipped her head to his shoulder instead.

"I share this with you on the way to saying I've decided we won't be…reinforcing her rest," he added.

"Mamie suggested a better use for the money."

Suspicion threaded through Geth. "Mamie?" She'd said nothing to Geth that afternoon.

He picked up the letter, which Geth had forgotten. "She wrote her cousin in Dayton a few days ago. The Women's Christian Association there has a girl's industrial school. They teach bookkeeping and stenography, and they come recommended. What I've put by will pay your class fees and board and still let you marry before I'm too doddering to give you away."

She jerked upright. "You're sending me away?"

Poppa drew back. "It's only an hour by train. I thought you'd be pleased. It's just the sort of adventure you usually beg for. And it'll help turn your mind from recent events." He squeezed her hand. "When you come back, if you like, you could work as a clerk. Or lady secretary. A few firms in town have hired girls and not men to present a lovelier face to their clients. I'm not overjoyed about you taking a job, but Mamie's convinced me it's thoroughly modern." He rose. "More importantly, business is full of well-paid bachelors."

"Wait, Poppa. I'd much rather stay here and start working now. My friend Sarah thinks she can get me on at the drapist's where she works."

"A drapist's shop?" Poppa asked. "Have we fallen so low?"

"Have we been higher? We're hardly society, Poppa. What's wrong with honest work?"

Her father patted his buttons. "Did Sarah tell you what they make at the drapist's these days?"

The question caught her off guard. "She told me they made drapes for theaters, linings for carriages, fancy jewelry boxes. Things like that."

"I suppose they still do. But the reason they're hiring is a new Champion contract. The fellow I met told me. Linings for caskets. Do you really want to sew for such morbid work?"

No. No, she didn't. She saw it as a stepping-stone only. But Geth wasn't prepared to fight that battle yet. "Well, I'd be with Sarah—"

He moved toward the stairs. "You'll make new friends in Dayton. That's more appropriate for you."

She jumped up to follow. "And then have to leave them again. Anyway, I thought industrial school was for…well, girls with regrettable pasts. Is that who you want me befriending?" He'd just called her a good girl, and now this?

"Oh no, I telephoned them from the station after Mamie suggested it," he said. "They're not a reform school, like some. They even take widows without other support."

"Then some starving widow needs it more than I do. I'll find something here right away," she promised. The drapist's had better work out.

He did not look convinced. "They'll hold your place until noon on Monday. We'll have to send confirmation by then. If you find an appropriate position here sooner, we'll discuss it. Appropriate, mind you. For now, come to supper," he said and descended the stairs.

Geth paced her room. Mamie probably meant well, and Geth had enjoyed the overnight outing to Dayton they once took together. But her father's wife simply may have decided the house was too small for two women.

Geth was here first. And if Granny Ableman's

advice didn't work, she couldn't run away from the Wind. It blew everywhere. Being alone in a strange town wouldn't help.

Besides, she needed to earn what she owed the old woman, and that couldn't wait until after bookkeeping lessons. Not now that Geth knew curses were real. She didn't want to anger an old woman who might cast a hex.

Chapter Twenty

After a silent supper Geth only picked at, she went back upstairs with a lamp filled to the brim. It wouldn't do for the flame to sputter out early.

The house grew quiet before she finished everything she could. The rest had to wait until morning. At sunset tomorrow, she'd un-cast her curse. While sitting in Granny Ableman's cottage, Geth's hope had waned. Now, after midnight, with an owl hooting nearby, she more easily believed this perverse rite might work.

She wouldn't need it to work if she'd realized sooner how she went wrong. Casting the curse was merely one part. She'd indulged in that drama to soothe herself, but even more to keep her focus on Will. To distract herself from admitting the truth—her entire engagement was a performance, one mounted in part to hide what she wanted and drown out the fear she'd never have it. Oh, not just what she wanted—indeed, who she was. Under the costume of good girl, good daughter, she yearned to be fearless, uncommon, and yes, dramatic. To reach for her desires instead of dreaming, and to win praise for originality, not compliance.

Perhaps no one wanted her without a costume. Her father, for instance, clearly preferred that she wore one. But Geth wanted to discover who she was beneath the stage makeup. She could always disguise herself again later. But "demure bride" was a role she no longer wanted to play—whether on stage with the Wind or with anyone else.

She hid away her supplies, scrubbed her hands beyond clean, and recited sonnets instead of prayers before she crawled into bed.

In the morning, Geth completed her charm. Sunset, when she'd use it, seemed far away, but she also faced another mission today—one delayed when Mamie stopped Geth on her way downstairs from her room.

"What on earth are you doing up there?" Mamie demanded. "It smells like you're boiling a dog."

Geth winced. The final steps of Granny Ableman's instructions had enhanced the rue's odor. The stench clearly hadn't remained upstairs as she'd hoped.

"Someone gave me a new tea to sample. I brewed it last night, but as you can guess, I didn't drink much."

"Is it still up there? The whole house reeks."

Geth turned back up the stairs, hoping Mamie wouldn't follow. "In my chamber pot. I'll dump it right now."

"Please. Then help me open windows and perfume the curtains. Let's hope the neighbors don't complain."

Geth took the opportunity to get rid of the horseshoe nail, too. Like the oak gall, it had served its purpose.

As they bustled into the parlor together, Mamie said, "You were a mouse at supper, and again this morning." She spritzed lavender water while Geth lifted sashes.

"I've been thinking about something Poppa told me about Mother."

Would her mother have found more patience with Geth if she'd kept her paints? Before Momma's death, Geth had recognized her mother's frustration—if not outright resentment. Along with the secret Granny Ableman shared, the sacrifice helped explain moods Geth had blamed on herself.

"Ah." Mamie didn't explore the topic, flapping it out the window along with bad air. "Aren't you excited about industrial school, though? I thought you'd be delighted to escape chores for a while."

"I don't want to work in an office." It sounded too much like a path Momma had tried—relinquishing one love, with the best of intentions, only to find the loss tainted the others.

Mamie threw open the front door, swinging it back and forth for a draft. "You can still come home and be married. The bookkeeping skills will help you manage your household." She smiled, part joke and part peace offering. "I dare say you'll learn enough about business to change your father's mind about women's suffrage."

If only Geth could change his mind about a theater life. Maybe one step at a time, like boiling a frog in a pot—from sewing curtains to sewing costumes to wearing those costumes. He'd see that no one step corrupted her morals.

In the meantime, she didn't have all morning to chat. She pushed the door shut. "Shall we air your room next?"

Though she nodded agreement, Mamie's hopeful smile waned.

The sun rose toward noon slowly. With the house finally aired to Mamie's satisfaction, Geth pulled on her coat before any factory whistles shrieked for noon. She hoped arriving at the drapist's shop just before mealtime might give her a chance to catch Sarah's boss and also say hello to her friend.

Geth opened her home's front door and froze. A toy balloon hovered just past the threshold, a disembodied red head. A length of grosgrain tied around the trumpet knot dandled over the planks of the porch.

The balloon bobbed. *"Good morning, my dear,"* sighed the Wind. *"A happy engagement gift for you."*

Mamie heard her gasp from the parlor. "Is something wrong?" she called.

Geth shoved forward, grabbing the door as she went to prevent Mamie from glimpsing the arrival. "It's just colder than I hoped. Back soon." She stepped onto the porch and jerked the door shut behind her.

Though she tried to ignore and brush past it, the ribbon's end rose to coil about her wrist like a snake. *"Do you not like my gift?"*

Hurrying down the porch steps, Geth tried to brush off the ribbon. "Are you longing to marry a child, that you bring me a gift meant for one?"

Dislodged from her wrist, the ribbon only coiled somewhere else. Maddening. Finally she wrenched it, hoping to pop the balloon. It merely bobbed and kept up with her, no matter how fast she walked. *"No—a young woman with a fancy for whimsy and theatrical performance. Have you been to a circus? There's one headed this way. That's where I picked up your present."*

"Stolen. I might've guessed."

"Set loose to be recovered by me for my bride."

Not sure if the Wind could hear her thoughts, she

tried to keep her evening plans out of them with blithe banter. "What would being your wife even look like? Would you lift me like a hurricane snatches up trees, so my feet never touch earth again? Or does the wife of the Wind stir pots of air soup and sweep blown leaves from the floors of your home?"

The balloon performed a loop-de-loop in midair. "*Such a poor impression of marriage. I have no home, not as you mean the word. Stay here or sleep where you will. I rest, but sleep is not something I need.*" The balloon bobbed around behind Geth's head to whisper into her opposite ear. "*But I can provide anything you desire. Your paper money is easily snatched. If you like to travel, I can bring you a horse, a carriage, a boat—*"

"And what do you get in return, may I ask?" As she drew nearer downtown and the streets grew busier, she remembered not to move her lips much. What would anyone think of her talking to a balloon? At her age, apparently carrying one looked bad enough. She pasted on an expression she hoped would convey she was taking the toy to a child. Not that she'd wish this demonic toy on anyone.

"*Other than a lovely companion?*" The balloon danced, the Wind sounding amused. "*There are only two things I demand from my wife. The first is tender friendship, of course. The familiar exchanges between husband and wife.*"

Geth swallowed—or tried. Her throat was too dry. "What does that mean?" she whispered. She didn't want to imagine.

"*Only that you leave your windows open so I might pass through and touch you without stealing in like a thief. I can come in regardless. But I'd like to be welcomed before stroking your hair or skin.*"

Geth's skin crawled. She'd certainly enjoyed summer breezes on her bare throat and arms, but that was before she knew how...*alive* the Wind was!

She barked a laugh. "So I'd spend winter with goosebumps. That's what you want? What is the second thing? Bear your child?" Ugh, what a thought. What might such a child look like? Milkweed fluff? A cloud? A twisted cross between a baby and this rubber balloon? Geth shuffled ridiculous ideas to avoid feeling the fear low in her belly or imagining how the Wind might sire a child in her womb.

"*I have no need for offspring. No need for more inner reaches than skin. I already enjoy being your breath. That's a deep intimacy, don't you agree?*"

Geth hated the relief that flooded her. It meant part of her could imagine giving in. Saying yes. Worn down by grief and frustration and shame, agreeing at last to the Wind's proposal.

Fighting that weakness, she said, "You still haven't told me your second demand."

The Wind went silent, though the balloon kept pace with her. Nearly to the drapist's shop, Geth veered onto a side street so no one at the shop could glance out and spy her with a toy.

"That bad?" she said. "Then my answer's still no. Now please let me be. You're keeping me from an appointment."

Finally a murmur came in response. "*Will you promise not to laugh? A kind promise?*"

Geth snorted. "I won't promise not to scream. But a laugh? There's nothing funny about this."

The balloon drifted around to face her. To lead her.

"*Quote for me*," said the Wind. "*What I want most is your voice. Tell me stories. Recite. Sing old songs.*"

Surprised, Geth fixed on the last part of the request. "I can't sing."

"*Oh, but you can. Every human can sing. Or don't sing. Just use your voice. Let the hilltops and fields be your stage. Tell me tales. Act for me. You've done so for years. You just didn't know anyone listened or how avidly.*"

Geth thought ruefully of the dozens of times she'd cast words to the breeze, even dropping a curtsy or flailing or weeping, depending on what the scene called for. She'd even noticed the gusts on Beech Hill seemed to calm once she began to recite. If only someone human enjoyed her words so well!

"But why? Why do you need me for that?"

"*I miss the songs. Poets no longer test their verses when walking, inspired by mountains and paths. A wagon no longer becomes a rough stage. Travelers have stopped carrying a book in one hand, reading aloud to companions to make the distance pass quickly. Few still tell stories around fires at night. And all praise of your gods is contained by a roof. I miss them, those voices, the human tunes of the earth. Some places are better than here for this music, but the time's coming when all your stories will be told by machines. You return the melody of humans to me.*"

Geth couldn't help but catch a hint of the Wind's sorrow. "Surely plenty of people still sing where you can hear. Children, at least. Jumping rope, caroling—"

"*Humans still sing while tilling soil or pounding railroad spikes, but much of that music bears misery and pain and is ruined by the snap of whips or the clanking of chains. I want better than that. Can you blame me?"*

Geth shook off the empathy she'd started to feel. "I'm surprised, I admit. But marry you? No. Impossible."

"Why?"

She grasped for a reason she shouldn't need. "For starters, my father would never permit it."

"He does not need to know. Is he aware of your curse? No, I thought not. This can stay between us alone. It requires only your word. Your devotion. Your honor. I can summon a token or ring if you like. Or an early summer breeze to bring trees into bloom? Or a tempest to send your kind into hiding while we enjoy nuptials in the storm's balmy eye. Let us set any terms you like."

Stuck alone with the Wind in the eye of a storm—Geth stopped imagining it. "I'm sorry," she said, not without sympathy. "But nothing could make me agree."

The balloon's ribbon slipped from Geth's arm. *"My price must be paid."* The Wind's voice gained an edge. *"You force me to be more…persuasive."*

Something about the Wind's tone alarmed her. "Are you making a threat?"

Bang! The balloon burst. But the shreds didn't fall to the ground. They whisked straight into the air, the ribbon still trailing. She watched until the thin twist vanished into the sky.

A factory whistle blew not far away. Startled, Geth remembered her errand. She hurried around the corner to the drapist's shop before the workers who took their luncheons at home finished flooding out through the door.

She thought the Wind had turned its attention away with the remnants of the balloon. Then it murmured again in her ear, "*Do you even notice how your breathing grows faster? I think I know how to convince you.*"

She couldn't answer with so many people around. But surely the Wind was only trying to scare her.

Chapter Twenty-One

A seamstress directed Geth toward the shop mistress. Mrs. Cheatham sat before an open luncheon pail at her table, which capped two long rows of longer tables filled with machines and fabric in burgundy, ivory, and black. Scraps and clipped threads littered the floor, the air thick with fabric dust. The stools before the tables stood empty, however. Geth had either missed Sarah out front, or her friend hid away in a lunchroom.

She greeted the shop mistress and apologized for interrupting her meal.

A severe-looking woman in a white waist and black skirt, Mrs. Cheatham didn't rise from her chair. "Miss Jones. What a coincidence."

"Is it?" Geth said. "Sarah Brannon told me I might get a position here. Perhaps she mentioned my name?"

"She did." The shop mistress removed a piece of pie from her box, unwrapped it, and took a large bite. While chewing, she looked Geth up and down. "We have positions available," she said once she'd swallowed. "And Miss Brannon is a reliable worker. I'd like to think of her recommendation as sound. But I must confess, Miss Jones, I have a doubt about you."

Geth glanced down at her clothes but found nothing embarrassing. "About me?"

Mrs. Cheatham took another bite of her pie. "I

overhead my girls talking this morning. Gossiping, which I do not allow, but in this case, perhaps it was useful. Someone saw you visit the Ableman woman." She peered up at Geth through her eyebrows. "I can't say I approve of such company, or the reasons why young women might seek it. Can you reassure me this isn't true?"

Geth's head whirled. Her mouth opened, but shock kept the words trapped inside until indignation helped her find a reply. "I—I'm afraid it is true, Mrs. Cheatham, but…I'm surprised at what you seem to imply. She's a kind but lonely old woman, no thanks to the rumors about her. I took her some sandwiches, that's all. She could do with more neighborly kindness. Or is that a subject for gossip here, too? Perhaps work here isn't as suitable for me as Sarah suggested."

Huffiness, whether righteous or not, did not seem to faze Mrs. Cheatham. "Neighborly kindness—I see. Commendable, even if ill-advised. As long as you don't make it a habit. Are you still interested in joining my girls then? Or not?"

Geth tried to get herself under control so as not to kill her chances. If she hadn't already. She looked demurely at her hands. "Yes, please, I am."

The woman plucked a needle from a pin cushion on her desk and thrust it at Geth, who took it. "Thread this. Quickly. Any thread within reach will do. If you don't see one, use a hair from your head."

Caught off guard, Geth blinked before bending to snatch a thread from the floor, glad she'd noticed the mess. In another heartbeat, the threaded needle was on its way back to Mrs. Cheatham.

"You move the thread to the needle, not the

reverse. Very good." She stabbed the needle back into the cushion. "I will need to make further inquiries about your character."

"Please. You could start with my pastor at Christ Redeemer or my former teacher at Northside School."

Mrs. Cheatham rummaged in her pail. "Why don't you call again Monday? At noon. Be prepared to spend the rest of that day in training if my inquiries are rewarded."

"Oh, but—" Poppa planned to telephone the industrial school Monday morning. She needed her job before then. "It's only Wednesday. Could I possibly begin sooner?"

"Monday, Miss Jones."

"Yes, of course. I will. Thank you."

Mrs. Cheatham waved a hand in dismissal. Geth moved away before finding the nerve to turn back. "Mrs. Cheatham, I believe Sarah told me the shop had a lunchroom? Might I see if she's there?"

Without looking up, Mrs. Cheatham pointed toward the hallway. "Second doorway on the left. Don't keep her over her time."

Geth escaped as quickly as she could.

Chatter flowed from the open doorway as Geth approached, but it hushed when she stopped at the door. Every pair of eyes in the room turned to her. Several women exchanged meaningful glances.

Her cheeks burning, Geth tried to ignore them and scanned for Sarah's face. Her friend squealed first.

"Geth! You came to apply." Sarah rose too fast, awkwardly, and hurried over. "I could spit in a bottle and sell it as tonic—that's how excited I am." Her smile seemed overwide. "Let's go outside. It's not raining, is it?" Casting a look over her shoulder, she said, "Mary, be a dear? Toss the rest of my lunch back in my pail?"

She pulled Geth into the hall and out the shop door. Once on the stoop, Sarah hugged her. "I'm so glad to see you. Did Mrs. Cheatham say yes?"

"Not exactly. It appears I have a reputation. She told me to come back Monday so she has time to learn more about me."

"Nonsense. She just likes to feel power over us." Sarah leaned back from their hug, and her smile fell away. "But…I did have to defend you today. Twice. Someone has started a terrible rumor."

"It's not exactly a rumor."

"It must be. I refuse to believe you paid Granny Ableman for—" She dropped her voice. "For something to stop you from being a mother."

"What?"

Sarah darted glances to check for eavesdroppers. "That's what they're saying. That Will only left after you…gave in to his lower nature. But 'not exactly a rumor'? What do you mean? If you're in that big a fix—well, I'd feel sad for our friendship, to start."

Geth sagged against the brick wall. "Goodness. I did visit her, I admit. But for nothing like that."

Sarah's eyes grew wider. "Whatever for, then? I'm glad to hear at least some of the story is wrong. Someone walking behind you as you left said she smelled rue. You can't miss it. And a main thing rue is good for is…fixing that kind of mistake."

Geth closed her eyelids until she felt Sarah's cool hands on her cheeks.

"Geth, Geth. I told them rue was good for coughs, too. My own mother has used it. And since your daddy has asthma, that had to be it. Please tell me that's why you were there?"

Geth gave Sarah a wan smile. "I'm trying to fix a mistake, all right, but not the kind I'll never live down. I hope. Maybe tomorrow I can tell you all about it and laugh. But your break must soon be over. There isn't time now."

Sarah glanced unhappily into the shop. "I suppose not. But I know you'll figure it out. I can't wait to laugh with you about it. And everyone will like you once you join us." She pecked Geth on the cheek. "Till tomorrow. Remember to come find me and tell me the whole thing. If you forget, I'll be on you like a tick in an armpit."

Geth chuckled despite her heavy heart. "Sarah, such an image! And I'm the one who gets gossiped about. But I won't forget."

As Sarah ran back inside, Geth turned away. She hoped that by this time tomorrow, she could speak as lightly as Sarah.

Chapter Twenty-Two

Not long before sunset, Geth left her house with a
warm loaf of bread wrapped in a cloth. She told Mamie
it had to be delivered that night for a charity bake sale
the next morning. In truth, she planned to present it to
Granny Ableman as a token against what she owed. If
she dropped it by after darkness fell, maybe this time
she wouldn't be seen.

But the loaf mainly gave her an excuse to go out.
She also carried, hidden under her coat, what she'd
started the previous day. She had to arrive at Old
Freedom to catch the sunset.

Skirting the very edge of the cemetery instead of
heading straight through, she kept a sharp watch for
Aaron or his father, glad darkness came quickly this
early in spring. It wouldn't do to be forced to explain
why she was there so close to dark. She hoped no sentry
watched for grave robbers just yet.

The graveyard seemed deserted. After finding, as
near as she could, the exact spot where she'd cast her
curse, she drew her charm from under her coat. She'd
soaked it all night with the oak gall and the nail, which
turned the yarn gray. Though the pouch dangled outside
her window all day to dry, it felt damp and clammy. As
a witching charm should, she supposed. It smelled like
wet sheep as well as the rue tucked inside.

She waited. She didn't have a clear view of the

western horizon. Trees got in the way. Only the shift in the light let her know the sun had begun sinking below it. Once she was sure, she poked Granny Ableman's bone knitting pin into the last stitch of her knitting and recited the words she'd been given.

"By this bone I undo what I've wrought,

Unmake a curse I should never have sought.

Brimming with rue, this bag and my heart,

Unravel ill work of my hands and my art."

She yanked the bone to rip the yarn, then pulled on the shredded tail to unravel her work, stitch by stitch. Her arm jerked and extended and jerked again. The yarn, crimped by her stitches, spooled out to tangle onto the grass. Geth turned counterclockwise to repeat her words in all four directions, one time more than when she cast her curse. The dusk under the tree deepened each time she turned. After completing a circle, she spun all four ways again, yarn piling around her feet.

As she unraveled toward the bottom of the pouch, rue leaves began spilling, catching in the yarn and dusting her fingers and dress. The knitting was ripped to the dried twist of skin in the last row of stitches when she spun a last time.

A motion to one side caught her eye. The loose end of the yarn had lifted from the grass. It snaked into the air like the string of a kite, but with no kite attached. Ghostly in the gloom, it swayed and danced as if mocking a snake-charmer's pet.

A line of her rhyme died on her lips. Though not a twig of the tree rustled, a shushing rose from the grass.

"*Do you think you can break our bargain with children's games?*" asked the Wind.

"My curse was a childish game, wasn't it?" As

more and more of the yarn flew into the air, the puddle of it near her feet entangled her skirt. Geth stepped back, but that only worsened the tangle. "It was rash. I want to take it back. Please."

"I'll stop hounding the one who wronged you when he's paid enough." The yarn quivered faster and began weaving around her. *"But you might like to know that someone he loves has caught what your kind calls 'bad air.' Taken ill. As for you, you can't be rid of me, darling. Not until you've drawn your last breath. Until then, you're as much wind as mud."*

Too keenly aware of the breath in her lungs, she murmured, "That's not true." As she spoke, air moved over the soft insides of her mouth—thin and begrudging, but a wind she controlled.

"No? You inhale by my goodwill," purred the Wind. An invisible current dragged at her lips, and Geth could not draw her next breath at all. Her lungs pulled and gasped against nothing.

She clawed at her collar. It wasn't tight.

"I sustain all the world's lives, from the mice in the field to yours. The air and everything supported by it awaits my command. But it'd be my joy to give breath to my bride with the knowing only lovers can share."

Suddenly aware of the air on her face, the cool pressure of it, Geth put her fingertips to her cheeks. Her lungs easily pulled in a breath.

She didn't waste it in words. So much yarn filled the air that it looked like a poorly made net. She tried to sidle away, to escape being caught. Her motion kicked up a gust. Swirling around her, it plastered the yarn to her body. She brushed strands from her clothing and stepped clear of the loops near her feet. They snaked back around, cinching tighter. One arm became trapped. Her other arm flailed and ripped at the wool. It was yarn, only yarn! Why couldn't she break it?

"Help," she called. "Help!"

"You don't need it," said the Wind. *"You need only consent."*

"No. Let me go!"

Yarn wrapped her throat in an uncomfortably tight constriction. Then the Wind stilled, the mood she dreaded most. It trembled with the weight of what might come next, too much like the sickly green of a tornado sky.

A murmur, as soft as a voice through a keyhole, reached Geth. *"From your own tangle, yes. But not from our bargain. We will marry tomorrow. You'll see soon enough."*

The yarn snare went limp.

Still draped like a fly trussed by a spider, Geth furiously raked the strands from her dress until both hands overflowed with the wad. She scraped a hole in the dirt with her heel and stuffed the yarn in. Not content with the shallow burial, she shoved a big rock overtop.

So much for Granny Ableman's witchcraft.

Geth sagged against the trunk of Old Freedom and leaned her temple against its ridged bark. As her fear departed, despair took its place.

She moaned, "Why can't you help me get free of this thing?"

Bare branches rattled quietly overhead. It was only a tree. No help here.

She watered Old Freedom's roots with her tears.

Chapter Twenty-Three

The Wind didn't return. Once she cried herself out, Geth pulled herself upright and retrieved the loaf of bread she'd set down under the tree. Fortunately, no pests had discovered it there. The old woman's advice hadn't worked, but Geth had been foolish to hope, and her frustration with one debt didn't pay off another. She could still leave the loaf on Granny Ableman's porch.

She picked her way toward the road at half speed, afraid of barking her shins in the dark. In the late twilight, the shadows and headstones all melted together. The stark black swaths recalled the superstition that stepping into a shadow the moon threw from a headstone would open her own early grave. She hoped Aaron was right and such lore wasn't true, but no superstition seemed laughable now. Not in the face of her plight.

She'd nearly reached the road when a breeze brought the sound of voices. For a moment she mistook the murmurs for the Wind, back to harass her again. But no—two different voices, both male, drifted toward her. Less ethereal than the Wind's.

They grew sharper. Geth eased toward a holly bush and crouched alongside it, hoping her silhouette would be lost in its shadow.

The words grew loud enough to catch, though the men interrupted and talked over each other.

"—what you promised. Hafta fend for my—"

"—you dolt. If I'd known you'd start—"

"—watching the richest ones closest. I'm the one who hangs if—"

"Lower your voice."

Geth hunkered, frozen. It didn't sound like a pleasant chat between watchmen, and neither voice was Aaron's. Frantically she scanned the dark, trying to figure out where the argument took place. No shadows moved to pinpoint the men's location. She couldn't sneak away without knowing where to avoid.

The noises started again with muffled laughter. Someone spat.

"Stop…paupers…the list." That voice, the quieter of the two, tickled Geth's memory. It sounded familiar. Could it be Aaron's father? Who else did she know who might lurk in Fernlawn after dark?

She rolled her eyes at that thought. She was here, wasn't she? But not on any respectable errand.

The gruffer voice came more clearly. "Do the hard work yourself, you don't like how I do it."

A slicing thud followed, like a shovel blade biting the ground.

"Wait. Wait." More laughter—Or no, not a laugh. Heavy coughing. She strained her ears for another snatch of the voice she might know—but from where?

"Better," muttered the voice Geth had heard first. "Oughta get you some tonic for that, Mr. Big. Or find yourself on the wrong side of my shovel. Wouldn't that be a joke?"

The familiar voice growled, "Do what you're told."

Footsteps. Geth tensed, barely stopping a panicked flight. Were the footfalls approaching or moving away?

Only a few sounded. They stopped.

Or their owner began stepping more stealthily, staying on grass and not gravel. And she wasn't sure if she'd heard steps from one man or two.

Geth didn't budge. Her legs started to cramp. Where were the men now? She didn't know how near they stood, where they went, or which way she could steal off. How long could she crouch before her limbs screamed to move? Her ears ached from straining. She heard clicks and hums that might've formed in her head. Certainly her heart pounded louder.

After a while, a distant frog croaked. The noise made Geth tremble. She couldn't wait here all night. Her father and Mamie were already worried, no doubt. Could both men have walked away so silently? Or did one or both lean against a tree even now, watching her shadow for a motion that proved she wasn't a bush?

She remembered Granny Ableman's loaf, nearly crushed in her grip. Moving slowly, as gently as a branch swayed by a breeze, Geth drew back her arm. She aimed far from the direction she wanted to take and flung the bread as high and as hard as she could.

A small thump came as it landed—or bounced off a gravestone.

She didn't breathe. No other noise followed. No feet ran away. None ran toward the thump to investigate, either. Could she trust that any observer was looking in the direction she'd thrown?

Her nerve snapped. Leaping up, Geth raced away. She found a straight path along a row of shadowed headstones. Grabbing her skirt, she ran with her knees lifted high, lest she trip and fall prone. With one sharp turn, she careened toward the road, terrified a shovel might swing to strike her.

She didn't stop running until she reached her front porch. Light blazed from the house—and small wonder. She'd been gone so long in the dark that her father had probably summoned the sheriff.

Geth paused on the porch, panting, to gather her wits. Flying in all upset would surely result in being forbidden to leave the house by herself.

She barely had time for that thought. The front door banged open. Mamie rushed to grab Geth, her grasp more like an attack than an embrace.

"Gethsemane, thank God. What took you so long?" Mamie's hair flew as she dragged Geth inside. Her apron was splattered with what looked like pea soup. A dining room chair lay upended. "I needed your help. Had to rouse Mr. Elliott. He sent for the doctor. Oh heavens, your father—and you gone!"

"The doctor? What happened? Is he all right?"

Mamie collapsed on the sofa and started to cry. Alarmed, Geth crowded close and took her fingers, but her stepmother was too frantic to take comfort from that. She wrung her apron, cradled her head in her palms, and clung to Geth, blinking tears from her eyes.

Geth resisted the urge to shake her and shout. "What? Mamie, tell me. Is Poppa…?" She couldn't say it. "Is he here?"

"Ohhh." Mamie's hands waved as if to slow her own gasping. "Doctor Hillis arrived just in time—he's in with him now—thanks only to providence, I have little doubt."

Geth stood. "In Poppa's room now?"

Her stepmother grabbed her sleeve. "Yes. Stay, though. Quiet and space, the doctor asked for."

Reluctantly, Geth settled again, though she couldn't stop darting looks down the hall.

Mamie took several deep breaths. "His asthma, you know. He's been doing so well—so long since an attack—and then, between one word and the next—oh." She hid her face in Geth's shoulder. "I hate to remember. That horrible wheezing. He turned quite blue, your poppa. Fell from his chair. I thought I was a widow right there. Nothing I did—I tried belladonna—nothing worked. He couldn't catch air. I flew next door for help and when I ran back…" Tears trickled down Mamie's cheeks.

Geth wrapped her in a hug, impatient for the doctor's report.

No sound came from her father's bedchamber. "It was kind of Mr. Elliott to rouse the doctor," she said, mostly to fill the ominous silence. "Though staying with you might've been, too."

Mamie finally regained control. "Oh, he offered. I sent him away. Forgive me, my dear. Here I go all to pieces. I held up till I saw you…" A scowl formed on her face. "If anyone should've been here, my darling, it's you. How frightened I've been, facing this by myself and worried about you half the evening as well."

Geth looked down. "You're right. I'm sorry. I…was detained. Please forgive me. Can I get you a glass of water? Or tea?"

Before her stepmother could answer, the doctor emerged. He shut the door carefully so that the latch barely clicked. "He's on the mend," he announced, looking gravely at Mamie and then, with more accusation, at Geth. "It was not what I feared. The tuberculosis—consumption—is in town. Still, he must rest for three days. Discourage him from talking. He may act confused. The stramonium can have that effect. He may even forget he had the attack. Keep him in bed nonetheless."

They thanked him, and Geth rose to see him out.

He handed her a slip of paper with a prescription jotted on it. "I'll stop in tomorrow. Get this for him in the morning. He can smoke it in his pipe for the next several evenings. For now, let him sleep. Send at once if the wheezing resumes."

As the doctor settled his hat on his head, he added, "Such a strange malady. Your father said something curious. 'The air seemed to taunt me, daring me to inhale. And laughter, laughter when I failed.' " Doctor Hillis shook his head. "Not enough oxygen to his brain, obviously. I'm glad I could help him in time."

Geth stood with one hand on the door after she closed it. The doctor's words echoed. She needed the strength of the wood to keep standing.

A door latch clicked behind her. She turned. Where she expected to see Mamie peeking in at her father, he stood looking out.

Mamie leapt off the sofa. "What are you doing up? Back in bed, Mr. Jones. Immediately."

He pouted. "But I told the doctor, I'm fine now. Not worn out like usual. My breath came back all at once. Strangest attack I've ever had."

Mamie would have none of it. She herded him into his bedchamber.

Letting her handle Poppa, Geth went to the kitchen. She needed to warm the despair from her bones.

Before the tea kettle boiled, Mamie bustled in to fetch water for Geth's father.

"I'm too worn tonight, but we'll discuss your behavior tomorrow," she said. "I'm starting to wonder if you're too irresponsible to go off to school. I expect you to be here in the morning."

"I'm sor—" began Geth.

"Good night." Mamie left without another glance.

Geth sighed, took her teacup upstairs, and began planning a wedding no one else would attend.

Chapter Twenty-Four

Before the sun rose, Geth cracked open her window. "Are you there? I want to talk," she grumbled into the draft.

The Wind didn't answer.

She tried several times before sitting back, thoughtful. Wasn't the Wind always present—outdoors, at least? It had certainly spoken even when the air around her lay calm. Or was it there right outside, silently gloating? Keeping the upper hand?

She closed the window. It could only be a matter of time before it piped up, probably in a startling way.

Mamie scolded Geth soundly when she went downstairs—mostly for staying out past nightfall alone, though Geth suspected what upset Mamie more was her departure from predictable behavior. Not shuttling directly from student to wife, she'd jumped the rails. What next? A train wreck?

Unable to explain a truth no one would believe, Geth resisted the urge to invent an excuse. They sprang to mind easily enough—star gazing, a visit to Sarah, trysting with a secret new beau. But lying and sneaking had improved none of her problems. Aaron's graveyard frankness probably served better, but when the truth was too strange, silence must do. She apologized to Mamie more than once and nodded contritely while her mind wandered.

In the excitement over Poppa last evening, she'd nearly forgotten what she overheard in the graveyard. Her horror rushed back once she'd slipped into bed. One of those voices scratched, scratched at her memory. So far she hadn't identified it, but she still ought to tell someone. Who?

She couldn't upset her father, not with him ill. Besides, he'd demand to know why she'd been there. So would the sheriff. If the police didn't suspect her of nefarious acts, they'd dismiss her as a silly girl seeking attention. That was the last thing she needed.

As her stepmother's ire wound down, Geth itched to leave. Fortunately, she had a good reason.

She drew the doctor's paper from alongside the tea caddy where she'd tucked it last night. "Please let me go get what Dr. Hillis suggested," she said. "I feel responsible, since his attack probably was prompted by fretting about me." Not to mention the blame due her maddening suitor.

Mamie took the slip to read it. "Oh, yes. He's been so ornery this morning, I nearly forgot." She handed it back. "I wish Doctor Hillis still dispensed his own drugs."

"Has Poppa sent word to the station? I could also let them know he won't be coming today." The station was not on the way to the drug shop, but Geth had realized who she ought to talk with. "Maybe he'll stay in bed more patiently if he knows they've stopped expecting him?"

"There's the thoughtful girl I've been missing." Mamie's smile made Geth feel guilty. "Hurry home. Perhaps if you read to him later, he'll rest more easily."

Geth hurried downtown quickly, catching a

streetcar for part of the way. She needed every possible moment of freedom.

She expected the Wind to shape the breeze into words, but again it stayed silent. Well, let it. If her attempt to reverse her curse last night had worked, merely taking a while—like bread set to rise—she wouldn't complain. She'd know soon enough.

Her errand to the drug shop didn't take long, and her stop at Poppa's office went even faster. After leaving the station, she crossed the tracks and saved time by tramping across a corn-stubble field, the only one left to a farmer who'd sold the rest for the railroad roundhouse. Reluctant to be seen, she stayed far from the farmhouse, but she heard the notes of rustic chimes from its porch as she passed.

With a start, she recognized a tune in the tinkling. She turned to stare at the dangling chimes. Although distant, they looked perfectly normal. But they were playing the song she'd picked for her wedding to Will.

"*Ah,*" said the Wind. "*Your expression suggests I remembered correctly. You're ready to accept my proposal, are you not?*"

Geth saw no dervish or rustling in the corn stubble where she could direct her outrage. "You could have killed him!"

"*But didn't.*" The breeze stroked her hair from her face, its touch soothing. "*And I have equal power to please you.*"

Geth scowled and kept marching down the rut between cornrows. "If I say yes, will you leave my family alone?"

"*I'll do better. I want you to be happy. Look.*"

An unseasonal milkweed seed floated before her

like a sheer butterfly. Sunlight glowed through it with pale iridescence. Two more and then a half-dozen joined the first, bobbing and keeping pace in her path. Geth found herself unexpectedly charmed.

"*I've made mistakes, I admit*," said the Wind. "*Scaring you when I meant to seem more like your kind. But I can also be warm. As sweet as a mist off a summertime lake. I will build you a glorious stone stage to recite from. A mountain swept level to bask you in sunlight. I care for you, Gethsemane. I value the ways you are different. Can you say that about the one who you cursed?*"

The Wind had a point, but Geth tried not to acknowledge it. "A wedding requires a ceremony. I want to be married in my church." Perhaps she could delay until she found a way out.

The Wind chuckled. "*Beech Hill would be my choice. Where we've spent such lovely times. But very well. Make arrangements—if you can. And don't blame me if, in my enthusiasm, I rattle windows so hard they break*."

The veiled threat silenced Geth, but not for long. For the first time, she felt not entirely at the Wind's mercy.

"I don't want you asking my father for my hand— I'll thank you to stay completely away—but I do expect a ring. One you've picked out yourself. I'll not marry a husband so lazy I have to buy my own gifts."

"*Hmm*," said the Wind. "*I'll take on that challenge*."

"A real ring," she added, recalling the balloon. "No cigar ring or ribbon or, I don't know, twisted vine. Gold or silver or jeweled."

"*I'll be pleased to present it. Anything else?*"

"Yes. A proper engagement. Six months at least. That's still a short—"

The milkweed seeds puffed into her face, catching in her lashes and nostrils and hair.

"*No. You'll not put me off that long.*" The chimes' tinkling fell silent. "*You prepared for a wedding that didn't happen. Use that. I'll give you two days of engagement. No more.*"

She plucked milkweed seeds from her eyelids. "I can't possibly arrange for my church that quickly."

"*Then Beech Hill must do. Unless you'd like another display of the ways humans need my goodwill?*"

"No. Fine. Two days—after you give me a ring."

"*Very well. I'll obtain one. By nightfall on the sun's day, we will be wed.*" With a quick sense of suction, the milkweed fluff still stuck on Geth's face lifted off like a flock of small birds.

"Wait. Before you leave—why didn't you come when I called this morning?" Geth crossed her arms to play pouty. "I expect a husband to be attentive. Not speak to me when it pleases him and ignore me the rest of the time. Isn't the Wind everywhere, all at once?"

"*Of course. But some of my business takes focus.*"

"Tornadoes, you mean, I suppose."

"*That, and the gust that fills the sails of a floundering boat. The breath that awakens the cherry blossoms. The thermal current that lifts an eagle to hunt for her chicks. Your previous suitor had work, did he not? Times when he couldn't attend you? So do I.*"

"I suppose." But she'd learned something potentially useful. "Maybe we can talk again later. I'd like to learn more about…my future husband."

The words pained her, but the Wind seemed susceptible to what it wanted to hear. "*Until then.*"

The milkweed fluff whisked into the blue.

Geth navigated the barbed wire at the edge of the field and stepped into a south corner of Fernlawn Cemetery, wondering if she were still being watched. Not that it mattered. If any path led out of the mess she was in, she could find it only by moving forward. She might as well do what good she could on the way.

Besides, she'd left more than yarn under Old Freedom last night, and she had to retrieve it. If it wasn't already lost.

Chapter Twenty-Five

Geth sneaked to the Holmes' small house from the rear, dodging a forest of wash hung on the line. She felt like a thief, but she wanted to avoid polite talk with Pris or her mother. The noises coming from the workshop suggested she might.

She found Aaron at work with a plane on the rim of a coffin. "Oh, hello," she said. "I thought it must be your father at work. Is he here?" She glanced around the shop, far too small for Mr. Holmes to be hiding unless he'd crawled beneath a pile of lumber, but she'd rather not stare at a casket under construction.

Aaron took a last swipe with the plane. "Hello, Geth." He ran his hand over the board to test it for smoothness. "I'm afraid he's out mending…sod. Can I help?"

"Mending? So, another theft last night?"

Aaron pulled a curl of wood from his plane and fidgeted with it. "Yes. But at least the town council has finally decided to pay for a deputy to watch here all night. It's not a nice topic, though—so what else can we talk about?" He gave her a warm smile as he flicked the wood curl away and picked up a drawing knife to continue his work.

Searching for words, Geth retrieved another wood curl from the floor as if it could tell her how to begin.

When she straightened, she realized the box Aaron smoothed was too short for a coffin. "Oh no," she said. "That's not for a child, is it?"

His smile broadened, which struck her as horrible until he finished his stroke and explained. "It is, but it's not what you think. It's a hope chest for Pris." He glanced up. "It's hope for me, too—that someday I'll be a carpenter for something other than coffins. I've already sold a few pieces. Cabinets and chests, mostly, but I'd like to make furniture, too. Sell enough to buy a few acres to farm. I know a thing or two about dirt." He winked. "But I'm not planning to dig graves forever. Want to see the lid?"

He turned to lift a slab of wood leaning against the wall. Carved swirls and a letter "P" stood out from its surface.

"Oh, that's lovely. I'm sure you'll do well. I just assumed you'd stay here." Hearing herself, she added quickly, "So many businesses run in the family, I mean." Her cheeks warmed with a blush.

He returned to his smoothing. "The council will have to find someone else when Pa gets too old. By then, I hope to have somewhere nicer to move my family."

Relieved he—for once—hadn't taken offense, Geth sank to a seat on a stack of boards. She brushed the wood curl against her cheek, struck by how something so hard as wood could also be velvety soft. She studied Aaron's face as he checked his work with a level. With his attention elsewhere, it was easier to admire the intensity of his eyes. The tiny muscles at their corners twitched as the bubble in the level settled dead center, no matter where he slid it to check. She envied his calm, his comfort in the silence. It wasn't difficult to imagine him either carving a cradle or freeing a calf from a fence. She wondered how his calloused hands might move over a muzzle or his own infant's ear.

With a start, she realized she was staring. Daydreaming, almost. She dropped her gaze to the floor. Spotting a gleam near her boot, she reached for it. A coffin nail.

"Oh. Could I have this?" When Granny Ableman had given her the horseshoe nail, the old woman had sighed, "A coffin nail would be better, but those are not easy to come by." This one might help pay Geth's debt. Even if it held as little magic as everything else Granny offered.

Aaron raised an eyebrow, then chuckled. "Go ahead. There's more in the can on that bench if you want."

Relieved of the burden of inventing an excuse, Geth slipped three more into her coat pocket before returning to her makeshift seat. The gentle smell of sawdust soothed her. She inhaled deeply and released the breath in a sigh.

Feeling Aaron's gaze, she glanced up. Sure enough, he was looking at her. His expression suggested he had all the time in the world. Instead of speaking, he lifted the lid of the chest into place to test its fit. To her, it looked perfect.

"Shall I put on a clasp that will lock, do you think?" he asked. "It's only meant for linens and such, but maybe a young woman likes a place to keep secrets?"

Geth toyed with the wood curl. "Whether they're good for her or not?"

"Not for me to say."

She summoned her courage. Blunt speech would be best. "I'm here about the grave robbers, Aaron. I overheard two men talking yesterday evening, near the gate, and I'm pretty sure that's what they were discussing."

With a look of alarm, he set down the hinge he'd picked up. "What were you doing here last night? What time?"

"Not long after sunset," she said, dodging the first part of his question. "I didn't see them, but I wanted to tell someone who might believe me. In case knowing it's two men could help. One had a gruff voice, but the other was…ordinary."

"Perhaps it was the sheriff assigning a deputy," Aaron said. "Though I didn't think they agreed to that plan until today."

"I really don't think so. They seemed to be arguing." Geth repeated as much of the broken conversation as she remembered. "And the softer voice sounded familiar, but I've racked my brain without figuring out whose it might be."

"I can't imagine you know a thief," he said. "But I'll tell the sheriff. Better say I heard them, maybe, and they ran away when I tried to get closer. Because you didn't answer my question about why you were here in the dark."

Geth studied her knuckles. She could feel Aaron's regard.

He waited a long time before coming around the half-finished chest to crouch in the sawdust near her knees. "It isn't safe, obviously," he said softly. "Is something pulling you here I can help with?"

The weight of his concern made tears rise to her throat. To distract herself, she folded the wood curl until it broke. She shook her head. "You wouldn't believe me."

Ever so gently, he drew the wood chips from her fingers. "Could we try? You can trust me to keep any secret. I'd like to help if I can. It's awful to see you so miserable."

He waited and waited. When she still couldn't speak, he sighed and rose to go back to his carpentry. "If you change your mind, anytime, I will listen. You might be surprised at what I'd believe."

Geth continued to stare at the carpet of sawdust as the scrape of his drawing knife started again. She dared to peek up. He kept his eyes on his work. The rhythm of his strokes lulled her.

"I owe you an apology," she said.

His fingertips glided over the wood. "For what?"

Geth looked around the workshop, at three colors of wood, at tools hung on a post, at a shelf piled with lead coffin fittings. The fittings murmured to her of regrets and lost chances.

"For ignoring you so long, I guess," she said. "For forgetting we were once friends. We used to have so much fun in the schoolyard. Sledding, building snowmen…"

His eyebrows twitched. "Wading the creek, playing roles—"

"Swordfights." Her smile faded. "After Poppa remarried, I got wrapped up in the changes, and then you left school…"

"And then you were being courted and going to balls on his arm. How could we still be friends?"

141

She made a face. He was right. Still, did his tone couch a faint accusation?

If so, it vanished as quickly as a passing fly. "We're friends now," he added. "No apology needed." He turned to sharpen his drawing knife with a file.

His broad, flannel-clad back made Geth feel safer. She blurted, "I'm in a terrible mess."

Aaron froze but did not turn around. "What kind?"

"I don't even know. The kind people call crazy." Geth covered her eyes with her hands, unable to continue even with his back toward her unless she couldn't see him at all. "You know how you said the Wind tells you secrets? It talks to me, too. It takes shape and prods me and won't leave me alone. Faces and whirlwinds and balloons and—"

Her voice caught. She pushed on, the sooner to finish. The sooner to suffer his judgment. "It says it wants to marry me and won't take no for an answer. I really don't know if I'm losing my wits or it's some kind of demon or God punishing me for my spite. I deserve it! I didn't know curses were real. And now—" She managed to hold back her sobs, but her breath came in gulps.

Firm fingers slipped over hers, drawing them gently down from her eyes. While she kept her lids shut, his hands closed over hers. Held them. Warm. Not soft but gentle.

"I don't think it's your wits." His voice, unexpectedly near to her face, seemed to wrap her and anchor her to the earth, to the scent of the wood, to the hard boards beneath her. He added, "But open your eyes. I have something I think I should show you. And then you can tell me exactly what's happened."

Reluctantly, Geth obeyed without meeting his gaze. Keeping one of her hands, he led her to the door of the workshop. After checking that no one outside would see them, he pulled her through the doorway and around the corner. She couldn't imagine what he wanted to show her, and her thoughts leapt from one wild guess to another, each more unlikely than the last. Some magic lantern that projected her phantom Wind, like a photoplay set loose from a nickelodeon? A cylinder talking machine that threw a voice only her ears could hear? A ghost named Wind that obeyed Aaron's summons?

They reached the back of the workshop. She stopped her thoughts cold when the guess that arose involved a quick, stolen kiss.

As if to prove that idea ludicrous, he let go of her hand and knelt at the corner of the workshop. He wiggled a loose brick in the foundation until it came free. A cavity behind it held a cigar box, which he handed to her. "Open it."

She obeyed. The box contained money, some of the bills rather large. When she looked at Aaron, confused, he put it back into its hiding place. "The Wind tells me secrets occasionally," he said. "Things that turn out to be true. Like how you recite on Beech Hill. But it mostly brings gifts. That's all been given to me on a breeze, drifting against my boots or right into my hands, while I'm working or hunting or walking somewhere. It's happened since I was my sister's age."

With the loose brick replaced, Aaron rose. "The Wind seems to like me. It's also brought chickens and game birds, a book and a hat and lots of warm clothes. And once, tickets to a circus set up at the fairgrounds."

He shrugged. "At first I just thought I was lucky. I tried to figure out where things belonged, or who lost them. I returned a few things when I did. Until one day the Wind told me to stop. Rather grumpy." He stared up at the sky. "For a while, I thought that voice must be God, but over time I figured it out." His gaze dropped to meet hers. "I started hiding the money when Pa accused me of stealing. I spend it on things we need and on furniture wood, but only when I can make up a good story about where it came from."

"Rabbit's feet?" she said.

His lips twitched. "Nettle tea, odd jobs, cabinet repair..." He grew somber again. "It sounds like the Wind fancies you, too...but not in a way that's so kind. Do you want to tell me exactly what happened? Now that you know I'll believe you?"

Geth bent close to whisper, "Can we go back inside?" She needed to hope the Wind wouldn't hear—even if the precaution turned out to be wasted.

He took her hand again on the way.

Chapter Twenty-Six

Geth arrived home out of breath. Her stepmother awaited on the parlor sofa, passing time with her darning, but she set it aside when Geth walked in. She glared up through her brows, disapproving without saying a word.

Geth handed Mamie the medicine parcel. "Why are you frowning? The druggist was busy. And I chatted a while with one of the clerks at the station. He assured me they're fine a few days without Poppa."

"That's not what I'm troubled about. You had a visitor while you were out."

Her manner sent Geth's heart to her throat. Had the Wind made demands of her stepmother, too? "Who?"

Mamie patted the sofa beside her and refused to proceed until Geth perched there.

"Eliza Ableman knocked on my door and claimed you owe her a debt. She refused to say exactly for what. I asked her to wait, but she wouldn't."

Geth gritted her teeth and tried to keep her face straight. She'd tucked a note with the bread she baked yesterday, calling it a token of faith for real payment to come. But of course, that loaf had remained in the graveyard. At least Geth had found the bone pin that morning, still lying under Old Freedom, before arriving at Aaron's workshop. She planned to return it to Granny Ableman, but it was already late. The old woman must've thought her a debt-dodger.

"I can't imagine what business you might have with that woman, considering the rumors that fly," Mamie added. "Please tell me you're not in any condition to bring shame on this family and kill your poor poppa."

"Never." Quickly Geth considered her options. Deny the whole thing? Lie about why she'd spoken to Granny Ableman? Claim privacy as a nearly grown woman? Mamie waited, her lips pinching tighter.

"I do owe her something," Geth admitted. "I didn't expect her to come here to collect." A thought struck. "But Mamie, haven't you ever noticed her at church? She's not a bad person. Just odd."

"Mmm-hmm. And?"

Geth opened her mouth but managed a partial truth only. "I heard she made tonics for female complaints." The rest was too hard to believe—but cursing a beau qualified as a female complaint, didn't it? "And I'm glad I went. She told me my mother once consulted her, too. If Mother could, why shouldn't I?"

"So that explains yesterday's stink?" As Geth nodded, Mamie added, "How big a complaint? You're not—?"

"Of course not," she said quickly. "It's been a difficult month is all."

Her stepmother took a deep breath. "I will not tell your father about this, not with him laid up in bed. But I ask two things in return."

Geth desperately hoped she could comply. "Yes?"

"One, we speak to Doctor Hillis next time. A real doctor. And two, you pay her immediately. By post, not in person. She wouldn't tell me how much you owed, or

I would've paid it to be certain she didn't come back."

Geth agreed, though she only had part of what she needed. She'd hoped to buy time with a job and put Granny off until her first pay. Instead, she'd have to give up something precious, even though its value far exceeded her debt. She could ask Mamie to loan her the amount, but the sooner her stepmother forgot the whole thing, the better.

Mamie's face softened a little. She shoved Geth off the sofa, but not unkindly. "Now go in and read to your poppa a while. You're not the only one driving me to distraction."

Her father's face lit to see Geth, and he asked her to read yesterday's newspaper to him. Geth chose a soothing selection of Mr. Whitman's poems, and eventually Poppa dozed, leaving her alone with her thoughts. Unfortunately, every time she tried to slip out, he snorted awake and asked for more verse. The afternoon waned before she escaped.

Mamie caught her as Geth headed for the front door. "Where are you going now?"

"I want to ask about a job on the candy counter at the Woolworth store." She couldn't mention a side trip to the Ableman house.

Mamie frowned. "I thought the idea about industrial school was settled."

Geth couldn't help blurting, "Are you trying to get rid of me, Mamie? Poppa said I could stay if I found something else before Monday."

Mamie sank into a chair. "Oh, my dear, is that what you think? No. My cousin might be disappointed. She's looking forward to having you visit. And it's the kind of chance I never had. But you must know you're my best company here."

Lovely. Now she'd wounded Mamie's feelings. But didn't she have feelings, too? Geth muttered, "Lately you're not acting much like you'd miss me."

Her stepmother heaved a sigh. "Lately I'm not sure I know who you are."

Geth stared at the miniatures on the mantel and wondered if her mother would say the same thing more sharply. "I also told Sarah I'd meet her when she finished work."

She'd almost forgotten that promise. Though she had no idea what she'd tell Sarah, she didn't want to let her friend down. And her appearance might nudge Mrs. Cheatham to a quicker decision.

Mamie eyed Geth while bunching her apron in her fists. "No. I'll collect Sarah later for you. She can join us for supper. How's that? You can go to the Woolworth's tomorrow. One night surely won't change their answer, and you need to spend some time here. If you don't want to help make supper, the rugs need beating, the windows need washed, and the wood really ought to be oiled."

Geth opened her mouth to protest. Mamie's face told her not to waste breath. "Fine," she said with a sigh. "I'll do rugs." The carpets weren't the only thing she'd like to whack.

Later, Mamie left to fetch Sarah but came home without her. "She couldn't join us for supper, but she promised to bring her sewing basket this evening. She said she has something to give you."

That piqued Geth's curiosity. It also made her think. She might have something to give Sarah, too.

Chapter Twenty-Seven

Sarah arrived at Geth's house after supper with her embroidery scissors in hand. "I thought I could help you pick a certain foul name from the work we did on your wedding linens," she said brightly. "Snip, snip—snip him out like a worm from a peach."

Though Mamie grimaced, Geth laughed. How could she leave such a friend, even temporarily, to go so far away as Dayton? She'd rather marry the Wind. Though she hoped, with Aaron's help, she still might escape that fate.

She ushered Sarah toward the kitchen. "Let's work by the stove. I'll go get those linens while you light a lamp." To forestall the question in Mamie's eyes, she added, "I can't seem to get warm today, but Poppa asked permission to leave bed long enough to enjoy his chair by the fire. So we'll cozy up by the stove."

Once their work sat before them and they stood alone, Sarah drew a letter out of her basket. "I wasn't sure you'd want anyone to see it, but here's a note from Mrs. Cheatham for you."

Geth's heart leaped. A job offer? She opened it quickly.

Miss Jones,

No need to return on Monday. I had dinner with my sister last night. Your name came up, as names do when one checks references. It seems you've been the talk of

Clifton School, where my niece attends. Something about stolen laundry. Perhaps schoolgirl gossip, but I can't take the chance. I have other applicants and can be selective. Perhaps another employer will be less exacting.

Sylvia Cheatham, Newhall's Industrial Drapist

Geth fought back tears.

"Bad news?" Sarah asked. "Her face made it seem likely."

Geth stuffed the letter into the stove's firebox. "Lynelle Cogglesmith has been calling me a thief all over Clifton Girl's School."

"Why would she do such a thing?"

Geth told her.

Sarah bit back a smile at the idea of flying laundry. "I'm terribly sorry you can't work with me. But don't worry. You'll find something else. Nobody else is going to lose their soup over schoolyard gossip."

"That's not the worst of it." Geth explained Poppa's plan to send her to Dayton.

For once Sarah did not have a chipper response. After a moment of slack-jawed dismay, she offered a hug and whispered, "You can tell me stories about it once you're back."

Geth plunked herself onto one of the chairs she'd moved near the stove. "I simply must find something else, fast. Never mind. I can't bear it right now. Tell me, am I still in the shop gossip, too?"

"Your fame has faded already, I'm sorry to say." Sarah picked up an embroidered pillowcase, squinted at the tips of her scissors, and snipped. "Today's talk was the consumption going around. You'll never guess who's gone to the new sanatorium."

"Who?"

"Gloria Cogglesmith."

"Will's mother?" If it were possible, Geth's heart sank even farther. Was that who'd caught the "bad air" blown by the Wind?

"I've heard you catch it from kissing." Sarah attacked the newly loose threads with her needle. "Hard to imagine of her, isn't it?"

"They also say you inherit it—oh." A thought struck Geth, one she'd searched for last night.

Sarah misunderstood. "Another way you're better off without her son, yes."

Geth stammered and shook her head to clear the thoughts piling up. Nothing Sarah could help with. She'd sort them out later.

When she glanced back up, her friend was studying her face. "I'm not seeing the laughter you promised yesterday," Sarah said. "Not that I should expect it, after that letter." Her thumb and forefinger rose threateningly. "But will you confess to me now, or should I pinch you to pieces before calling a priest?"

"You might need a blessing soon anyway," Geth said grimly. "But first, will you do something for me?" She removed a loosely tied handkerchief from her sewing basket and tucked it into Sarah's hand. "Mamie's getting strict about letting me out. Will you take this to Granny Ableman for me?"

"Ah, you want me in the gossip tomorrow." Sarah giggled before she realized Geth meant it. "Oh. Goodness." She reached for the handkerchief.

Geth tried to take it back. "You're right. I shouldn't have asked."

"No, no, I can—" They both tugged on the cloth,

which fell open. Coffin nails and the bone knitting pin spilled out, along with a note. So did Geth's silver thimble and her moonstone brooch.

Sarah picked up the bone pin. Her eyes widened. Geth bent to scoop up the nails, and both of them reached for the brooch. Geth grabbed it first. Her friend thrust the thimble into Geth's hands as well but closed her fingers on Geth's as if to help hide their contents.

"Isn't that your mother's brooch? I certainly hope the rue worked, for that price."

"It didn't. But I still owe her, and I need to pay now, before she makes things with Mamie even worse. I'm hoping she'll accept these to hold until I can give her money instead. Or if she feels she must, sell them for what she can get." Geth pulled away to hide the valuables in her handkerchief again—and to conceal her glistening eyes. Even seeing the brooch again hurt.

"Will you please tell me what's going on?"

A breeze whined through tree branches outside. That drone, once so innocent, now carried menace. Geth double knotted the handkerchief, her knuckles pale against the fabric. Sarah shifted her stool to Geth's side. Slipping her arm through Geth's elbow, she leaned against her, ensuring neither of them could easily return to needlework.

Geth stared at the grime lodged between the floor planks. At last she said, "Do you remember when we talked about joining a convent together?"

"St. Clare in Columbus. Of course. I considered it right up until Alfred proposed."

"You did?"

Nodding, Sarah nudged Geth. "But don't tell me you've signed on as a novice. I could see you as a

Mother Superior but no silent sister, and I doubt you can leapfrog the last to the first."

Geth drew a deep breath. "No. You'll think I'm crazy. I'm not. I'm not marrying God, but it may not be so different." Her voice dropped. "I think I have to marry…some kind of demon. Some spirit controlling the wind."

It took a while to overcome Sarah's disbelief and confusion as Geth laid out the fix she was in. Her friend kept suggesting a simpler explanation—a prank, a nightmare, a fever, a ventriloquist act, even a new Spiritualist trick.

Only the last idea made Geth hesitate. "Poppa says wall-rappers are charlatans. But if it's an afterlife spirit, who's the medium?"

"You? With a talent you never knew? It started in the cemetery, right?"

Geth ran the tip of her needle along her finger, leaving a scratch. Sarah's idea frightened her more than an unwanted demon. Might other dead voices start speaking to her? "What difference does it make if it's a ghost or the Wind?"

"Well…I think there's a Psalm that says the latter comes from God," Sarah mused. "So maybe it's an angel. A test of some kind, like Gabriel appearing to Mary."

"Then I should obey it." Geth stabbed her needle under a stitch to remove it. "But I can't see how I have a choice. Not if I want to keep Poppa alive. Did Gabriel steal anyone's breath?"

"Good point." Sarah turned her face to the ceiling. "An exorcism won't fix a force of nature, I suppose. A priest could handle anything else."

Geth rested her forehead on her knuckles. "An exorcism. Oh, Mrs. Cheatham would love it. But you have more faith in Pastor Duncan than I do."

"You're the one who made me think of nuns." Sarah squeezed her shoulder. "There must be some answer. You'll find it."

"I've read a few plays with trick weddings," Geth mused. "The bride hides under a veil so she's not who the groom thinks until after the vows. By then it's too late. But those tricks always turn out in the end, the bride and groom well matched after all. Not with a bride getting away. Besides, who'd wear a veil to be mistaken for me?"

"Hmm." Sarah pulled at her lip. "A witch might like to marry the wind. Easier to ride a broom through the night, I would think. Have you asked Granny Ableman?"

Geth snorted. "Ha. No. And she did not volunteer. But if she's a witch, she isn't a good one."

"I suppose not." Sarah took the knotted kerchief, which still sat in Geth's lap. "But I might ask her when I take care of that errand for you."

"Maybe she'll tell you I'm losing my mind. Which do you think would be worse—being locked in a madhouse or an unholy marriage?"

"Hmm. Maybe the madhouse. Did you read Nellie Bly's story about the one she sneaked into? But those can't be your only choices." She stuffed her scissors and needle and one pillowcase into her basket. "I'd better get home, but I'll take this to do in the evenings. And I'll think hard about how to help. You consider telling Pastor Duncan. Will you?"

Geth promised, but she imagined every soul in her

church looking at her as though she were possessed—
and avoiding Mamie and Poppa as well, to be safe.
Witches might not be tied to stakes anymore, but
shunning burned, too.

As she lay awake that night, she decided she'd
rather become Mrs. Wind. It felt inevitable. A snide
twist in her stomach said she couldn't do better
anyhow. The note from Mrs. Cheatham seemed like one
more reminder—Geth was too improper, too ill-fitting,
too *something* to become any gentleman's darling. The
Wind wanted her, though. No one needed to know of
her unholy match. She'd look like a spinster. Granny
Ableman managed all right, didn't she?

She comforted herself with a small silver lining—
Gethsemane Wind sounded better than Gethsemane
Cogglesmith. Gethsemane Breeze had more melody
yet, but she couldn't grow friendly with such a
frightening force.

Then again, she'd heard whispers about more than
one man seen beating his children or wife. Except for
the whispers, no one treated such brutes any different—
not even their children and wives. Apparently people
got used to whatever they faced.

Including industrial school?

Geth threw off her covers and felt her way to her
linens box. The program from the Rose City Theater
still rested on top. She riffled its pages, unable to see
them but catching a shiver of the excitement sparked
last time she'd looked.

She didn't want to sew linings for coffins anyway.
The drapist's job simply sounded more likely than her
real goal. Could she skip that half-step and approach
Mrs. Augusta Morton directly?

She had little to lose. If she could borrow it briefly, she could show the cape she made Pris as a sample. But how could she find a woman she didn't know before Poppa sent her off on a train to Dayton?

She crawled back into bed. Maybe an idea would come in her sleep.

Perhaps the Wind could direct her. Put that hissing voice to good use.

Turning over, she pondered another voice and the realization jogged loose by Sarah's gossip—the familiar voice in the cemetery reminded her something of Will's. It wasn't his, she was sure. But it might've belonged to his older brother. She'd only met Randolph twice, but their similar tenors had struck her.

She couldn't tell anyone. Even if she'd been certain, no one would believe it. Especially not coming from her. The idea that a Cogglesmith might be digging up graves was too much.

Of course, so was the idea of marrying the Wind.

Chapter Twenty-Eight

Moments after Geth stepped into the outhouse the next morning, something large bumped it. She gripped the edge of the seat as if her hands could keep the outhouse upright. Hadn't the neighbor boys grown out of this prank?

The bumping continued.

"Stop!" Geth cried. Maybe boys weren't to blame. Was the Wind so immature? Her marriage might be even worse than she thought.

A voice jeered through a knothole. "Pull up your drawers and pull down your blouse, come out with a leap or I'll tip your outhouse."

Geth laughed, recognizing the voice. "I'd like to see you try it," she called. "Unless you've got an ox with you."

She opened the door to find a smirking Sarah who said, "I wanted to start your day with a laugh."

"Says the girl who thinks one day of becoming a nun and steals into back gardens the next. Laugh accomplished. But don't you have work?"

"Yes, which is why I've got to be quick." She thrust the knotted handkerchief into Geth's hands. "I rose early to do that errand for you. She took the pin back, and the note and the nails, but said your debt was already paid. Yesterday."

"By whom?"

"She wouldn't say. I thought you must know."

Geth looked into the sky. The weather was still. "Maybe the Wind blew money to her?" It helped Aaron that way. But why pay for advice meant to free her from it?

The answer clicked into place. "Oh. I did tell someone else I owed her. Do you remember Aaron Holmes from school?"

"Spooky Holmes? Goodness, why? Was he there at her house, selling gruesome things for her cauldron?"

"Oh, ha, I'd forgotten that nickname. Poor Aaron, he's not like that. I run into him at Fernlawn sometimes."

Sarah pouted. "So you told him before you told me? I'm insulted." She stuck out her lip with exaggeration, but hurt glimmered under the jest.

Geth slipped her arm around Sarah. "Be glad you don't have a grave there to visit," she said gently. "You're my dearest friend, Sarah. Don't think you're not. But you're always at work. Am I allowed other friends?"

Sarah's eyes narrowed. "Friends? Is that all? Is he still good-looking, or spookier than before?"

Rolling her eyes was the safest reply, but Geth hesitated too long. Sarah pounced. "Aha. Fine. Throw me over for a square jaw and shoulders. Here I thought you were broken-hearted. You've moved on like grass through a spring-pastured horse." As Geth hushed her, she sobered. "But a gravedigger, Geth? You might as well walk out with a railroad tramp. I can't imagine your father approves."

Her words made Geth wince, even though her reaction when Aaron first asked her to tea had been similar. "Did you miss how the fruit of one of town's finer families nearly left me on the church steps?" she said. "There's your tramp, I submit. But it isn't like that. It's complicated."

"Complicated. Mm-hmm. I expect more, my friend, but I'll be docked if I'm late." Sarah kissed Geth's cheek quickly and trotted toward the gate. "But see? You should've let me help sooner. It's barely dawn, and we've already mended one problem. As for the other—I asked Granny Ableman if she wanted your place."

"Shh." With a glance at the kitchen window, Geth hurried after Sarah to ensure she kept her voice down. "And?"

"She told me the Wind can't be fooled by a veil. It's a power of sensation and sound, not of sight."

That made sense. Geth sighed. "It was never more than a wishful idea."

"But we'll fix that up, too," Sarah said. "You wait."

In the silence left by her absence, Geth stepped uneasily back into the outhouse. She didn't want to be indebted to Aaron—no more than to the old woman. If he'd paid, he shouldn't have. Not without speaking to her.

Once she finished what she'd come to the outhouse to do, she whispered into the rustling boughs of the plum tree. "That wasn't you who sent money to Granny Ableman, was it?"

Neither the plum tree nor the air stirring it answered. How quickly she'd come to believe it might do so! As Geth returned indoors, she spared a moment of wonder—she'd expected a reply from a tree.

But that moment didn't linger. Will's departure shocked her in part because everything she'd believed about him had proven wrong. Along with a few things she'd believed of herself. Since then, the world had grown even more puzzling, more threatening—and more thrilling, too. She had no idea what might happen next.

Terrified but enthralled, she'd never felt more alive—or closer to utter disaster. Those feelings seemed one and the same.

Chapter Twenty-Nine

Geth spent part of the morning flipping through her mother's Bible, looking for verses about casting out demons. Jesus made it look easy, handling it in two or three lines of verse. She doubted Pastor Duncan worked with such efficiency.

As she'd hoped, however, when she showed no interest in leaving the house, Mamie loosened the reins.

"Are you still set on trying Woolworth's today?" she asked Geth. When Geth said yes, Mamie added, "Shoo that crow off the porch when you go, then. Before it leaves droppings for us to scrub off."

Geth had noticed the crow bobbing on the porch rail through the window that morning, but only when she stepped out did she see something caught in its beak. At her motion, the bird fluttered down from the railing. After two stilt-legged hops toward her, it opened its beak. A scrap of dirty fabric fell out. The crow cawed and flapped off.

The bit of ripped cloth tangled around something metallic. Geth pinched the cloth and raised it for a better look. A silver ring set with a large purple stone dangled there.

The Wind whispered, *With this ring, I thee will wed.*

Geth flinched, flinging the scrap away by instinct. It tumbled across the porch, the ring clunking—but then the fabric whisked into the air back to her, flopping against her skirt.

"*You asked for a ring. Please accept. I insist.*"

Reluctantly, Geth picked up the cloth again. She hadn't expected the Wind to meet this demand. "You startled me, that's all." She worked the ring out of the tangle. Though the amethyst's prongs were encrusted with dirt, the ring looked costly, no mere trinket. In another time or place, she'd have admired it.

"*Put it on.*"

Clamping her teeth, Geth slid it onto her middle finger. It fit loosely.

"*It favors your hand. But is that the correct place to wear it?*" asked the Wind.

"It's too big for my ring finger. Besides, we're not married yet." That battle was probably already lost, but her stubbornness wouldn't be silenced.

"*Before noon on Sunday. As you agreed.*"

"Two days," she mumbled. Could anything happen in that time to save her?

"*Will your friend attend you?*" asked the Wind. "*The one you spoke with this morning? You've told her of me, have you not?*"

Geth bit her lip, unwilling to say Sarah's name. If the eavesdropping Wind knew about Sarah, she might not be any safer than Poppa. "I don't know."

She stepped hastily off the porch. As though she could escape.

"*Invite her. She may not hear me, but she can bear witness. Our union need not be secret. Your choice.*"

She turned down the street. "We'll see. I'm done talking now, if you please. Your business occupies you? So does mine."

With a chuckle, the Wind tweaked her earlobe. "*Very well. Until later, mistress.*"

"Oh, wait." She'd nearly forgotten. "Do you know Mrs. Morton? Augusta Morton, that is. A seamstress of renown, I believe?"

"*I know every human. And eventually, their secrets. And I sometimes spread the renown.*"

Geth tried not to look avid. "Can you tell me where she lives?"

"*You have business with someone of renown you can't find?*" the Wind teased.

She thought quickly. If she must be bound to this thing, the more she knew about it, the better. "My wedding dress needs an adjustment I can't make myself." Could the Wind hear a lie?

"*Mmmm.*" Geth couldn't tell if that murmur held doubt or approval. "*That busy woman keeps to her brick house most days. Wisely.*"

Geth wrinkled her nose. Bricks fronted half the houses in town. "An address? A street name, at least?"

"*I pay small attention to human labels—petty divisions and counts, most of them. Near the feet of the tower of water. Which despises being imprisoned, you know. Shall I accompany you to guide you?*"

"No, no. I'll find her."

The postmaster must know. Or most anyone near the water tower, which stood just off Evans Street. Rising nearly one hundred and sixty feet, it gave the fancy new homes built well south of the levee good pressure despite their distance from the river. She refused to ponder the Wind's other comment. She didn't want to know about unhappy water.

"That helps, thank you," she said. "You can leave."

"*I'll blow you sweet nothings until we speak again.*"

"Please don't." But a slight tickle at Geth's neck and a sense of departure implied the Wind had already left.

As she waited on the streetcar platform, the ring felt loud on her finger. She wanted to take it off but feared the Wind's reaction. Instead she twisted it so the stone faced toward her palm, where no one could notice and ask about it. Later she'd hang it around her neck on a ribbon, easily hidden under her dress, on the excuse it might otherwise slip off her finger.

It took some asking to find Mrs. Morton. Two men scowled and brushed past her without a reply. Each time she inquired, whether answered with an ignorant shrug or hasty directions, Geth grew more apprehensive. When she reached the house that must be correct, halfway down an unfamiliar block, she stood across the street a long while to summon her nerve.

At last she shook herself. "For heaven's sake," she muttered to herself. "Act One, Scene One. Outside a house. The heroine strides to the knocker and raps."

As she approached the porch, the door opened and a curly-haired gentleman stepped out, still settling his hat on his head. Bounding down the porch steps, he stopped short when he saw Geth in his path.

"Good day, sir," she said, performing in a play of her own. "Is this where I might find Mrs. Augusta Morton, seamstress to the stars?"

He gave Geth an unsubtle look up and down. She stared him right in the eye to counter his rudeness.

He smirked like a boy caught with a frog in his pocket. "That it is, lovely, but the scenery's fresher out here." He tipped his hat and stepped around her to go on his way.

Before she found a response, a gust of wind knocked his hat from his head.

He chased the hat as it tumbled. "Argh. Cursed wind," he muttered.

Geth couldn't resist. "On the contrary. I have it on good authority, sir. The Wind does the cursing, not the other way 'round." With an impertinent smile, she turned her back to glide toward the door.

A woman now stood in the still-open doorway. "I'm Mrs. Morton. How may I help you?"

Geth had expected a working-class woman, with pins stuck in her collar and a tailor's tape for a necklace—a more artistic cousin of Mrs. Cheatham, perhaps. No. This stately lady was impeccably dressed, complete with a hat over her greying hair and a bearing that belied experience as a dancer. She was also, however, a member of Amity's colored community. Geth often chatted with the train station's porters, laughing at insights about her father they shared, but the dark face on the stoop caught her off guard.

Surprise kept her gaping for only a moment. She hurried forward. "I—Forgive me for appearing with no introduction, but I saw a notice in a theater program. I think. Are you seeking an apprentice? Like me, I mean?"

She should've stopped there, but her tongue took control, spilling words that didn't appear on her script. "I'd love to sew costumes, or help with fittings, or hem, or—or anything you do for the theater, really. Even tidy your workroom, or iron, if you need it. I can bring a work sample—"

Mrs. Morton raised a brown hand to stop her. "What is your name, Miss…?"

Geth told her, hoping the rumors hadn't gotten this far. Did gossip cross the race lines in town more readily than most friendships did?

"Well, Miss Jones, let us see. The sass you just offered one of my loyal clients may have disqualified you." Mrs. Morton's full lips fought a smile. "Cyrus pitched a look at you over his shoulder that gives me to believe he'd know you if he saw you again. How the man would react if he did, I can't say."

The lady's tone was not unkind, but Geth crumpled. "Oh, I—that wasn't sass, was it? I'm so sorry, I didn't mean…" Her voice died. Cyrus. Not Cyrus Ray, the businessman who made photoplays right here in town? That's what Will told her once, anyhow. Photoplay actors might need special costumes…and appreciate talent wherever they found it.

Had the Wind ruined this for her, too? She'd never have opened her mouth if the man's hat hadn't soared.

She peered down the street. He'd passed out of sight. "I'll apologize to him. Which way did he go? I'm quick, I can catch him—"

"Save your sorries, Miss Jones. It's no matter. I'm afraid you're too late." Mrs. Morton plucked a stray thread from her skirt and released it to the now-gentle breeze. "I'm well set for apprentices, thank you."

Geth watched the thread drift to the dirt. "Oh. I see. Well. I wish I'd come sooner…"

The woman's gaze cut from the thread to Geth's face. "Your…enthusiasm commends you, but I don't see a place for you here."

Geth took her meaning. As much as she longed to,

she could not disagree. She managed a weak smile. "I suppose not. Thank you for your time. And...and your work." Geth had pinned so many hopes on this chance she hardly knew how to turn and go home. Mrs. Morton helped by nodding smartly and closing the door in her face.

Geth walked slowly away. Her ears rung. She imagined the knots Poppa would've tied himself into if she'd run home to announce she'd found the perfect job. And oh, by the way, she'd report to a Negress. Her father took pride in his fairness and his Anti-Mob Committee, but it likely did not stretch that far. Not in a town whose last lynching happened only five years ago.

"You might've warned me," she murmured, more to herself than the Wind. She'd have tried just the same but made a better impression, with more time to plot how to persuade her father.

Busy elsewhere, perhaps, the Wind didn't answer. But a reply of her own struck her. If the Wind's power drew mostly on sensation and sound, as Granny suggested, could it even tell the difference between shades of skin? Surely it overheard talk on the topic, but that didn't mean it took note otherwise. It heard and felt, sensed direction, knew many things, and perhaps enjoyed senses people did not. But without eyes, how much could it see?

Geth let the beat of her own footsteps numb her. She'd answer that question soon enough, she supposed. By asking her husband. Light wedding night chat.

Once back in the business district, she stopped in the F. W. Woolworth's, where she bought a length of ribbon before leaving again without asking about work. She might as well simply make Poppa happy by attending industrial school. Keeping books probably paid better than selling wine gums. And the train ride to Dayton surely would be the only wedding trip she'd ever receive.

There seemed no point in visiting Pastor Duncan, either. She couldn't imagine how to start, what to say. Could she order an exorcism like a roast from the butcher? Asking for herself—and not a family member vomiting nails—seemed too rational for anyone possessed by a demon.

Geth had nearly returned home, her steps slowing, when something large dropped from a tree into her path. Startled, she recoiled. "Do you always have to be so dramatic?"

But the vast swoop of blue wasn't caused by the Wind.

Chapter Thirty

Pris Holmes straightened where she'd landed and brushed twigs off her new cape. "I'm sorry," she said. "I wanted to glide like a flying squirrel in my cape. Anyway, I thought you liked it when we were dramatic at school?"

Geth recovered her balance to walk forward again. "Oh, Pris. I thought you were…someone else."

"Who?"

"Never mind. Did you glide?"

Pris twirled her cape as she fell in beside Geth. "Not very well. But I was waiting for you anyway."

"For me? Why?"

Pris handed her a folded note, written in carpenter's pencil on a scrap of butcher's wrap.

I have an idea. If you're brave. But I'm not sure I should say it aloud. Meet me at the pond on Moss Lane and I'll show you. Let Pris know what time you can come. Aaron.

Geth refolded the note, feeling the girl's gaze.

"Will you do it?" Pris asked.

Geth cast her a sidelong glance. "Does that mean you read it?"

Pris squirmed, but her act wasn't convincing. "I hoped for a love note, but you don't look sweet on it."

"Priscilla Holmes, your brother and I are old schoolmates. Nothing more. As a matter of fact, I'm

169

unhappy with him at the moment."

The girl studied the roadside for a few paces. "Because of the witch money?"

"You know about that?"

"I took it to her." Pris jumped over a pile of horse droppings. "She gave me a dried plum."

Geth opened her mouth to protest before remembering that she needn't discuss her private business with a nine-year-old girl. "Then I'm not too happy with you, either." She walked on, leaving Pris.

"Why not?" Pris called. When Geth didn't answer, she added, "But what should I tell him about the note?"

Geth halted to stare at her boots without turning back. She needed all the help and ideas she could get. "Yes," she said at last, directing her words more to the ground than over her shoulder. But she could feel Pris, who'd crept up to hover behind her. "Within the hour." Then Geth stepped away quickly, tucking the note into her sleeve. The handwriting felt scandalous there—but comforting, too.

Even the words "if you're brave" in the note weren't enough to tamp down a warm glow. She'd almost forgotten how hope felt.

That was the only reason for her anticipation, of course. Wasn't it?

She sat on a log near the pond, dampness soaking into her dress, for what felt like a long time before Aaron approached. When she spied him, he put a finger to his lips. No one, not even a deer, lurked nearby, but she nodded. She harbored the same suspicion about who might overhear.

When he came closer, she spied a school slate in his hand. He passed her log and gestured her nearer the water's edge, where he crouched and slipped the slate into the water. Keeping it under the surface, he tilted it for her to read as he wrote on it. She had to bend over his shoulder.

Maybe only two places Wind can't reach. 1) Underwater.

She nodded. He flipped the slate over.

Alarmed at the second place he spelled out, Geth drew back. "How does that help?"

"Shh. Wait." He reached in with a slate sponge and scrubbed both sides clean, splattering pondwater before writing more quickly. The water muffled the slate pencil's awful scratching.

She read as words formed. Nothing he wrote reassured her. "Aaron, no. I'm not that brave."

He kept writing, but Geth turned away to slump onto the log. She should've known meeting him only wasted time.

When he realized she'd stopped watching, he deflated and erased the slate again before joining her on the log.

"I appreciate you trying," she said. "I really do. But the day after tomorrow, I'll marry the Wind. It won't be much different than aging into a spinster."

Aaron watched water drip off his slate. "Is that what you want? Or just what you think you deserve?"

"Neither. I just don't have a choice."

He looked up. "There's always a choice. Will showed you that, didn't he?"

Wounded, Geth gaped. "That was uncalled for."

"It's exactly what's called for. You're making the exact same mistake."

Geth stood to leave in a huff, but Aaron caught her

sleeve. "Don't get me wrong. Will was cowardly toward you, and what's more, a fool. Any man's a fool to turn away from your spark—other than one who's afraid you'll be stronger." He rose so his eyes could connect with hers better. "Only weaklings resent strength in anyone else. That's why Will ran away, and half the town knows it. He saw he'd never be able to tame you."

His words were honest. Too honest, as usual. Geth pretended not to hear all he said. Not to hear his—No. Sympathy, that's all it was. She soundly dismissed anything more in his tone. Anything too big. Too frightening. It struck somewhere too raw.

Not trusting herself, she tried to be flip. "So you're an expert on the living as well as the dead?"

"Don't believe me? Then you don't know what folks think of Will. Oh, he's smart. I'm sure he's much smarter than me, and I don't mean book learning. He's canny. He'll probably end up a judge. But he has to be canny, because beneath that, he's scared. Scared he can't live up to his father and scared he'll never escape his big brother's shadow." His voice dropped to a murmur. "He's even more scared than you."

She jerked her sleeve from his grip. "Stop. Enough."

"No, it's not." He slapped his slate on his thigh. "Why can't you see you're better than that, better than a life with a bag of hot air—a simpering law clerk or a whirlwind of leaves? You keep taking the deals you get without fighting for what you deserve. Let alone want."

Geth crossed her arms to contain an impulse to strike him. "If you knew me as well as you think, you'd know I'd be angry about you paying my debt."

He looked away, sheepish. "Oh, I knew you'd be mad. That's why I didn't ask. But the Wind caused the debt. It's only fair the Wind's money paid it."

His boyish shame softened her heart, but she growled, "I'll replace it as soon as I can. I don't want to be in your debt."

"I wish you'd be in my debt more. I wish—" He caught himself, shaking his head. "Think about my idea. It's worth trying. What's to lose?"

"Everything, if something goes wrong. Including your family's livelihood, maybe. I told you, I'm not that brave."

They scowled at each other.

Relenting first, Geth touched his arm. "Honestly, Aaron. I appreciate you trying to help. I do. I just— Your father wasn't choked breathless. Mine was. If it keeps him safe…" She lifted a shoulder, forced a wan smile, and turned toward home.

She got a half-dozen steps before he trotted after to stop her. "Wait. Another idea. It might make the first one look better." Holding his slate so she couldn't see while he wrote, he scratched and scratched before turning it toward her.

If you were already married, the Wind couldn't. Taken.

Geth made an impatient noise. "Well yes, I suppose, but who do you suggest? Unless our cowardly Will's had a wild change of heart and is folded up in your pocket?"

Aaron held her gaze for a moment too long before looking away. "Never mind."

Oh. That was stupid of her. Geth closed her eyes, torn between an apology, a laugh, a list of objections, and "Yes, please." None seemed correct.

"Go home, Aaron," she said gently at last. "And thank you. I'll sleep on all your ideas, I promise."

The amethyst ring, swaying on the ribbon she'd bought, tickled her chest as she turned toward home. Pressing her hand to her throat to stop it, she spied a tower of black clouds rolling toward town. A distant growl of thunder promised an early and uneasy night.

Chapter Thirty-One

Wrath of God?
FREAK FUNNEL CLOUD
RIPS STEEPLE FROM CHURCH.
No injuries reported.

Amity, OH—Heaven seemed to express displeasure with one of town's largest churches yesterday evening just past 7 p.m., when a funnel cloud descended without warning to tear the steeple from the First Lutheran Church of Christ the Redeemer on High Street. In a stroke of mercy, no one was injured, although the pastor and a local girl cowered in the building throughout.

"The roar was overwhelming," reported Pastor Ernest Duncan, who has served at the church for six years. He and a parishioner took cover under a pew when they heard roof tiles smash. "We're just grateful the green glass windows were spared."

Although many citizens noted the evening's storm clouds, no reports of rain or damage elsewhere have been received. At press time, the steeple had not been found in any nearby fields, but Duncan expressed hope that some portions might be discovered in repairable condition. He

has canceled tomorrow's services but said the
damage should be covered with canvas by next
Sunday. When asked about plans to get his flock
back in the Lord's good graces, the pastor
offered no comment.

Geth dropped the paper on the breakfast table. "Whew. I wonder who the 'local girl' is." Maybe she wasn't the only person the Wind was trying to blackmail.

"Terrible, isn't it?" Mamie said. "And shame on the reporter for making it sound like God's work."

Geth took her bowl and spoon to the washbasin, her oatmeal mush barely touched. "Mamie, you can't blame the devil for everything bad while still claiming God is in charge." Her own faith in the latter had weakened considerably lately.

Mamie spooned sugar into her tea. "Of course I can. He works in mysterious ways. Including allowing Satan to test us." Her spoon clinked in her cup. "I suppose we can sleep in tomorrow. But perhaps the time should be spent taking up a collection to fund the repair."

Geth jumped on the idea. "Why wait? Shall I go door-knocking to the neighbors right now?"

Mamie gave her an arch look. "Some other Samaritan can do that, I think. I don't know why you're suddenly so eager to get out of the house, but I'll not make misbehavior easy for you. I owe that much to your father."

Geth said, "I know you care, Mamie, truly, but can I remind you I should've been a wife in charge of my own life by now? I'm too old to be grounded."

Mamie sipped her tea primly. "You were childish enough Monday to sneak away while I used the outhouse."

Monday—a lifetime ago. Geth dried her bowl in silence before announcing, "I'm going up to my cell. Let me know when the solitary confinement's repealed."

Mamie sighed.

Once in her bedchamber, Geth dragged her chair to the window, which she opened to lean on the sill. Partly she hoped to hear from the Wind. If not, the sharp notes of the cardinals might help her think more clearly about yesterday's conversation with Aaron.

Before long, the murmur of the breeze became a more meaningful croon. "*Where is your ring, my sweet mistress?*"

The air stroked her fingers. She drew the ribbon from her bodice and explained.

"*It can be adjusted to fit, can it not? Tell me the price and I'll get it for you.*"

She folded her arms. "You took the steeple off my church, didn't you?"

"*I didn't hurt your friend or the man she spoke with. You see how I care about you?*"

Startled, Geth searched the air for a place to focus her anger. "My friend?"

A male cardinal fluttered from a nearby tree to the roof over the porch below her window. It recovered its balance, tottering, as though it hadn't expected the move. The bird was as good a direction to face as any, and the Wind's voice shifted as if the bird were speaking. "*The one who came to you yesterday. The one you call Sarah.*"

Geth gasped. Sarah—the "local girl" in the paper? The terror in the church last night gained new meaning. "You eavesdropped on her?"

"She spoke about you. I meant to show her more strength than any ritual performed by your man of the church. I've enjoyed centuries of exorcisms. Most are little more than make-believe games. So you both can stop wasting your time."

The cardinal bobbed nervously, eyes darting under Geth's glare. Taking pity on the bird, Geth shifted her scowl to her window ledge. She wished her friend hadn't said anything to the pastor but was grateful no one got hurt.

"You can let this bird go, if you brought it for me," she grumbled. "It seems you hear my thoughts."

The cardinal flew. *"I don't need to,"* the Wind murmured smugly. *"I've been studying humans since they began forming words. Your breathing, your gestures—even your smells give you away. And I've grown fond of a few before you. But your lives are tragically short."*

Geth made a face. In addition to marrying some inhuman spirit, she'd be the latest in a line of consorts.

"You're the one I want now, though," added the Wind. *"Will we marry in your church under a blue sky tomorrow? I wouldn't dream of bringing us rain."*

She couldn't tell if the Wind might be teasing, but the church was never more than an attempt to delay, and Pastor Duncan probably thought she was crazy. "Hardly. I suppose Beech Hill will do."

She banged down the sash. Careful to hide the ring back inside her dress, she headed downstairs. "Mamie," she called. "I just remembered that last night Sarah mentioning an appointment with Pastor Duncan. She might've been the 'local girl' in the paper! I'm going to make sure she's all right."

Her stepmother met her near the base of the stairs. "I certainly hope not. But you can't go just yet."

Geth grabbed her coat. "I'm not asking, Mamie. Sarah's my dearest friend."

"That's not what I mean. There's someone at the front door for you."

Her tone halted Geth. She'd seen nobody come down the street—but she hadn't focused beyond the cardinal.

Mamie nodded grimly. "Make it short, keep it quiet, and remember your father's recuperating."

Geth hurried through the front room, expecting to find the door open. It wasn't. Was Aaron outside, too dirty to set foot indoors? Pris would've come to the back door, where she sometimes brought eggs, and Mamie invited most everyone else in.

She swung the door open. The visitor stood on the porch, shorter and far more wizened than Aaron Holmes.

Chapter Thirty-Two

Geth exclaimed, "Granny Ableman! I'm sorry my stepmother kept you out in the cold."

The old woman grinned. "You might as well join me, my dear. It's plain she'd rather not welcome the likes of me into her house."

Forced to agree, Geth stepped forward. She lurched as the door caught behind her.

"Oh, no you don't." Mamie's hand halted the door. "The door fell to, that's all. The frame's out of square. Come sit, both of you, while I put on the kettle." She rolled an eye at Geth, who would rather talk on the porch. In private.

Geth caught Granny Ableman's eye and pressed a finger to her lips, hoping the old woman found some discretion. Granny winked and waltzed past to a seat on the sofa. The tension zinging through Geth stopped her from sitting. To take control, she asked, "Is anything wrong? My debt's paid in full, I believe."

"Indeed, and my thanks. I like people who pay with cash money." Granny fingered the doily on a parlor table. "Lovely bit of lace, isn't this? Like a bridal veil, nearly?" She shot Geth a sharp look. "If the Wind caught it just right?"

A clank from the kitchen did not fool Geth. She leaned her temple against the side of Poppa's book cabinet as if the best, safest words could seep through the wood to her. "I suppose it is. Every debt must come due, mustn't it? Whether we like it or not. Bad things happen when we…don't do the honorable thing."

Granny nodded. "Mmm." Her wrinkled lips pursed. "A good reason to be careful when making new vows. Rely on an advisor to sort through the words."

Geth gave her a quizzical look as Mamie bustled in with three teacups and a pot on a tray.

Addressing Mamie, Granny said, "Ah, tea. I've done many things in my years, yes I have. Healing, midwifery, advice for the lovelorn, and all with particular teas to apply. But would you believe I've married new couples, too?"

Geth imagined Granny Ableman conducting her vows. "Oh?" She didn't like to picture a ceremony. But she'd best start preparing herself.

Granny rambled on. "I don't know a wedding tea, but I might invent one. Weddings happen somewhere most every day, don't they?" Her eyes darted around Mamie to Geth. "I'd hate for a nice girl to make a second mistake."

Mamie frowned as she set out the cups. "Do you refer to my stepdaughter's broken engagement? Please don't. The subject is painful."

"Oh, shame on me. And shame on a cursed engagement, hee hee." Granny put her empty cup to her lips to stop her giggles. It didn't work. She blew hard on the cup's rim as if to cool it. "I'm sure the tea will be hot, when it gets here. Where's a cooling breeze *engaged* these days, eh? When you need it?"

Geth hoped she was following the hints properly. "Beech Hill, I think. It's usually breezy up there. I'd try wedding tea, if there is such a thing. It sounds nice for a

181

Sunday morning, perhaps."

"Not more of that smelly brew you gave her before." Mamie covered the other two cups with her hands as if Granny Ableman held a steaming pot ready to pour. "Not Sunday or ever. We'd have to refuse any more tea, I believe."

Granny cocked one eyebrow at Geth. "Yes, tea today is quite enough, surely? And an honor for me. By my witness. But no vows to obey. Hah!"

The kettle whistled in the kitchen. Mamie didn't move. Her eyes darted between Geth and Granny Ableman as though she suspected they were up to no good but could not pin it down.

Geth pointed to the kitchen. "Shall I—?"

"Yes." Mamie watched her go.

Geth fetched the kettle quickly. When she returned, Mamie perched on the edge of her chair, her head tipped toward Granny. The two women murmured.

"—not a bad girl, but—" Mamie broke off, straightening.

"Wild oats," declared Granny. "They sprout in all fields but come to nothing. You'll see. Don't spread 'em by trampling them. They'll just go to seed."

Mamie nodded. "You're probably right."

Granny held her cup out toward Geth. "Of course I'm right. Tea."

Geth poured water from the kettle into the teapot. "It hasn't steeped yet." As steam rose, she added, "What more can I get you, Miss Ableman? For your…tea, I mean. Sugar, cream—nothing more?" She hoped the woman didn't expect another payment for whatever came Sunday but couldn't figure a more direct way to ask.

"Nothing, nothing. I take my tea black, thank you. Strong. Like four nails." She winked.

Soon Mamie poured from the teapot, and they sipped, suddenly quiet. Geth wove a vision of an unholy wedding where she repeated lines fed her by a two-penny witch. She'd assumed her vows with the Wind, if she made them, need be little more than "I do." Capitulation.

But now that she thought about it, many brides repeated long promises—want or wealth, sickness or health, obey and forsake and submit. Nothing she wanted to say. Afterward, a wedding night with a loquacious draft, cut off forever from love. But maybe Granny could defend her from some detail of commitment even worse than the one she'd already backed into.

The lump in Geth's throat kept her from swallowing her tea. Aaron's daunting idea might warrant a second look. Maybe even his offhand proposal. That'd put an end to industrial school.

It might also put an end to her father. How could she anger the Wind?

Granny drained her cup and clacked it onto its saucer. "Pleasure. Now I must be away."

"But why did you come?" Mamie asked. "How can we help you?"

Granny shook her head as she stood. "Nothing more, nothing more. Just making a call. I'll likely see you on Sunday. In church or out. Church bells, fire bells, wedding bells, hah! Someone may need me down the road, too. Marriage grows tiresome, eyes stray, hearts cool." She nudged Mamie. "Even good men lose vigor. You wouldn't be the first to ask for my help."

183

Mamie bristled. "I hardly think anyone needs that kind of help."

Geth mashed a smile between her lips, sure the old woman provoked Mamie on purpose. She couldn't help a begrudging respect.

"Time will tell if it's true." Granny moved toward the door. Geth leaped to show her out and watched her hobble away. Then she clung to the door, faint with smothered tension and the effort of speaking to Granny in riddles.

"Close the door and good riddance." Mamie gathered the tea service with movements so brisk they threatened the china. "You said she was odd, but batty's more like it. I couldn't make heads or tails of half what she said."

"Christian charity, Mamie. Remember the steeple. It might be a sign we need humbling."

Mamie's prickly demeanor collapsed. "You're right. But I do hope she won't come again."

"Me, too. Now I'm off to make sure Sarah's not horribly shaken. I promise to bring you a report." Geth left before Mamie could object.

Sarah only worked until noon on Saturdays, so Geth didn't have long to wait before workers spilled out of the shop. She asked the first woman she caught whether Sarah had come to work that morning.

"Oh yes, she'll be along." If the shop chatter today revolved around Sarah or exorcisms, the woman gave no indication to Geth.

Her friend appeared soon after. Geth rushed to greet her. "I'm glad you're all right. Were you at church last night?"

"Shh." With a haunted look on her face, Sarah

pulled Geth from the crowd. "Nobody knows. I didn't want questions about it. Let's get away from so many ears." They hurried down the street toward Sarah's house, one of many small homes clustered like mushrooms on town's boggy east side.

A block later, Sarah asked, "How did you guess?"

Geth shook her head. "I didn't. The steeple thief told me." She arched an eyebrow. "You didn't think that was a coincidence, did you? You asked about exorcism without telling me first?"

"I know, I shouldn't have. I'm sorry." Sarah glanced to be sure nobody overheard them. Nobody human, at least. "I thought it might ease your mind if Pastor Duncan agreed to do it in secret. I never imagined—well. I suppose we got lucky. It was terrifying. It's been hard to act normal all morning."

Geth wrapped her arms around her friend, who trembled. "I'm sorry I dragged you into this. Now you see what I'm up against, though. What did he say?"

Sarah shook her head and resumed walking, keeping her voice low. Geth had to lean in to hear. "Nothing that made sense to me. It sounded like a train crashed through the wall to turn us both into mush."

"No, not the Wind. Pastor Duncan, I mean. Did he believe what you said about me?"

Sarah grimaced. "I didn't get far or even mention the Wind. When I told him I had a friend with a problem, he said he knew of only one authentic possession in the last forty years—and I should speak to the doctor, who could fix hysteria better."

Geth didn't know whether to laugh or get angry. "Did the roof blowing away change his mind?"

"You could ask him, but I doubt it." Sarah

shrugged. "I'm your best friend, and I barely believed it. Until I crouched under a pew while Pastor Duncan begged God to take the altar or organ, not him." She forced a smile. "So much for his faith in Heaven. I take it back, though—don't ask him about it. Next time a tornado might wreck the whole block."

Geth sighed. "I know. I don't want anyone hurt."

They continued in silence until Sarah said, "Will you go through with it, then?"

Geth took a while to answer. The nearer a wedding drew, the more torn she felt. Left without a choice, she still hated to submit without a fight.

"Would you do something for me?" she asked at last. Her neck crawled as though someone were watching. "I can't say it aloud." She put her lips to Sarah's ear, cupping one hand to catch any leaked sound. "Aaron has this idea," she whispered. "Will you come with me to see him? Help me decide if it's mad?"

Sarah nodded. They changed course without words.

Yesterday the idea sounded awful. Outlandish. Today, with the church missing its steeple and a crone musing Geth's wedding vows, Aaron's idea felt like her only hope.

Chapter Thirty-Three

Working out the details of Aaron's idea took forever as they wrote out key words, which they couldn't say aloud lest the Wind overhear. It went faster when Geth suggested they sneak into the school to use the big blackboard and chalk. Every student knew of the broken lock on one window. Only the teachers wondered how rude drawings appeared on their boards between the end of one school day and the beginning of the next.

Skulking around the outside of the school, they confirmed no one had repaired the bad lock. Aaron shoved up the sash and quickly climbed through before helping to pull Geth and Sarah inside. They ducked into the first classroom with chalk on the rail of the blackboard. The three soon grew accustomed to deciphering half-written phrases, choosing words carefully, and speaking in broken chunks to save time.

As they all stood together with chalk on their hands, Geth said again and again, "Oh, I don't know. What if—?" Then the classroom fell silent again but for scratching chalk, the swish of an eraser, and the occasional groan in reaction. No laughs.

By the time they climbed back outside, Geth's friends had persuaded her to try the idea. But first she and Sarah had to weave a story for Mamie that would allow Geth to remain out all night.

The plot put Sarah in high spirits. Of course, she had the easiest role. Once they left Aaron, she teased Geth. "I think it's kind of romantic," she said. "Like the play we read in school a few years back. Remember?"

Geth groaned. "Sarah, I'm nervous enough as it is." *The Most Excellent and Lamentable Tragedy of Romeo and Juliet* did not turn out so well. She stopped walking. "I can still change my mind. And I should. Too big a risk." Their plot might rouse the Wind's fury.

Sarah pulled Geth on their way. "Ooh, I'm sorry. Bad example. Come on." She lowered her voice. "Aaron was right when he said…you know. The whole rest of your life. It's worth trying for…a play with a happier ending."

Geth grumbled, "It'll have to end differently, since Aaron is not—" She mouthed "Romeo."

Sarah gave her a sly look. "No? He'd be if you let him, I think. This is a risk for him, too."

"Yesterday you compared him to a railroad tramp."

"Yesterday I didn't know how his muscles have grown. He could definitely carry you over a threshold."

Flushing, Geth dismissed that idea with a wave. Then she paused to watch a boy play with a whirligig, blowing on it to make the arms spin.

An idea formed. "Sarah," she said slowly. "Do you still have that kite?"

Her friend nodded. "I hung it on my wall for the memories. We had such fun with it."

"Will it fly, do you think?"

Sarah studied her face, trying to guess Geth's intent. "I suppose so."

For now, Geth only nodded. They could pick up the kite later.

When they arrived at Geth's house, Sarah persuaded Mamie to let Geth spend the night at the Brannon home with her. "If you knew my nightmares last night!" Sarah exclaimed. "Feeling Geth beside me will help me forget the threat of a roof crashing down on my head."

While Sarah recounted hiding under the pew, Geth collected a few things in a small carpetbag—not because she needed them but for the charade. She also helped herself to her stepmother's sleeping tonic, tucking a few crystals into a handkerchief. They might help shorten a daunting night.

If she got that far. A lot needed to go smoothly first.

****

By mid-afternoon, she and Sarah climbed Beech Hill where they took turns, one holding Sarah's old kite while the other ran down the slope, trying to pull it aloft. The Wind didn't help. The air lay too still for flight.

Finally Geth took the kite while addressing the sky. "Don't you want to come play? Come amuse yourself with us. Take our kite, or…or brush back my hair. And I want to introduce Sarah. She'll attend at our wedding."

Sarah's gaze darted as if she expected a tiger to bound up the slope.

Geth waved the kite gently, not trying to launch it. She began singing, inventing words about a kite too lonely to fly.

Shortly, the Wind lifted the kite from her hands, jerking at the string Sarah held.

Sarah squeaked. "Oh!" String spooled out. The kite

189

ascended to the end of its leash, where it danced figure-eights by itself. Geth finished her song and went quiet.

"*Here I am,*" said the Wind in the burr of the kite's jittering paper. "*You see how I came when you called? But I already know Sarah.*"

Sarah's eyes grew round.

"Do you hear?" Geth asked her.

"I heard my name. That's enough." She shoved the string spindle into Geth's hands to clutch her and crowd close.

"*Sing more,*" said the Wind. "*I'll amuse you with your kite.*"

Geth repeated a verse while the kite switched to loop-de-loop antics. The string sometimes slackened, but the kite never fell.

"That's amazing," breathed Sarah. "You could win contests."

"*Sometimes I do,*" said the Wind, a bit smug. Sarah stiffened. Geth could tell she'd heard at least part of that answer.

"You enjoy playing children's games, don't you?" Geth asked. "Kites, balloons, whirligigs."

"*Don't you?*" said the Wind. "*Don't all humans?*"

"Sometimes. In fact…" Geth took a deep breath. She'd get only one chance. "I wonder if you're good at another game. My favorite. Hide and seek. Do you know it?"

"*Of course. It's too easy. There's no place you can go where I cannot find you.*"

"You may know where I am, but can you follow to tag me?" Geth's voice held a challenge. "I can think of at least one place you can't go."

"*There's nowhere I cannot reach, including your*"

lungs. I showed you that with your father."

"You can't follow me into my dreams."

The Wind huffed without words. Sarah looked nervously between Geth and the kite.

Geth took a chance for a taunt. "Do you even know what dreams are, since the Wind never sleeps? Or is that something you can't understand?"

"*You don't truly leave when you sleep. And I can rouse you from those dreams, if I like. That's the same.*" Geth heard a new note in the voice—petulance.

"No, it's not." Geth dismissed the argument with a wave. "And that's just one example. I bet I can find a few more."

"*What? Tell me.*"

"Let's play the game instead. Do you know the rules? I'll make you a wager on it. Sarah can attest to it for us."

The Wind's chuckle sounded forced. "*You will lose. But what wager?*"

Geth dared not hope. Had she found a weakness?

"The one who is 'it' cannot watch while the other players hide, you know. So you must leave town between now and sunset. Attend business elsewhere. No cheating."

"Right. No cheating," Sarah warned.

Geth's courage failed as quickly as it arrived, and she ducked as if expecting the kite to land on her head.

"*I won't need to cheat, lovelies. What wager?*"

Geth pursed her lips as if considering. "Hmm. If I can hide well enough that you can't find me by dawn, our marriage tomorrow is off. You forfeit."

The Wind dropped the kite to rollick around her and Sarah, tugging hair and skirts. Arms thrown over her head, Sarah crouched against Geth who calmly reeled in string.

Agitated breezes fluttered about them. "*You already agreed and accepted my ring. So what do I get when I win? I will find you.*"

Geth shrugged, feigning a lack of concern. "If you win, we'll marry at sunup without further protest. I'll sing or recite for you daily—and make up a ballad about you so good others will sing it, too. I promise. With Sarah as my witness."

Sarah slowly straightened. "I'll sing it."

The Wind told Geth, "*That's small gain for me. You owe it already.*"

"You think so? You're mistaken. Here are the stakes we can play for. If you won't, I vow silence for the rest of my life. Like a Cistercian nun. Ask Sarah—we once talked of similar vows. You can steal my breath, but you can't drag my voice out of me. Not if I choose to stay silent."

The Wind stilled.

"Oh," Sarah murmured. "I hope you know what you're doing."

A small cyclone kicked up before them, a frustrated knot in the dust. "*You can't. You'll forget. Speak to Sarah, your family. Would you abandon their fellowship to spite me?*"

"I can talk to them in writing. A thing you can't feel or hear. You're the only one for whom I'd truly be silent."

Holding her breath, Geth exchanged glances with Sarah. Was she wrong? If the Wind knew the messages they swapped in the classroom, it also knew where she intended to hide and the thinking behind Aaron's original plan. He had written in chalk, "Would you still marry Will if he came back, asked?" At the obvious answer, he added, "If you don't appear for your wedding, Wind can't find you, it'll be humiliated. Who wants a wife who embarrassed her groom and might again?"

"Wind could still insist," she'd replied, her chalk squealing.

"Could. But what's to lose?"

Lives, Geth feared, if she made it too angry. Tornadoes could wipe entire towns off the map. But the Wind also claimed to care about honor. If it agreed to a bet, the risk of disaster might shrink.

Now, on Beech Hill, she marveled at the silence. The longer the Wind didn't answer, the more her confidence grew. "Do we have a wager?" she prodded. "Will we play this game?"

"*You will lose.*"

"So be it. At least I have a chance, which is more fair than never speaking to me until you could blackmail me. More fair than not naming the price of a curse until after I cast one."

The Wind whipped around them. Geth and Sarah clutched each other for balance.

"*I resent how you question my honor,*" it growled. "*I spoke to you before, many times. I cheered your verses and sang harmony with your songs. You never listened. I spoke the morning you mention, in fact. I soothed you and celebrated your lucky escape from an unworthy beau. Your ears were too full of your own convictions to hear. Your heart too certain no audience appreciated you, too sure you deserved what you got. Too deluded you knew the whole world and what's possible in it. I took up your curse to surprise you, to show you how little you understand.*"

The words made Geth bow her head. They struck home.

"*And what about your honor?*" it added. "*Will you finally live up to your words if I win?*"

She closed her eyes against the weight of her future. "Yes. I promise."

Sarah squeezed her hand.

"*Then I bid you adieu, per your rules,*" said the Wind. "*The sooner to find you again.*"

"Not before sunset," Geth reminded it. But she recognized now when the Wind left—how much thinner the air felt. A subtle change in its warmth. And a lightness at the back of her scalp that told her someone or something no longer watched.

"Is it gone?" Sarah whispered. When Geth nodded, her friend dropped to the grass. "Heaven preserve us. Every time I thought, oh, you're a convincing actress, spinning an imaginary world on a stage, I caught a few words. Or felt its pestering hands. How do you stand there so calmly?"

Geth grimaced. "Practice, I suppose. Let's go. Before—"

She stopped herself. The wager might turn out to be fruitless. Their whole plan might fail. But regardless, she'd saved herself many unpleasant hours. She didn't want to suggest the Wind could still change its mind. Who knew how far her words reverberated?

Chapter Thirty-Four

"You're early," Aaron said, when Geth appeared at the door of the Holmes family's workshop, her carpetbag in hand. "What happened?"

She ducked inside and gestured for something to write on, which she scribbled on quickly to explain the wager.

He nodded. "Good."

"Maybe," she whispered, wishing to be invisible. As she hurried across the cemetery, the air had felt eerily still, the breathlessness before a storm. But even with a shawl wrapped over her head, she'd never felt so conspicuous. "This way we'll know sooner. By dawn."

He took the carpenter's pencil and below her lines wrote, "Wouldn't keep your threat to go mute, would you?"

Grimly, she nodded. She might as well practice.

He regarded her, his lips poised as if to argue. Shaking that off, he raised a hand to tell her to wait. He slipped out the door and returned with a wheelbarrow, bouncing it over the sill. A wadded canvas filled the barrow.

He pivoted the barrow to face the doorway. "I'm afraid this is the best I can do for a chariot. But it's a common sight, if anyone's watching." He lifted the canvas and extended his other hand to help her climb in. "You won't have to hunker beneath for long."

Geth winced. "What else has that canvas draped?"

Aaron faltered. "I cleaned it as best I could." He flashed a wan smile. "Pretend we're practicing for a race at the fair?"

Geth abandoned cautious words. "Can't I walk? If the Wind cheats, if it's watching and listening now, I'm already doomed."

"It doesn't need to cheat," Aaron said softly. "If it commands the birds like you said, they can point out the last place they saw you. Here. Better if they don't see where we go now. Anyway, you need something to sit on and keep off the chill."

Geth cast about for a more pleasant idea. Like his sister's hope chest, which looked nearly finished. Hiding in a box with a happy future appealed, but she couldn't fold up that small. Besides, the extra weight would make things harder for Aaron.

With a sigh, she sat in the barrow, drawing up her legs to curl tight over the carpetbag on her lap. He drew the canvas over her gently, but the scent of dirt filled her nostrils.

"Stay still," he advised. "I'd hate for a spill."

She knocked her knuckles against the barrow to answer, unwilling to think about their destination. The other place Aaron thought the Wind couldn't follow—a grave.

Not in the ground. She wasn't *that* brave. He'd suggested that first, in their chalkboard session at the school, with some notion of a bellows and tubing contraption to allow her to breathe. When she refused and pointed out the Wind could follow her breath, he'd posed a back-up idea—the Martinson tomb. The descendants of one of Amity's founding industrialists owned a family mausoleum as large as a chapel. It sat in the cemetery's choicest location, surrounded by yews. Aaron could get the key.

"When a Martinson dies, carry new coffin in, they don't want to see dust on the last one," he'd written on the chalkboard that day in a shorthand version of speech. "I go in, wipe up. Air like swamp gas at first. Proves Wind can't get in. But after aired, door shut again, has good air to breathe. Long enough."

"How do you know that?" Sarah wondered aloud.

"Stole key. Spent night on a dare," Aaron wrote. "With Ben Houk. We were thirteen."

"I told you he deserved the name Spooky," Sarah crowed.

In the classroom that day, it felt like a prank that, while daunting, might pay off. When the Wind took Geth's bet, she felt success within reach. But now, as she bounced in a barrow like an oversized pumpkin, the plan sounded like torture. She resisted the urge to fling off the canvas and call it off only because of the risk Aaron was taking. If one of the Martinsons found out, his father might lose his job—and the family their house. If Aaron could stay so determined for her, she owed him her very best try.

The trip across the lumpy grass and gravel paths of the cemetery took an eternity. The barrow bounced harder as Aaron sped up. Its rattle didn't drown out a shout. "Aaron."

Geth knew that voice, even muffled by canvas.

Pris yelled, "Aaron, wait up." Running feet.

"I'm busy!" he yelled. In a murmur, he added, "Don't move." The barrow came to a halt, but he did not set it down.

His sister arrived, breathing hard enough for Geth to hear her. "Whatcha doing? What's that?"

"What do you care? You don't do any work around here." Geth cringed at the unfamiliar edge in his voice.

"Oof, don't bite my head off," Pris said. "I just wondered. You got the keyring in your pocket? I need the oil can from the shed. My wagon wheel squeaks."

Geth heard his hesitation, so Pris probably did, too. "Did you look on the hook? Where it belongs?"

"It's not there. I figured you had it."

"Pa must, then. I don't."

"I asked him already."

"Maybe it's lost," Aaron growled. "Or ask Ma. Or look on my workbench. Maybe I left it there. Now let me get something done, will you? Get lost."

Pris didn't reply, but Geth imagined her face. The girl must have obeyed silently. The barrow moved again.

"It figures," he muttered. "Bad timing."

Geth wanted to suggest he'd been harsh but didn't dare let words escape the canvas.

"Don't worry, I'll make it up to her soon," Aaron added. "Before she sets Pa in a panic."

After a long rumble, the barrow stopped again, followed by the scrape of a door against stone. Even without sight, Geth knew they'd reached the mausoleum. Its shadow felt cool through the canvas. When the barrow tilted again, its wheel rolled smoothly, and the chill deepened. An eternal winter lingered within the walls of the vault.

When the motion ended once more, she started to brush aside the canvas.

"No," murmured Aaron. "Not yet."

The door scraped again. She heard the scratch of a matchstick.

Aaron lifted the canvas away. "All right now." He held a lit oil lamp. Its wobbling flame threw more shadows than light, and the sick, sweet scent of decay laced the musty air.

"Sorry," he said. "I couldn't leave the door gaping. But I aired it as long as I could earlier." Outside, the afternoon felt unusually still, but the air here seemed weighted, cold and thick on Geth's skin. Drawing breath felt like dragging dirt into her chest.

She darted a glance to each side. The corners of the vault swallowed much of the lamp's brightness. Shadowy niches or shelves lined the wall. Most bore coffins, but a few held darkness instead, symbols of deaths in the future.

Aaron offered a hand and helped her out of the barrow. "Try not to look. Watch me instead." He pulled out the canvas and plumped it into a pile on the stone floor. He reached into one of the unoccupied niches and removed a jar of water, a sweater, and an apple.

"I thought these might help." He placed them at the edge of the canvas with the lamp and a tin of matches.

Distracted, Geth tried not to stare at a wet leak along the base of a coffin. "Thank you. I brought Mamie's sleeping tonic. To make the night shorter. But now that I'm here, I'm scared to take it. Did you really fall asleep here with Ben?"

He sank to the canvas. "We both did. You can, too. Here." Still holding her hand, he pulled her down alongside him. "Nothing here can hurt you." His eyes locked on hers. "I'll take a long watch tonight. I'll come by more than once and tap a stick on the door. If you tap back three times, I'll let you out. But you're brave. You won't need to. Stay quiet instead. The Wind won't find you here, I don't think. Will Sarah distract it?"

Geth nodded. "She's going to sneak to the church after dark and pretend to speak to me like I'm hiding under the altar or in the sacristy. Or in the churchyard, if she can't get inside. She may not fool the Wind, but it can't hurt."

"So you'll win the bet. I'll be here when the sun rises to help hold the Wind to its word."

Geth struggled to keep her nervous eyes on his face. "Why are you risking so much to help me, Aaron?"

His steady gaze pulled at her until she could return it. She realized abruptly he still held her hand. "Do I really need to say it?"

She blushed and looked into her lap.

"I will if you want. If it'll help you feel braver." He squeezed her fingers. "I'd like a chance to be the one you marry, Geth. I know that's a long way from what you might want, but I'm sure I'm not the only one. You deserve a loving husband, not a sly twist of air. I'm fighting the Wind for whoever's lucky enough to win you. And just hoping that man might be me."

Geth abruptly found it harder to breathe. Some answer seemed called for, but the leap in her heart did not come with words—only joy and an equal measure of terror.

At last she said, "You're always so honest. It's…unnerving, Aaron."

"Maybe you got too used to someone who wasn't."

She looked up at him. "Maybe I did." She might've been that truth-skirting person herself—a girl who only expressed how she felt by pretending to be someone else. Frank graveyard candor was better. More pure.

As they gazed at each other, a heat spread through Geth to chase off the vault's chill. She wished to keep that warmth with her—to keep *him* with her. But someone had to open the door from outside. As it stood ajar now, a crack of light glowed where Aaron could grip the edge to pull it open for himself. That crack of light must close tight before sunset. Without crushing a truth he'd revealed for her.

He raised his free hand to trace her cheek with the tip of one finger. "I have to go," he murmured, the words more distant than the sparks his touch left on her skin. It raised the hair on her neck. "Before Pa misses me. But take your tonic, Geth. Sleep. I'll be back before you know it, with morning."

He released her hand and rose. "You can win this, Geth. You're stronger than you realize."

She trembled from the cold, Aaron's presence, or both. "Girls aren't supposed to be strong," she replied. "People don't like it."

"Not the people who matter," he countered. "And the Wind clearly agrees. But hush now. Hold your breath, maybe, while I open the door. Or duck under the edge of the canvas. Just in case."

Careful not to upset the lamp, she pulled the canvas over her head but peeked out.

His fingertips pried at the door. For an instant she feared they'd be trapped there together. The idea held a strange attraction. But the heavy door shifted.

She stopped peeking, unwilling to watch him leave. It would feel like he was going forever.

From beneath the canvas, she heard, "Whatever

happens—you make me proud to help."

The barrow rattled as he pulled it outside, then the door grated again. It shut with a thud like eternity falling. Geth huddled under the canvas a while. The close warmth of her exhaled breath smelled better than the odor of rot. The rough canvas beat sitting alone with the dead.

At a sudden image of the lamp flame igniting the canvas, however, she threw it off fast. The vault looked smaller, not larger, without Aaron in it. She pulled his sweater into her lap to give herself something cheerful to see. Not a sound from outside seeped through to her ears—no bird chirp, horseshoe clop, or roar from a train. She almost missed the sound of the Wind.

But not quite.

Hearing her heartbeat like never before, she wrapped herself in a second shawl from her bag and toppled prone on the canvas, Aaron's sweater nestled under her cheek. Comforted by the boyish smell of it, she gripped the match tin in one fist so she couldn't possibly lose it, drew the lamp closer beside her, and blew out the flame to begin her long wait.

Aaron's gaze, and his electric touch on her face, returned more than once in the dark.

Chapter Thirty-Five

Time didn't pass for the dead. Geth had surely turned thirty, a spinster entombed, before she heard a slight tap on the door. She resisted the urge to leap up and pound to get out. The tap sounded so much like a stick or branch blown against the door that she suspected the Wind of a trick.

Hours later, she waited for another comforting tap. She wanted to tap back, just once. To show she still lived. To connect with Aaron outside. To prove she existed there, living and warm, more than simply part of the darkness.

No second tap came. To pass time, she recited poems and monologues in a whisper, filling the shadows with imagined words. She lit the lamp once before blowing it out, simply to ensure she hadn't gone blind. She struggled to get used to the absolute darkness—blacker than moonless nights, blacker than sleep. Stars and flashes appeared in her eyes, so desperate to see they invented sights for her.

Mamie's sleeping tonic no longer appealed. She was too terrified she'd never wake up, that swallowing it would be the last thing she did. After a while, the stink stopped insulting her nose, and she had to tell herself the air didn't grow more stale with each breath. But it did. Had the vault aired long enough? Would relighting the flame burn her last chance to inhale? Her death grip on the match tin, and sometimes the lamp, became the one sensation that kept her from screaming.

That, plus the fuzz of Aaron's sweater.

She imagined herself growing old there, older than Granny Ableman. Older than death. A mummy like the one displayed at the county fair, shriveled and gaunt and no longer human. Her fingers ran over her arms to remind herself it wasn't true. She pictured Poppa and Mamie, surely dead now and buried beside Mother's grave, not far away and yet out of reach. Sarah, married and gray with a grown brood around her, telling them stories on spooky nights of a friend who vanished one evening never to be seen again. Aaron, dear Aaron, who forgot about her, earned fame as a carpenter, sent his sister to college, and fell for some lucky student he met on a visit. Geth would have been better off marrying the Wind. At least then she still could have friends.

Without her realizing it, these daydreams lulled her to sleep. She woke with a start at a bang on the door. Over and over, *bam-bam*. No tap. Shouts rolled outside. She fumbled the lamp and broke a match without striking a flame.

The door ground open. The glare of morning sunlight dazzled her but was immediately blocked by a man shoving in past the door. A thin one. Not Aaron. Geth skittered backward off the canvas like a frightened spider. The effort made her gasp before a rush of fresh air underscored how labored her breathing had grown. Blinded and blinking, she wobbled to her feet.

The skinny male figure proved to be Aaron's father. "Mercy on his soul, what's he done to you, girl?" He reached for her.

She recoiled. "Where's Aaron?"

"No, Pa, it ain't like that!" Pris followed her father into the doorway. "It can't be."

"You hush and go home," he ordered. "This is nothing suited for you." Turning back to Geth, he softened his voice. "You all right, Miss Jones? Please say you are. Did he lure you here? Hurt you? You can tell me, by God. I'd take a horsewhip to him sooner than I'd turn a blind eye to any harm he's done you."

"Oh, I—I'm fine, Mr. Holmes, really. Aaron's done nothing wrong. Nothing like what you must think." As her shock wore off, Geth bent to the floor, gathering shreds of composure with her shawls and Aaron's sweater. Her joints felt stiff from her night on the stone, but she moved as fast as she could, stuffing the lot into her bag.

"What in Kingdom Come are you doing here, then?" He whirled on Pris. "And how did you know? I was fixing to tan you for lying. But this…"

"I'm afraid, uh…a prank?" Geth replied.

"Told you, Pa," said Pris at the same moment. "Aaron grabbed me before they took him and told me to make you open it. Somehow." She smirked at Geth. "I knew he was up to jakes yesterday."

"The sun's up, then?" Geth moved toward the door to see for herself before fully hearing the girl's words. Her instant of victory fading, she stared at Pris. "What do you mean, 'took him'?"

"He got arrested this morning. Before daybreak. Maybe an hour ago." Pris glared at her father. "Took me that long to sway Pa."

"Arrested? For what?" Geth pushed out past Pris. He must be out there, laughing, enlisting his family for a joke at her expense.

He wasn't. She gaped for some explanation—had the Martinsons discovered the trespass?—as his father dragged out the canvas and lamp.

"Arrested for robbing graves," he growled. "Which I called nonsense an hour ago. If Aaron wanted to steal from the dead, including their bones to sell to some school, he's smart enough to do it before the casket gets buried so he doesn't have to dig it up in the dark and rebury the durned thing again the next day. Now I find you here, I've got to wonder. What else don't I know about my son's doings?"

Geth's mind still churned over two words—robbing graves. "But that's silly," she said. "Did they have evidence?" Neither of the voices she'd overheard in the dark cemetery belonged to Aaron. Of that she was certain.

"Got a tip, said the sheriff. When he banged on our door with deputies and handcuffs this morning." Mr. Holmes eyed his daughter before shutting the vault door and turning the key in the lock. "Kinda like another tip to check the Martinson vault." He turned a sour look on them both.

"I'm sorry, Mr. Holmes. I know this was wrong. I can't explain, really. Not so you'd believe it. But don't blame Aaron. Please. It's my fault, not his." Even her worry about his arrest couldn't quench a small thrill—the Wind hadn't found her. The trees shook enough in a light morning breeze to assure her it stirred not far away. Those branches probably trembled with fury.

She took his arm. "He's helped me more than you know," she added. "Please, think first of him. You can yell at me later. We need to free Aaron."

"And how do you figure to do that?" His father's

concern quickly curdled to anger, though not directed at her. He flung down the canvas. "I can't pay a lawyer. I can only hope the sheriff finally adds two and two and gets some number other than five. Half the nights we were robbed, Aaron sat up watching with me, but a father doesn't make a good alibi."

A suspicion began to form in Geth's thoughts, planted by the shuddering leaves. Anxious to test it, she released Mr. Holmes's elbow to stuff her carpetbag more firmly under her arm.

"Let me talk to my father," she said. "He'll know how to approach the sheriff. And help Aaron." She gathered her skirts in her free hand and ran before he could object.

Chapter Thirty-Six

As soon as she left Pris and her father behind, Geth
tipped her face to the sky. "I won!" she cried. "You
couldn't find me. Admit it. No wedding. We
outsmarted you. And I know you must be listening."

She waited, expecting a tantrum—a whirlwind of
dust, a gust knocking her down, an uprooted tree falling
on her. When nothing interrupted the lovely spring
birdsong, she added, "Don't be a sore loser. We still
can be friends. You've said things that sound like—
well, like you're lonely."

The sigh of the breeze sounded forlorn. Against her
better judgment, empathy welled within her.

"I wouldn't mind reciting for you now and then,"
she offered. "Just not as your wife."

A low hoot swelled around her. "*Whooo...Who
outsmarted who?*"

Her empathy dwindled. "You had something to do
with Aaron's arrest, didn't you?"

"*Why would I care about human crimes?*" But a
chuckle followed the words.

"What did you do?" When no answer came, she
tried provocation. "Frustrated, were you? Or jealous.
Poor thing. Or trying to spite me?" A thought occurred
to Geth that hadn't before. "Wait. You must know who
the thieves are. Don't you?"

"*Few things escape my notice,*" said the Wind

airily. "*Whether worthy of interest or not.*"

She stopped. "Would you tell me?"

At last the Wind became visible for her, a maple seed pod spinning like a wheel in her path. "*What would you do for me if I did?*"

Geth ignored the answer that rose in her heart. She had to think carefully first. What good would it do her to know? Who'd believe her, and why? Poppa offered more likely help. Especially since the Wind apparently took a role in getting Aaron locked up. "A tip" for the sheriff, indeed. A disembodied voice from the shadows, perhaps, or a buzz that seemed to come over a telephone line but hissed directly into an ear.

"Never mind," she said. "We'll have time for that later. I wanted you to acknowledge I won our bet."

"*Perhaps the game's over. Perhaps not.*" The seed pod fell to the ground.

Geth headed to Sarah's house first. Her friend would be anxious. Wouldn't she? While in the vault, Geth imagined Sarah outside at daybreak to greet her. A needle of disappointment rose inside her now. Why hadn't her friend come? What if Pris hadn't prevailed without help? Geth might have suffocated to lie dead once the door finally opened.

She banished that thought. Sarah had planned to stay up half the night trying to mislead the Wind. Maybe her father caught her sneaking out. Geth would be lucky if she knocked on the door and Sarah's parents didn't chase her away.

Her worries proved wildly wrong. Sarah's whole family stood in their yard while two men helped her father upright a carriage that had crashed through their porch rail and into their house. The crumpled carriage listed, with one wheel broken. Glass and splintered wood littered the ground.

Sarah spied Geth and hurried to meet her. "You're out. Did it find you?"

As Geth shook her head, Sarah lowered her voice. "I was dressing to come, and then this. Before sunrise." She gestured at the commotion. "I couldn't find an excuse. I'm so glad you're safe I might lick you like a poodle. And you did it! Despite my visions of you smothering in there. Was it awful?"

"Yes. But it worked. Did the horses run wild?" The pair seemed calm enough now, loosed from their traces. No blood. One of Sarah's brothers held their bridles.

"Yes." Sarah nodded. "They spooked out of nowhere, it seems. At least no one was inside, and the driver not badly hurt. Our poor house, though. I'm grateful none of us sleeps in the front."

Geth moaned. "This is my fault."

Her friend smacked her arm. "The whole world doesn't spin around you, you know. Accidents happen."

"But you're not the only one. Aaron's in jail."

Sarah frowned. "For what?"

"Robbing graves. That's the Wind's work. I could tell by its laugh. If it wasn't for Pris, I'd still be with the dead." She shuddered, offered a brief explanation before adding, "I bet the Wind spooked the horses this morning. To punish you for helping me."

Growing pale, Sarah gripped Geth's arm. "I thought it already had. I wasn't going to say anything, but it trapped me in the church last evening for hours— the front door wouldn't budge, and the side doors were locked. When the pastor came around to lock up before bed, he told me the sign had blown against the door.

Jammed it. The Wind taunted me all the way home."

Geth hugged her. "I'm so sorry."

"It was a badge of honor last night," Sarah replied. "But this—my family…"

"I know. I've got to stop this."

They watched the men drag the disabled carriage to the side of the road, where it awaited repair or a wagon to haul it away. Sarah's mother prodded her home's broken siding where a strip of wallpaper curled through.

Geth kissed Sarah's cheek and turned to leave. "Don't worry," she said. "I know what I need to do."

"Don't do anything rash. You won the bet."

Geth clenched the handle of her carpetbag as if it were a weapon. "Not the battle, though. Not just yet."

"Wait." Sarah grabbed her. "So Aaron doesn't know you're out? He must be frantic."

Geth bit her lip. "I'm not sure. He told Pris—"

"But what if their father hadn't listened to her? Can we get word to him, do you think?"

"I don't know. I'm hoping Poppa will go with me to speak to the sheriff."

Sarah wrinkled her nose. "Might only be deputies working on Sunday. And a cell full of drunkards. Poor Aaron—can a visitor see him, do you think?"

"I'm hardly acquainted with the rules at the jail." Hearing the snap in her voice, Geth caught her temper. "Sorry."

"No, no, me either. Listen. You get your father. Meanwhile, I'll try the jail. If nothing else, I can shout outside the windows."

"Don't you get arrested, too."

Sarah's eyes lit. "That sounds like a challenge.

Let's leave together. I'll tell my mother you came to invite me to that church near your house, since the service at Redeemer was canceled. And you'll loan us some quilts to keep out the draft until the damage is fixed. Can you spare some?"

"Of course. But don't you need to stay and help with the mess?"

"That's what brothers are for. I'll make a cork out of quilts. With your help."

Geth hung back while Sarah fibbed to her mother. She regretted the way she'd corrupted her friend—never mind Sarah's delight at the sport.

The pair stayed together only until they reached the street that led to the jail. In way of goodbye, Sarah mused, "If I were an actress like you, I'd play a crime victim and shout, 'Geth is free' once inside."

"Don't. They'll lock you up as a madwoman. Or drunk. Is lying to a deputy a crime? I'm not sure I should let you go."

Sarah giggled. "I can't act well enough. But I have other charms. And a few tricks I can use."

Geth took her hands. "I'm afraid of that, too. Please, Sarah. I can't stand if this gets any worse. I'd rather have Aaron worried, but safe, than put you in more danger as well."

"Pfft. You don't have enough faith in me. I won't do anything foolish, I promise. Just coddle some deputy's ego to make him my hero. You wait."

"Don't do anything the Wind can take advantage of, either."

Sarah grew thoughtful. "Yes, good point. I'll try."

After they parted, Geth fretted. How could she stop the Wind from venting its rage? She didn't think reason would work. It wouldn't even answer her now. She called several times. No response.

Something about Sarah's last words stuck with her. Wasn't everyone the hero of their own life and story?

There might be a story Geth could still weave to gain the upper hand with the Wind.

Chapter Thirty-Seven

Geth found Poppa teetering on a stepladder in front of the house, nailing planks over the parlor window.

He heard her footsteps and glanced over his shoulder, threatening to topple the ladder. "Ah, Geth. I feel better you're here. It's so strange." He finished pounding a nail. "Somebody shot out the window last night, along with the one in the kitchen. The hooligan's bullet burst in here and out there. That's how it appears, anyhow. We did not hear the shot, just the shatter of glass. Thank goodness we lay snug in bed."

Geth knew better the cause of the damage but let her father place blame where he would.

Mamie appeared at the side yard with another plank. "We nearly leapt from our skins at the clatter but couldn't properly fix anything before daylight." She peered back the way Geth had come. "You're home before I expected. Did you and Sarah fall out?"

"No. You'll never believe what happened." Geth told them about the carriage accident. She'd never dare to invent such a story but recounted Sarah's as though she were there. "I came home to ask if we can loan them some quilts."

"Of course. Though we may need a few for ourselves while we keep the fire roaring until the glazier arrives. But she didn't come with you to get them?"

Geth pinched herself for not foreseeing that question. "She'll come once the mess is cleaned up. Or I'll drop them off later. But guess what else, Poppa? Sarah's brother had news—Aaron Holmes got arrested. For the graveyard thefts. Can you imagine a more ridiculous charge?"

Mamie rested her plank within Poppa's reach. "It's about time they caught someone."

"Mamie, how could you? He's not guilty, of course. Why go to so much trouble when he and his father could wait until the last mourner left and take what they wanted before filling the grave? With no one the wiser. Why make extra work for themselves?"

Her father set another nail. "The criminal mind is not always wise." His hammer banged.

"Balderdash," Geth replied. "He's my friend. I know he's not guilty. Please, Poppa. Won't you speak to the sheriff with me?"

Poppa chortled. "And say what? You're the better detective? Did gossip keep you and Sarah awake all night long? You're delirious, darling. Or in shock from the accident. Go inside to bed."

"Or make yourself useful, at least," Mamie added. "Hold this for him while I get the next."

Geth lifted the new plank for her father. "I could vouch for his character," she insisted through the hammering. "And don't they have to say what the evidence is?"

"Not to anyone but a judge." *Bang.* Poppa scowled. "Should I be alarmed you believe you know this person so well?"

"Don't be silly. We spent years in school together, and he lives just down the road. Of course I know him."

"Hmm."

It took twenty minutes of pleading and at least that many nails, but once planks concealed both window frames, Poppa gave in. "It won't accomplish a thing, except annoying the sheriff on a Sunday morning at home," he said. "But I don't mind annoying him slightly. You have a point about the logic of this incarceration, on a matter that should've been solved long ago. He may need a reminder of the next election."

Geth threw her arms around him to thank him. She'd threatened to visit the sheriff alone but had no idea where he lived and no reason to hope for the Wind's help this time.

"Are you sure you're up to it?" Mamie asked. "You're only just out of bed after your asthma attack."

"You didn't mind when you wanted windows boarded up, Mrs. Jones."

Mamie huffed, but Geth and her father soon went on their way.

When they arrived on his porch, Sheriff Cornell made clear his door would've shut in her face if she'd appeared by herself. Instead, he begrudgingly invited them in. They sat in his well-furnished parlor, Geth alongside her father on a low sofa while the sheriff held court from the tallest chair in the room.

"Let's keep it brief," he told them. "I don't like to mar the Sabbath with my work, and I've already done much this morning."

Poppa smiled. "I wasn't aware the criminal set took Sundays off." Geth worried he might enjoy himself too much, their visit doing Aaron more harm than good.

But Sheriff Cornell returned a thin smirk, perhaps accustomed to political sparring. "For all the success of its industrialists, Amity remains small enough for its sheriff to welcome his neighbors. Correct? So what can I do for you folks this fine day?"

Geth explained what she'd heard about Aaron's arrest. "His family said you got a tip. From whom, may I ask? He's a friend of mine, and I assure you, he's wrongly accused."

The sheriff kept his eyes on her father and answered as though she weren't there. "Arrests aren't usually made public until the arraignment. But I suppose I can tell you—as a favor, you understand—the tip came anonymously. Someone spoke to one of my deputies from the shadows as he made his rounds downtown last night."

A voice in the dark. Just as Geth thought. And it didn't belong to anyone who could testify in a court. "Then how do you know that anonymous tipster isn't the robber himself?" she blurted. "Don't you need more proof than that?"

Poppa put his hand on her knee to hush her. "What my daughter means, from our untrained perspective, is to point out you've arrested a person for messy and obvious crimes he could easily commit before filling the graves, without anyone knowing the thefts ever happened. Unless he's guilty of an excess of stupidity, an anonymous tip sounds less like good cause and more like a grudge. Or a drunken clod's prank. Or, as she said, an intentional red herring. But we'll be grateful if you enlighten our innocence on these points of law— since an educated citizenry forms a bulwark against crime, don't you agree?"

The sour look on the sheriff's face made Geth want to kiss her father. She sometimes considered his social club visits a way to avoid talking with her. She realized now they nursed a hidden flair for politics—or even acting, though he'd protest if she pointed that out.

"What an interesting ring you wear, Miss Jones."

Startled, Geth glanced at her fingers, confused, before it dawned on her what he'd spotted. During all her bouncing in barrows and reclining in crypts, the ring from the Wind had slipped out of her dress. It hung in plain sight on its ribbon.

Sheriff Cornell pounced on her flustered reaction. Rising, he stepped toward her. "Amethyst, isn't it? May I admire more closely?"

Geth eyed her father and stammered, "I suppose?" Poppa's tiny frown said he hadn't noticed. Until now. To prevent the sheriff from grabbing at her, she lifted the ribbon over her neck and extended it to him.

Barely glancing at the ring, the sheriff gave a crisp nod. "May I ask how you came by it?"

"Someone gave it to me, a few days ago." Words tumbled from her as if to drown out additional questions. "A friend, I mean, that's all. Nobody important." Aware of her father's keen gaze, she stopped her blathering only with effort.

The sheriff's fist closed on the ring. "The same friend you're here to defend?"

"No," Geth said, too hard. Too relieved at the truth.

"Because strangely enough, he first came to our attention with an unlikely story about overhearing the thieves in the graveyard. He waited remarkably long to report it, since a deputy patrolled nearby that night."

Geth tried not to wince. That report was her fault.

"Then we found hidden money, most likely ill-gotten, when we went to arrest him—"

The sofa seemed to drop from beneath her. Aaron's stash in the cigar box did look suspicious.

Sheriff Cornell didn't pause. "—and now your ring matches one on a list of stolen goods. Grave goods, I'll add."

With a gasp, Geth clutched where the ring had lain on her chest—grave dirt, a dead finger, a desecrated corpse. She should've guessed when the crow dropped it. That dirty fabric. Like somebody lost it.

Indeed, someone had.

She barely heard the sheriff say he'd need to keep it. Evidence. Her head cleared when he asked her a second time to name whoever gave it to her.

"I don't know," she replied. "That's why I can't tell you. But it wasn't Aaron, I promise. Anonymous—that's it—an anonymous gift. I found it, truly. On my mother's gravestone. Left there with a note that said, 'From a friend.' "

"Ah. A secret admirer, maybe." His voice dry, the sheriff clearly did not believe her. "Our anonymous tipster indeed gets around."

Geth's father stood. "Well, yes. Anonymous—a troublesome concept." He pulled Geth to her feet alongside him. "We're happy to contribute that evidence, sheriff. My daughter only wants it restored to its rightful owner. Or, er, the heirs. Also, we appreciate this time from your Sunday. We'd best be off now, leaving you to important crime-fighting work."

Hearing her father retreat so fast pricked tears into Geth's eyes. For herself and for him.

"I think that'd be wise," the sheriff said.

Geth flinched when his gaze slashed from Poppa to her. "But don't go far, Miss Jones. Stay close to home.

My deputies may need a word with you. Or that note, if you have it."

She murmured, "I don't think I kept it," while her father tugged her toward the door.

They trudged in silence nearly all the way home. At the start of their street, Poppa said without stopping, "The sheriff deserves my vote after all. I didn't know you wore some fellow's ring. Stolen and defiled or…otherwise. Near your heart but hidden from me?"

"No, Poppa. It's not what you think." Despite her efforts to catch his eye, he wouldn't look at her.

"What is it then, Geth? Mamie's worried. Now I'm worried, too. Was it Aaron who gave it to you?"

"No. That's the truth."

"Then who did? Is it Will? Are you holding out hope he'll return? Or did it come from an even less savory tryst?"

Miserable, Geth let a sob escape her. "Poppa, no, neither. I did…sort of…find it. The Wind blew it toward me. I thought someone lost it. 'Finders, keepers,' I mean. I never dreamed it might be stolen."

"That's not an attitude I expect from a nearly grown woman. We should have posted a notice in the newspaper for it, tried to find its true owner." He sighed. "But it sounds like whoever lost it is well beyond reading the paper."

Geth shuddered. "Will I be arrested too?"

Poppa finally relented to put his arm over her shoulders. "I don't think so. He had fun scaring you. Just when I thought things were going so well and we'd have your friend out of chains within hours. But you may have to testify. Don't be surprised. You'll tell the truth if you do. The whole truth. You hear me?"

She nodded. Testifying in court might delay industrial school, but she didn't dare mention that now. And that gleam of a silver lining meant nothing if the horrid ring strengthened the case against Aaron.

When she and Poppa reached home, the boarded-up window looked different—less like a childish, sore-loser gesture, and more like the pillage of a war she still needed to win.

Chapter Thirty-Eight

Geth barely stepped into the house before Mamie announced, "Someone's skulking around the back garden. More than one someone, I think."

Poppa's eyes bored a hole into Geth, who tried to ignore him. "Who, Mamie?" she asked. "How do you know?"

"I saw them, of course. One quick glimpse out front, then another in back. At first I thought it was Sarah, here for the quilts, though I don't know why she wouldn't knock. You're both too old for the pranks you used to play." Mamie cut her eyes at Geth. "But a better view showed the figure moved like a man. I called out. Whoever it was slipped away. Are you running a smuggling ring from my home, Gethsemane Jones?"

Geth laughed despite all that had happened. It felt good. "Yes, Mamie. I distill rum in the bathtub at night. Our saloon opens next week in the outhouse. Do you want a cut of the profits?"

Her stepmother did not find this funny.

Geth's father wasn't much amused either. With a scolding glance, he announced, "I'll go take a look."

Geth followed him on the chance Sarah hid out there and needed defending. But nobody lurked in the yard.

After checking behind the plum tree and shed, Poppa asked, "What do you know about this?"

Geth exaggerated only a little. "Nothing." Sarah may have brought a report from the jail. Or Granny Ableman may have come in search of a wedding after finding Beech Hill deserted. But neither of them looked masculine. Had Mamie caught a glimpse of the Wind? Or perhaps the skulker was someone else altogether.

"Excuse me, Poppa," she added. "While I step into my speakeasy outhouse." She mostly wanted to gather her thoughts—and postpone the moment her father told Mamie about the amethyst ring.

He swung the door open for her, pretending to be chivalrous but taking a long look inside before letting her pass.

She sank to a seat on the privy and dropped her head in her hands. She couldn't let Aaron pay such a price for helping her outsmart the Wind. Even if a judge eventually set him free, the reputation might dog him for years, putting an end to his carpentry dreams. She had to do something. What?

Only one thing was certain to help—the arrest of the real thieves. If that were simple, the sheriff would've already done it. But Geth might have one advantage the police didn't. She spoke routinely with someone—something—who knew the scoundrels.

Of course, she'd just made that something angry.

As she steeled herself for what she must do, she used the outhouse for its original purpose. When she reached for the Sears Roebuck catalog, a thought struck her. The pages before 100 were already ripped out, but she flipped to 200, then 300, then—yes. A note was scratched in the margin of page 400, like the secret messages she and Sarah traded as children, "invisible ink" written with the tip of a nail.

Hard success, waiting on hill if you can.

Geth tore the page out and used it before cracking the door to peek out. The yard was empty. Her father had gone back indoors. She should too, before she raised deeper suspicions.

She didn't. Glad she'd rushed into the backyard with Poppa without removing her coat, she slipped from the outhouse and out of the yard.

As soon as she couldn't be heard from the house, she called to the Wind. Pleaded first. Then demanded. It refused to reply.

"I know you're listening," she growled. Leaves and grass shivered all around her, and she occasionally felt an unseen finger tweaking her nose or chin. "I acknowledge your power. Satisfied? Now I want to make you an offer. Stop pouting and come talk like an adult." When that also failed, she recited a poem, replacing the last stanza with, "If you'd like to hear the end, speak to me as a friend."

The Wind wasn't lured. By then Geth had climbed halfway up Beech Hill. She kicked a stone in frustration. She wanted to meet Sarah and find out what happened at the jail, but she longed even more to get Aaron out. And for that, she needed the Wind.

While her mind worked, her gaze wandered—then stopped. The Evans Street water tower stood across town, considerably taller than Beech Hill. The tower couldn't free Aaron from jail, but it helped put more than one rascal in—and the stairs that ascended to the base of the tank must be the windiest location in town. Surely there the Wind couldn't ignore her.

Ophelia. Cleopatra. Lady Macbeth. Snippets of plays echoed in her head as she abandoned the hill to hurry toward the tower. She'd tell Sarah later why she changed course. Geth couldn't waste time in explanations. Or risk being overheard and outfoxed by the Wind.

She focused now on the acting role of her life—on a stage perfectly suited for it.

Chapter Thirty-Nine

Geth's plan nearly stumbled before it began. The iron staircase that spiraled around the tower was locked with a gate at the bottom. That gate wasn't there when the mayor dedicated the tower, releasing ticker tape from the platform up top. But back then, two years ago now, no one had yet climbed it to throw pumpkins, advertising circulars, or cow patties onto the streets below.

Luckily, the blacksmith who forged the new gate worked so intently to keep drunkards and troublemakers off the stairs that he hadn't considered who else might attempt it. A girl in a corset only had to slip one leg at a time between the bars, turn her head, wiggle, and not mind snagging her dress on the rust.

The tower's height soon posed a new obstacle. It was one thing to hoist herself into an apple tree or look down on a street from a widow's walk. It felt wholly different to keep mounting up, around and around, ever higher. With the birds. No risers linked the metal stairs except at their edges, so the ground showed beneath, flickering and making her question her eyes. So much empty air...so easy to slip. Geth hadn't ascended even halfway before she slowed, leaning against the tower in a shaky half-crouch while clutching the railing with cold fingers. Those fingers grew increasingly stiff. Though she kept creeping upward, her heart rose faster than her body until it crowded her throat.

The Wind indeed played here. Though the air was calm when she slipped through the gate, now it gusted and grabbed at her hair and clothing.

She forced her feet forward and cried, "You see what you've driven me to?" Another step. And one more. *Keep going. For Aaron.*

The breeze blustered through the ironwork with a "*hmph*."

"You wouldn't attend for my poems or a song, but now I have a story," she said. "Just for you. There once was a girl who made a mistake. She felt bitter and vengeful and said something she shouldn't, and she found herself betrothed to the Wind. Sound familiar?"

The Wind calmed suddenly. The hiss through the stairs softened to a dubious hum. "*Mmmm.*"

"She didn't want to marry the Wind. So first, the girl hid in a box, but she couldn't inhale deeply enough from inside. 'This is no good,' she said to herself. 'I must have the Wind to keep breathing. But I don't want to marry it. What should I do?' She told a friend, who tried to hide her in church, but the Wind stole the steeple and bells, and all other sounds in the town along with them. No noise, no voice rang out anywhere. Silence.

" 'This is no good,' the girl said again, though nobody heard when she spoke. 'We must have the Wind to bring sounds to our ears. But I don't want to marry it. What should I do?' "

Geth took a few more steps up, promising herself not to carry on with the story until she reached the top. The very tip-top. *Press your foot to the iron. Clutch the rail. Step up. Again.*

Anticipation grew tangible in the air. "*What happens next?*" the Wind asked at last.

"There you are. Thank you. It's true what they say about you, isn't it?"

Geth's soles on the metal stairs made them ring in the hush until the Wind said, grudgingly, "*That I'm ill indeed if I blow no good?*"

"No. That you're fickle. And not only with me." Geth climbed faster now. It wasn't merely that she felt less alone. In a battle of wits, she had to think sharp. Which made it easier to forget the swath of sky now below her, that whole yawning distance to fall. "Aaron thinks you like him, you know. But your tip caused his arrest, didn't it?"

"*Even a favorite may need to be punished. What happens next in your story?*"

"The story? Oh, let me see." She fell silent again to command attention. The story worked to lure the Wind out of its silence. Now she had to keep weaving the spell and entice the Wind to her bidding. "The girl got an idea. She put on her best dress and pulled on a lace tablecloth as a veil, and she went to meet the Wind for her wedding. Can you guess what happened next?"

"*The Wind gets what she owed it?*"

"Too easy. When the Wind bent near its bride, the girl whipped off her veil, caught the Wind in the lace, and trussed it up tight. A neat trick."

"*Pffft,*" said the Wind. "*I cannot be bound. Certainly in nothing as flimsy as lace.*"

"It's a story," Geth said. "Not life. But I tricked you, didn't I? First, you tricked me into a bargain. I tricked you back out of it. Show the grace to admit it. We're even."

"*I disagree*," the Wind grumbled. "*I could level this tower to prove nothing between us is even.*"

Geth's stomach knotted. "I know. But you're interrupting the story. Shall I finish or not?"

A long silence. "*Go on.*"

"Tangled in lace, the Wind roared and raged, but the veil was stronger. Falsehoods often are, or appear so, at least. The girl and her friends rejoiced at her freedom.

"But then came a terrible drought. With no Wind to suck water out of the seas, clouds didn't form. Rain didn't fall. Crops died, rivers dwindled, mill wheels didn't turn. Steam engines ran out of water for steam. No more clothes, no more bread while the Wind lay there, trapped."

"*You see? I am more important than you know.*"

Pleased, Geth ignored that. The Wind couldn't resist taking part in her story. The more it cared what came next, the better her chance of success, just like the Arabian story of The Thousand Nights.

Like Scheherazade, Geth carried on. "So the thirsty girl admitted, 'This is no good.' She untied the Wind. It tore through her town, blasting through windows and upending wagons. The young woman stood and weathered its fury, her skin chapped, her dress torn, her hair in a tangle. When the Wind's raging ebbed, she called to it, saying, 'Come. Calm yourself. I will keep our crooked bargain.' After she put her veil back on, she offered her hand. 'Only first you must do something for me.' "

"*I've already done something for you. Your curse.*"

"It's a story. It's egotistic to see yourself in every tale." At last Geth reached the top of the stairs, where the legs of the tower propped up the tank. The steps ended in a narrow platform that circled halfway around. "But I do have a choice to give you."

She forced herself forward onto the platform, both hands gripping the cold metal railing. It seemed too low to stop her from tumbling over and too thin to bear weight if she stumbled against it. Her knees wouldn't quite straighten. Trying not to look down, she stared at her knuckles. They gleamed, tight and bony. But her hands were not large. Beyond them wavered roofs and treetops and the hard, hard earth below.

She gulped. The pumpkins thrown off for the tower's first Halloween had splattered orange goo for a block. Pulp. And one stem. That's all that was left. No candle stubs, no carved faces, no telling one from the next.

"*Gethsemane. Do you hear me? Why do you not answer?*"

She flinched, her ears no longer stopped up with fear. "Yes, I hear. Could you…would you blow more gently? It's dizzy up here."

The breeze eased immediately, its voice dropping so she had to listen sharp to catch words. "*Why are you telling me this story now? Are you saying you'll keep our original bargain?*"

"It was your bargain, not mine." But in her hours of thinking the previous night, she decided she'd acted little better than Will. Will had quit town to avoid marrying her. But hadn't she abandoned life itself, nearly, by hiding out in a tomb? Once jilted, she'd now done the jilting herself, resolving little except to shift her fear for herself into fear for Aaron. The latter, considerably more helpless, felt worse. Guilt plagued her. She'd hurt those she loved—and even felt bad for the Wind. As with the girl in her story, mostly others had suffered. She could not risk more harm. Perhaps it was time to embrace her mistakes and accept the role she'd auditioned for when she chose the cemetery as the stage for her curse.

"*You said a choice*," insisted the Wind. "*What choice?*"

Geth took a deep breath and looked up at the sky. That dizzied her too, but at least she couldn't fall that direction. "Get Aaron set free for good. I don't care how—but knocking the jail down won't be enough. You know who the grave robbers are. An 'anonymous tip' can serve justice this time. If you do that, I'll meet you as soon as he's free and finish my story the moment we're married. My gift to you, who wanted my voice. If you care how it ends, if you value my telling, do what I ask of you first."

She let go of the railing to throw one arm wide and shout. "Then I'll make the best wife the Wind's ever had! Stormy and gentle and lilting by turns. Fierce. And sweet. As befits your companion. I'll live up to my deepest ambitions with you, performing all the great roles for your pleasure. Even if no one else thinks I am sane."

"*Oh-ho, that's the Gethsemane I admire*," the Wind cried. "*A change of heart—but what brought it? Surely more than a story.*"

Wobbly by then, she pressed herself back against the tower and stared at the horizon. "It's not a change but a realization. I care more about Aaron than what happens to me. Maybe…that's one way to love."

She hadn't meant to say that part aloud. But her

exposure, so far above Earth and anyone else, forced her to be honest. With the Wind. With herself. One kind of acting put an end to another.

The Wind stayed silent for so long Geth asked, "Are you still here?"

"*Yes.*" The murmur sounded thoughtful. "*What's the other half of the choice? Something more easily done?*"

Geth closed her eyes to shove her fear back and summon her best skills as an actress. Now was no time for honesty. Not exactly.

"If you won't help Aaron, when I know you can, I won't take the stairs down. I'll throw myself off. Let's see how powerful you really are. You want me? Catch me. Set me down easy. You snatch things and throw things in every tornado, but you never put them down nicely. It appears that you can't. You face limits too, don't you? You're not perfect, either. If you choose wrong—well. I won't have to marry an inhuman groom and spend the rest of my life shunned by everyone else, who won't understand my devotion to you. I won't have to watch the ruin of Aaron's life, either. And you'll never hear the end of your story."

The Wind barely breathed. Nor did she.

"*You wouldn't,*" it murmured.

"You think not?" Geth's eyes flashed open as if to strike the Wind with her stare. "You don't know Lover's Leap? There are dozens of them. Maiden Rock, just upriver? Sorrow Gulch? Breakheart Bluff? You've heard me rehearse Ophelia, I know. It can't be less painful to drown. A fall will be faster—with no turning back." Carried away, she rattled the railing.

And gasped at its flex. Her heart lurched. Her

knees buckled and threatened to slip her under the railing.

The Wind gusted hard, shoving her back toward the tower. "*Done, done!*" it intoned through the ironwork, as in the graveyard after her curse. "*Done. I chose doing what I can for Aaron.*"

Choking on fear, Geth sank to a seat. More stable there, she managed a scoff. "No. You have to do better than that. When he's free, I will go to Beech Hill for a wedding. Not before."

"*Will you descend now?*"

Geth was not sure she could. Her legs felt like water. And she didn't want the Wind to spot her weakness.

"I think not," she announced. "Perhaps I'll stay here until Aaron is free to make sure you meet your commitment."

"*Don't,*" pleaded the Wind. "*It's true—if you fall, I cannot catch you. The harder I tried, the more your fragile body would break. If you descend now, however, I can help keep you steady before turning to the business you want me to do.*"

The idea of it pressing her into the stairs didn't comfort her much. "Just go do that, please. I don't want Aaron behind bars a moment longer."

"*As you wish.*" The Wind whisked away. In the calm that remained, weak sunshine helped soothe her.

Once her legs seemed to regain their bones, Geth started down, scooting at first on her seat like a toddler. Her performance had nearly sent her to her death—but it worked. With nothing to hold over the Wind after their bet, she'd still drawn it into negotiation. And convinced it—again—to do as she asked.

Of course, the rest of her life would be strange. And lonely. The rumors about her this week were only a start. But Sarah stood by her, at least for a while. Maybe Aaron too, until he found someone more normal to marry.

He could be a carpenter, though. Or a farmer. Not a convict. And Geth could stop wondering if the next blustery sky might flatten a building where someone she cared about lived. It happened each year, just not in Amity. Yet.

Moving slowly, so slowly, snug to the stairs, gradually restored her confidence. She rose to her feet and descended more quickly. If Poppa sent her to Dayton for school, so be it. Maybe she'd audition for plays between classes. At that distance, how would he stop her? The Wind didn't mind if she acted. It cheered. On the other hand, if she stayed here at home, she must wait until Poppa joined Mother in heaven before she could try for the stage.

Ah, Mother. Geth imagined how she'd rant if she knew. Engaged to the Wind! Not "improving her prospects." But surely the angel who once lived as her mother had given up the perfect portrait of Geth long ago—the miniature, yes, but the life-sized canvas, too. The real Geth, the one blurred by errors and actions, hoped her mother found joy painting God's violets and sunsets and only looked down now with amusement.

As she neared the ground, Geth found the nerve to admire the view. She could spy the top of Beech Hill during parts of the spiral.

Abruptly she increased her measured pace down the stairs, alarmed by what she saw on the hill.

Chapter Forty

A puzzling scene greeted Geth on Beech Hill. Granny Ableman stood on the boulder Geth used as a stage, waving a potato sack through the air as if trying to catch butterflies in it. Sarah watched from a seat on the stone behind her, her chin in one hand. She jumped up at Geth's approach.

"What on Earth?" Geth asked.

"I'm not sure if she's mad or a genius," said Sarah. "When we first arrived here, we both heard the Wind. She spoke to it, and it answered."

"Cranky to find no bride, maybe," Granny added. "You said today, right? Now she's here and it's not. But I heard it. What power. To hear—such a privilege." Her eyes narrowed craftily. "To harness, still better. There might be a way."

Geth and Sarah exchanged a glance. Madness seemed to be winning.

"Don't you know the spell?" Granny asked.

"I'd have called it a nursery rhyme," Sarah replied.

Granny scowled, shook her head, and recited, " 'Catch lightning in a bottle, lure the wind inside a sack, or toss a rope around the moon to turn an evil back.' Sack's empty, though." Looking it over, she sighed. "Maybe another chance later."

"Don't make it mad." Geth turned to Sarah. "What happened at the jail?"

Sarah threw out her arms with a groan. "That was harder than expected. But I let Aaron know you were safe. He looks…well, scared, to be honest. But sound."

"They let you see him?"

Covering her face with her hands, Sarah peeked out through her fingers. "I made it a game, but it got out of hand. Don't think ill of me. Promise?"

Geth tugged at Sarah's forearms in vain. "Of course not. What happened?"

Her friend leaned close to whisper. "I let the awful deputy kiss me. And ugh, imagine a man buying a horse. Running a hand over its hindquarters, ha." Shuddering, Sarah turned away. "It grows worse in the telling."

"Oh, you needn't have suffered so much! Aaron would've found out eventually. His peace of mind doesn't count more than your honor." Geth rubbed Sarah's back. "But thank you. Would your fiancé, Alfred, be upset if he knew?"

"He'd laugh and demand equal treatment, not that Freddie will find out from me. Or you either, please. His kisses aren't horrid. This was. But I won." Triumph lit her face. "The deputy walked me to the cell, and I told Aaron myself. Honestly, the men whistling might've been worse. I turned redder than a fishwife's thumb before I escaped."

"I'm glad you did." Geth felt enough guilt. But Sarah had enough wisdom to make her own calculations.

"That's why I left a Privy Post for you," Sarah added. "I couldn't face your good Mamie so soon after that. I'd have died if she saw me, with that wretched kiss on my lips. Anyway, when Mrs. Ableman came down the street too, I, er…thought it'd be better if she didn't knock, either."

Geth thanked her with a hug. "I hope your deputy keeps his mouth shut. Rumors about one of us are enough."

"I think he will. A hubbub broke out as I left. A telephone call from the sheriff. Wouldn't it be lovely to have telephones, too? Put an end to our Privy Post quick. Anyway, when it came, the deputy went straight as a poker and nearly shoved me out the door. Like the sheriff watched him somehow."

Geth tried to match Sarah's cheer. The call from the sheriff probably referred to her ring. She'd be lucky if she didn't face a stolen property charge. The Wind might have to free her from a jail cell, too.

Granny nudged Geth. "Pardon for interrupting the hen party." She pulled a small book from her sack. "A wedding—or not? Got my prayerbook here." She waved it.

"No." Sarah turned to Geth. "I tried to explain."

"Not yet," Geth told Granny. "But probably, yes."

Sarah shoved Geth, not entirely in fun. "What did you do?" She planted her fists on her hips. "If I wasted that kiss, I may never forgive you."

Geth assured her it wasn't wasted but didn't want to share details with Granny right there. "I'll explain later. Come get those quilts from my house. There's no more we can do until Aaron's set free."

Sarah's eyes scoured her face, trying to read more from it.

"For now, things are fine," Geth declared. "Granny, I'm sorry I've wasted your time."

Granny peered down her nose. "Nonsense. I'll stay

here a mite. In case the Wind speaks again. Or find me at home when you need me."

"I will. Soon, I hope."

Sarah growled and poked Geth in the ribs.

Ignoring her, Geth gestured to the sack, so much like the veil in her story. "You might pull that sack over your head and sing softly. The Wind likes a song and might be drawn close beneath it. Then you might catch it. But don't be surprised if it's wily."

Granny started to draw the sack over her head before eying Geth, suspecting a trick.

Geth smiled and pulled Sarah away down the hill.

"What do you mean, 'soon, you hope'?" Sarah asked.

Explaining her new attitude came more easily than Geth expected. She'd barely begun when her friend's face crumpled.

"Oh, Geth," Sarah said. "I knew I could see your heart better than you do. Yesterday in the schoolhouse made it so plain. But to sacrifice this way? For love, really? No."

"I never said I loved Aaron." But a memory of his touch in the vault flushed through Geth, stealing all force from her protest.

Sarah continued, "He won't allow it, for one thing. You underestimate him. Like you underestimate me."

"He doesn't have a say, I'm afraid," Geth replied. "He's behind bars."

"Hmm," was all Sarah said before a shriek behind them made them spin. Granny hobbled fast down the hill, screeching, the sack at arm's length in one fist.

"I've got it, I think! A piece, anyhow." The potato sack churned like a bag of raccoons, threatening to burst from her grip around its throat. In fact, the sack seemed to drag Granny and not the reverse. "Aaiiii! Great idea, girl. Who knew?"

While they gaped, Granny burst past them toward town, looking for all the world like an elderly bank robber fresh off a heist.

Only Geth heard the chuckle that followed her down the hill. The Wind added, "*Thank you for such rare amusement.*"

Chapter Forty-One

At home, a storm of righteous anger greeted Geth. She thought for a moment Poppa would turn her over his knee, even with Sarah watching. Mamie knew about the amethyst ring. Now Poppa accused Geth of intentionally tormenting them.

"That's not true." Tears sprang to her eyes. "I know I've been frustrating. Truly, I'm sorry." But she had no explanation, no defense she could use, other than a slant on the truth. "An evil spirit hangs about me, I think. On some days it gets the better of me. But I've nearly tamed it. Give me a chance, and you'll see."

Poppa dismissed her apology. Sarah meekly suggested that Geth sneaked away this time for a good cause—concern for a friend.

Advising Sarah to mind her own business, Mamie piled her arms with quilts. "Take these and go home." She shoved Sarah toward the door. "And don't you dare ask for Geth's help. Or try to visit her later. I'm sure the poor influence runs the other way, but she uses you too often as an excuse to vanish."

Sarah threw a sorrowful glance back at Geth, who blew a good-bye kiss and wondered if she'd be married by the next time they met.

Once the door closed on Sarah, Poppa's wrath took a turn. "Go upstairs and pack," he commanded. "When I call the industrial school tomorrow, I'll advise them you'll arrive on the afternoon train."

"So soon?" Geth's voice wavered. "You just threw Sarah out. Am I denied any proper goodbye?"

"Send her a letter," said Poppa.

"What about the sheriff? He said to stay close."

Poppa's face grew even redder.

Mamie forced him to a seat. "Calm yourself, Bertram. Your asthma." She turned to Geth. "Perhaps Sarah can join us for supper tomorrow. We'll put you on the train Tuesday morning instead. That will give your father time to alert the sheriff and pledge any needed return for the court." She eyed her husband, who harrumphed at being contradicted.

"Maybe I'll return to advise him today," he grumbled.

Geth wisely said nothing.

"Go upstairs," Mamie told her. "We'll decide before morning. You'd best write that letter, in case."

Geth spent much of the rest of that day leaning out her window and hoping for word from the Wind about Aaron. Though it sometimes patted her cheeks, it chose not to speak. Only once, near bedtime, it murmured while pushing her back from the window. "*Patience, please. Your request is not easy.*"

Morning brought Geth more glares than embraces, but her father postponed her departure a day.

"Thank you." She hugged him, nearly spilling his tea. "I'll earn your trust back, I promise."

As if marking that vow, a clanging approached up the street.

"Not another fire?" Poppa wondered. He untucked his napkin to rise from his chair.

"None of the factory whistles blew," Mamie said.

Running by habit to the parlor, they looked out the window to see nothing but planks. Mamie opened the door and they spilled onto the porch. Amity's three-horse ladder truck moved at the end of the street. Geth saw no smoke or flame, though.

"Looks like it's headed to Fernlawn," said Poppa. "But what's there to burn? Are the grave robbers dabbling in arson now, too?"

Geth leaned her temple against the chill of the porch post. The Holmes house and workshop were built all of wood. If those caught fire, they'd be ash before the flames could be quenched. And she couldn't imagine how burning their house could prove Aaron's innocence. Had the Wind turned on them both?

With her eyes closed, she heard Mamie say, "But where's the tanker? They can't put out fire without water. Perhaps it's only a demonstration."

Geth knew not to ask about following the truck. She only moaned, "Please, could we not guess? The Holmeses are friends."

"I'm not sure they make suitable friends," began Poppa.

Mamie interrupted. "We'll send up a prayer and hope they are safe. Come back to breakfast, you both."

Geth couldn't eat, only clutch her teacup through her family's cruel lack of concern. She got Poppa to promise to bring news, if he could, when he came home for luncheon. He was shrugging on his coat to leave for the station when somebody banged on the door.

She moved without thinking until her stepmother stopped her and said, "I'll answer, thank you."

Geth peeked from the hall as Mamie crossed to the door. It might not be a neighbor with gossip about fire but a deputy there to arrest her. She withdrew to the kitchen, where Poppa lingered, and considered another flight out the backyard. It wouldn't slow the police for long if she escaped, but the next train to Dayton sounded better than jail. Not much, but a little.

"Is Gethsemane in? I'm so hoping she'll help us."

The voice, hoarse and breathless, trembled with alarm but drifted clearly from the parlor. Geth and her father swapped a glance.

Placing the voice, Geth ran back to the parlor. Aaron's mother stood at the door, looking flustered. A twig was stuck in her hair.

Mamie shook her head. "Geth is indisposed," she said curtly. "Perhaps I can help? Is it fire?"

Mrs. Holmes spotted Geth, her gaze darting past Mamie. "Oh, no. There's no fire. It's Pris, my daughter—"

"That's good news," Mamie said, as if the woman weren't frantic. She threw a glance back at Geth. "See? All that worry for nothing."

Mrs. Holmes looked confused but talked so fast she barely drew breath. "I don't know if you heard, but yesterday our son was arrested." Her hands rose to forestall a response. "He's innocent, I assure you. We know he'll come home. But Pris has herself all upset. People said hateful things, heartless things this morning. And she's starting to understand how long a trial will take."

Poppa, who hovered at Geth's shoulder, murmured, "The wheels turn slowly, no doubt. But he'll still be her brother when justice is served."

Mrs. Holmes flashed a strained smile. "But that's not the problem. She climbed into the old Freedom

Tree. You know it? So high we're scared she'll fall and be killed. Not even the ladder truck reaches, and the men fear they're too big and heavy to climb after her without breaking the limbs holding her up."

Her eyes pleaded with Geth as she finished, "Aaron's the one she really responds to, but she looks up to you so much, dear Geth. She adores you. I hope you might come and talk sense to the child. Dismiss her superstitions about an old tree and persuade her to come down before my poor heart gives way."

When Mrs. Holmes swooned against the doorframe, Mamie rushed to support her, throwing a look of bemusement at Geth.

"Can I?" Geth grabbed Poppa's arm. "Please. Can't you see this isn't my doing, not an excuse to get out of the house?"

Poppa and Mamie exchanged a frown.

"Oh, say yes," Mrs. Holmes begged. "Please. It may not work, I know. But Geth's my best hope. Pris deplores her schoolteacher, and her father and I have already shouted ourselves hoarse."

Poppa cleared his throat. "I'll accompany you. It's so close to the station. My clerks can manage a while, I am sure."

As Geth spun to grab her coat, Mamie caught up with her. "Success or fail, you come back directly."

"Of course. I swear with all my heart, Mamie. Come with us if you want, but you needn't, I promise. I hope only to help."

Geth hurried with Mrs. Holmes to the cemetery, Poppa huffing to keep up behind. On the way, she searched for words to convince Pris that Aaron soon would be free.

By the time they strode beneath the old iron gate, she hadn't found them. None she could shout with the girl's parents beside her. And even if she'd been alone with the girl, the truth—the hope she couldn't share—might only tempt Pris to climb higher and make her own demands of the Wind.

Chapter Forty-Two

The ladder truck still sat under Old Freedom. Its crew spread a rescue net alongside. Firemen took turns trying to persuade Pris to climb down or jump into the net. When Geth saw how high Pris clung to the tree, the bough bending and shivering under her weight, the fear she felt on the water tower rushed back in a wave.

"Go away!" the girl yelled to the men below her, the distance thinning her words. "Not getting down 'til Aaron is free. Go bust him outta jail, if you care."

Before she reached the tree, Geth tipped her head to the sky. "Please, Wind," she called. "Be still and don't shake the branches. For me?"

As Mrs. Holmes and her father both gave her odd looks, Geth shrugged. "It can't hurt." She ducked under the branches, jockeyed for a partial view of Pris, and called her name as loud as she could.

"Why you here, Miss Geth? Won't do no good."

"Risking your neck won't do Aaron good, either. What would he say if he knew?"

"He'd tell me to stick to my guns. It's unfair."

Geth had to admit that sounded like something Aaron might say.

"It's got to help," Pris insisted. "If truth and freedom and justice are real."

Unwilling to say they might not be, Geth thought back to the stories she told Pris and other students in school. "What will you do when it's bedtime? Tie yourself to the branch like a sailor in the crow's nest of a ship?"

"Don't have a rope." Pris sounded petulant. "Just won't sleep."

"We could run one up the fire ladder, like lines up the mast." Geth pointed. "Come down that far to get it. All right?"

"If she came down that far, they could grab her," murmured Mr. Holmes.

"Wait, though. Don't spook her," Poppa advised softly. "One thing at a time."

Pris considered it while they all held their breath.

"Nah," the girl said. "It might be a trick."

Her parents groaned, but Geth grinned and threw her arms wide. "You're probably right. Like a pirate. You remember *Treasure Island*, don't you?"

"What about it?"

"X marks the spot, of course. You passed the X, Pris—the blaze on Old Freedom. That scar. That's where this tree gets its power. Don't you know? For treasure, you go to the X on the map. If you want freedom for Aaron, go to the X on the tree. You're wasting time otherwise."

The adults around Geth exchanged puzzled glances. But when Pris said, " 'Zat true? Are you making it up?" their expressions turned hopeful.

"Not only am I not making it up, your brother's the one who told me. That blaze is the eye and the heart of the tree. That's where you should've stopped climbing."

"Really?" Pris shifted to look down the trunk. She eased herself back down her branch. Every shiver and creak made the onlookers jump. Before long, Pris admitted, "I don't know if I can get down to that X."

"What I was afraid of," moaned her mother.

"Well, that's a pickle," called Geth casually. "What if…what if I touched the blaze? If you're in the tree and I'm at the blaze, and we both beg Old Freedom to help Aaron, do you suppose that might work? Like a captain could order a sailor to dig at the X without digging himself?"

"What on earth?" muttered Poppa. "Don't make matters worse."

But Geth explained her idea, and a fireman agreed to try it. Geth warned Pris so the ladder's motion didn't make her suspicious. The crew moved it into place, leaning the ladder against a thick branch near Old Freedom's trunk. Then they helped Geth to the base of the ladder. She planted her soles on the rungs. A fireman came behind her, uncomfortably close, to steady her on the ladder.

The ladder, though not nearly so tall, scared her as much as the tower stairs had. It swayed under their weight with each step. Even with the man behind her forming a protective cage of his arms, her fists gripped the rungs so tight they hurt.

Fortunately, Old Freedom's blaze wasn't terribly high in the tree. A dozen steps up, Geth could reach for the scar.

"I'm at the X, Captain." Her face lifted toward Pris. "Now let's do this together."

From this angle, she thought she could tell Pris how to move each hand and foot to come down. The girl got up there, so clearly reversing her climb mostly required confidence. Geth's mind raced, weaving a story to draw Pris down to touch the blaze, too.

She did not even begin.

"Oh. Oh!" Pris yelled. Her branch shook, making those below flinch. "Miss Geth, that X is working already!" The girl stared out of the tree, laughed, and beamed down at Geth. Before anyone knew what she was talking about, she reached with her feet and slid on her belly, climbing and slipping in equal measure back down her branch. Once past the nearest large fork, where the branch bent less under her weight, she scrambled down even faster. With the right motivation, she was not stuck at all.

"Pris, careful!" Geth cried. "I'm glad you want to touch the blaze, too, but more slowly. It won't help Aaron if you fall."

"He doesn't need my help now." Pris came down fast. Soon Geth and her fireman would be in the way. She turned her head to ask about backing down when Pris screeched. She'd slipped.

The girl dangled briefly from both arms, her feet flailing for purchase. As the onlookers shouted useless advice to stretch a leg right or left, Pris's fingers gave way. She dropped. Geth instinctively ducked as human limbs thudded on tree limbs above her. The girl fell like a penny in an arcade pin game, bouncing from one branch to the next. The fireman lunged forward. He crushed Geth to the ladder as Pris struck them like a forty-pound sack of potatoes. Geth shrieked and clutched a rung for dear life.

"Owww," wailed Pris. When Geth opened eyes she didn't know she'd squeezed shut, one of the girl's legs was hooked over Geth's head and another rested on the branch alongside the ladder. The fireman caught her small torso between his left arm, the ladder, the tree trunk, and Geth.

"Don't move yet," he said, far too calmly. "Anyone."

"It hurts though," Pris whimpered. Voices shouted below.

It took a few moments to sort out body parts, and Geth saw nothing of what went on behind her, but the fireman nudged Pris to a less precarious rest and then pulled her down to fold her over his shoulder. Pris started to cry.

"Can you cling here yourself while I haul her down?" he asked Geth. "Don't move. Just hold on."

"Yes, I'm sure," she replied.

"That's a brave girl." Several bouncy moments later, he returned to usher her down.

"She's bruised, maybe a few broken ribs," he informed her. "But no bad knocks on the head, it appears, and she'll live. A happy-ending story for the firehouse tonight."

Geth stood on the ground, being patted for soundness by Poppa, before she saw what made Pris so excited. Aaron approached across the cemetery. From the treetop, his sister spotted him first. The people now knotted around Pris and her mother still hadn't noticed him coming.

Abandoning her father, Geth ran to meet him. She resisted the urge to fling her arms around him. "Aaron, you're out! But what—how?"

He caught both her hands, shooting a concerned look at the tree. "What's going on? Did I hear a scream?"

"Yes. Pris fell, but she's mostly all right. Thanks to

a fireman's strength. You are, too?"

"Well, I'm here." A wry grin lit his face. "And awfully glad you are too, considering where and when I last saw you. Though I don't understand what's happened since. I had some bad moments thinking how I left you, all alone in the dark…"

His mouth remained poised to continue, but their gazes locked first. Geth barely drew breath, stretched between the warm grip of his fingers, the pull of his eyes, and the memory of his touch in the vault. The commotion at the tree fell away. Heat roared up her neck into her face.

In a murmur, he finished, "I should've stayed with you. And touched more than your cheek."

Geth wanted to tell him she thought the same thing that whole night. She was too scared of words, even a whisper, breaking the luscious tension between them. It buzzed through her skin and ricocheted back to him—a vibration, felt but not seen. As if he stroked her mind and her heart with his eyes.

At a *clonk* of the firetruck's ladder, his gaze flicked toward Old Freedom and back. Very softly, he said, "Do I need to be jealous of a fireman now? Isn't the Wind enough of a rival?"

"Oh…" She looked away and gently pulled her hands loose, tingling too wildly to stand square on her feet. She longed to sway against Aaron. But not with Poppa nearby. At the thought, her lips curled in a smile.

It faded quickly as she recalled what Aaron's freedom meant.

"Don't tease me," she said. "There's a lot you don't know. But say hello to your family. Pris needs the doctor, I guess, but first she'll want to see you close.

Hug you tight." A pain stabbed her chest as she turned. Relieved by her father's hasty approach, she ran to meet him and let Aaron make his way to his family.

She didn't have the heart to explain what she'd traded to see him again. Or why it mattered so much for her to keep her word this time. To break it would mean losing part of herself, an authentic part she'd only recently found, and what remained wouldn't be worthy of him anyhow.

Chapter Forty-Three

CAPTURED
Ghoulish Thief Foiled at Last
Implicates Local Heirs

Amity and Xenia, OH—A deplorable crime spree plaguing Amity ended last night when authorities apprehended a member of a grave-robbing gang caught red-handed in nearby Xenia. Divine retribution played a role as the thief, one Frank Fulsome of Philadelphia, was downed by an oak branch broken off by the wind—a hazard lumbermen know as a widow-maker. He lay pinned on the spot with injuries until a watchman heard cries for help. It appears the villain, too beholden to greed, shifted his operation down the railroad line after the arrest of a suspect in Amity made further grisly heists there foolish. Under questioning—and the considerable discomfort of a great branch on his legs—the real thief confessed.

The original suspect was freed.

Later, Fulsome gave up two partners in an attempt to reduce the wrath of the law. As this reporter heard him shout from a cell, *"I won't stay mum for any rich dandies. Not for what they gave me, the one who did all the work."*

In a twist worthy of a sensational novel, the thief alleges he took orders from the sons of an Amity industrialist—Mr. Frederick Cogglesmith, the owner of Champion Ironworks. The firm recently patented a burglar-proof casket.

Amity's Sheriff Cornell explained, "The brothers concocted it as an unholy sales scheme—a campaign of fear to sell the invention and build up their inheritance." Needless to say, they can't inherit from prison.

The elder son, Randolph Cogglesmith, appears to be the criminal mastermind and has already been apprehended. A manhunt continues for the younger brother, who allegedly converted stolen goods into cash. Attentive readers will note the junior Cogglesmith quit Amity unexpectedly not long ago, no doubt to more easily transfer goods that might have been recognized locally.

The founder of Champion Ironworks, Mr. Cogglesmith senior, has disavowed both sons and any knowledge of the plot. He declined to reveal casket sales figures or any new plans.

Arraignments and trial dates are pending and will be reported here as information becomes available. Amity's sheriff also dismissed a rumor that any Amity deputy was involved.

Her jaw sagging, Geth looked up at her father. He'd thrust the paper at her when he returned home for luncheon. His foot tapped impatiently while she read.

"You dodged a worse fate than being left at the altar," he declared. "But I'm pleased to see that criminal error, not a superstition based on a tree, was responsible for the release of your friend. I admit the coincidence made me wonder." He made a beeline for his meal, hastening to add, "Not that your help for Pris was any less worthy."

Geth managed a smile. That success wouldn't keep him from putting her on a train in the morning. But at least now she could leave confident Mother's grave remained peaceful.

To her surprise, she did not hear from the Wind right after the adventure with Pris. Its silence came as a relief. It would've been awkward to speak with her fiancé while poor Mr. Holmes walked her home. She'd hoped Aaron might step into his father's place, a last chance for her to walk alongside him and imagine things turning out differently. But Aaron had not volunteered. The only farewell he'd offered was a puzzled expression and a silent lift of his hand.

Still, after luncheon she thanked the Wind profusely from her window, both for Aaron's release and his sister's rescue with her limbs mostly intact.

The Wind responded immediately. "*You are*

welcome, beloved. Don't be surprised if the old woman takes credit. She thinks she righted a wrong with the bag of wild air it amused me to give her. I'm glad you acknowledge the truth. And I want the end of my story."

"And you'll have it," she said. "I can't get to Beech Hill, though. We'll have to take our vows here at my window, I think. Or in Dayton. Poppa's putting me on the train in the morning. Unless—" Geth thought quickly. The Wind could possibly deliver a landslide to block the tracks and delay her departure. But the chance of a derailment, of someone being hurt, was too great. "Never mind. I assume my move there is no obstacle for you?"

"*No. But why not the hill where you first caught my attention?*"

"Because my stepmother won't let me out of the house. And I'm sure you don't want a delay. Sarah's coming for supper to say goodbye, though. Mamie arranged it this morning. I'll whisk her up here for a few minutes tonight." Granny Ableman might be disappointed, but there was no point in putting it off. Geth now accepted her impending marriage to power. Something like Titania in *A Midsummer Night's Dream*, or maybe Prospero commanding Ariel in *The Tempest*.

She avoided thinking about Aaron at all, except as a carpenter someday.

"*Let me handle your family,*" purred the Wind. "*We'll marry on the hill at sunset.*"

"Don't hurt them. Don't you dare."

"*Never, for your sake.*" A breeze as warm as

a draft from an open stove brushed Geth's cheeks. "*I'll deliver a lovely spring evening.*"

"I don't have your stolen ring anymore," Geth warned. "I wouldn't wear it if I did." She didn't hide her annoyance. The Wind already knew her temper ran hot and cold. "How could you give me that, when you knew its source?"

"*In poor taste, I admit. I rushed too much to woo you. I'll bring something better this evening.*"

"What about Granny Ableman? Do you mind if she does the honors? She's lonely, and it makes me happy to see her so enthused. Even if she exaggerates her own skills."

"*Write a note for me to deliver to her.*"

Geth jotted a few lines to Sarah, too, to make sure she arrived before dark. As she tossed the notes from her window and the Wind carried them off, she smiled at the advantages of her new role.

Nonetheless, she stared out the window a long while, squeezing one hand with the other to bring back the feeling of Aaron's warm hands gripping hers. She pressed those sensations deep into her skin, sealing that memory to last her whole life.

Within an hour, an unseasonably balmy wind warmed Amity so well the plum tree in the yard began blooming. Petals drifted in through her window. Poor Mamie's hay fever acted up early. Sniffly and red-eyed, she asked Geth to start supper while she took a nap. A lullaby soon whistled through the boughs of the plum tree, and Mamie's snores rolled down the hall.

Guessing how long she might sleep, Geth put

on a nice dress—not the one she'd planned to wear a week ago for Will, but a silk to swirl in the breeze. She slipped into her wedding slippers and pinned on her mother's brooch. Poppa's hydrangeas didn't even boast leaves, but before she left home, Geth clipped plum boughs to carry as her bouquet. She made the mistake of brushing her cheek with a blossom. Its velvety touch, too much like a certain fingertip, brought tears.

Well. Brides ought to be weepy, right? It made their eyes shine.

She met Sarah, who ran up breathless, on the porch. To her surprise, Sarah didn't try to talk her out of the wedding. And Poppa apparently lingered at work, though for all Geth knew, he snored in his office louder than Mamie did in the house.

She grasped Sarah's hand. As they set out for Beech Hill together, she considered the final lines of the story she owed her bridegroom. Her wedding—planned, canceled, rescheduled but feared, dreaded, avoided, and finally embraced— started at last with a rustic procession over roadsides and grass. No rose petals lay in her path, and no music played, but Geth held her untimely plum blossoms high.

Chapter Forty-Four

Granny Ableman stood in position when Geth and Sarah arrived on Beech Hill. The old woman cocked an eye at her. "You make a lovely bride, girl. Wasted, maybe. You're certain?"

Geth nodded. "You'd do it, wouldn't you?"

"I would now. Not at your age. But we're different, you and I."

Geth smiled. She noticed the fluttering grass and suspected the Wind of eavesdropping.

"Don't know if I'll hear it today," Granny added. "Haven't so far. Maybe turning back evil to get that young man out of jail—and you're welcome—used up my luck with the Wind. So I'll trust you to hear the vows it makes. But common-law marriages do the job, anyway. It's not vows or the prayer book that matter. It's being true to each other, you know."

Geth stared over town at the water tower. "And to yourself, I suppose."

"Life's only good when that's the same thing."

Sarah gazed around the hilltop as if expecting the Wind to take physical shape.

Geth tilted her face up. She persisted in thinking of the Wind in the sky, though obviously it went everywhere—nearly—and she felt certain it was already present from the light touches grazing the small of her back, through the hair she'd left loose, over her

259

cheeks. She wondered why it didn't speak up. Drawing out the victorious moment, perhaps.

"We're ready," she called.

"Not yet," Sarah said. "Let me pin this on you." She pulled a velvet rose from her bodice and fussed with pinning it on Geth's collar near Mother's brooch. Her fingers fumbled and took an inordinate time.

"*A beautiful bride*," whispered the Wind in Geth's ear when finally Sarah stepped back.

"There you are." Geth glanced at Granny Ableman, whose eyebrows shot upwards.

"*I've watched speechless with admiration*," said the Wind. "*Shall we begin?*"

Granny looked side to side and shuffled her feet as though trying to decide which direction to face.

"Anywhere here is fine, Granny," Geth said gently.

The old woman raised her prayer book but did not refer to it. "Here we stand on Beech Hill to bear witness." Her tone, unexpectedly regal, rang over the hilltop. "We have come together in the presence of—"

"Wait." A male voice.

Geth whirled. Aaron appeared behind a tangle of bracken as he strode up the back of the hill. "I don't see your father. Don't you need someone to give you away?"

Geth threw Sarah an accusing glance.

"You bet your bosom I sent word to him," Sarah said. "Two seconds after your note fell in my lap."

Geth turned away from Aaron. She couldn't bear to see his kind face, let alone think of him as handing her off. If he touched her, she'd burst into tears.

"Please, Aaron. Don't make this harder."

He stopped a few paces from her and cocked his

head, listening. "I don't hear an objection from the groom."

"Oh, the objections have not even started," Sarah muttered. "We've got a list, if Granny gets that far, and I, for one, will not hold my peace."

The Wind rushed around them. "*Sshhh. Allow this event the dignity it deserves.*" Buffeted, Sarah cringed but sidled closer to Geth. Granny wobbled, too. Defiant, Aaron planted his feet.

"*Before we proceed, I want the end of the story that's due me,*" the Wind added. "*In lieu of a dowry or ring from the bride.*"

Disconcerted, Geth fumbled for words. "All—all right. Let's see…I think I left off with the young woman offering her hand—"

"*Just so,*" said the Wind. "*And she said, 'First you must do something for me.'*"

Three of the humans on the hill looked confused, and Geth wondered how much they heard the Wind's voice. But she smiled. "Oh, yes." She stepped back into the control she possessed on the tower. Since then, she'd accomplished so much, and with self-assurance came calm. "The girl felt her fingers entwined by soft air, and she said, 'First you must teach me to sing like the breeze, that I may be a partner worthy of you. Even if my song is of sorrow.'"

"*But she already sounds lovely,*" the Wind said.

"Honestly," Geth confided, "she secretly hoped singing lessons would delay her wedding."

"*Ah,*" said the Wind. "*Predictable. I should have known.*"

Sarah began, "Geth, I don't under—"

"Stop," Geth said severely. "Let me finish." She

didn't know what Sarah and Aaron planned but she wouldn't allow them to risk everything. Not in some misguided attempt to save her from herself that would probably hurt someone else.

She took an audible breath to find her story again. "So. The girl sat on a hilltop while the Wind taught her songs. After seven days and seven nights, the Wind came to rest. 'That's all I can teach you,' it said.

"The girl understood the Wind so much better now—its furies and rages, its lullabies, and its unpredictable sighs. By the time the lessons were done, she'd come to know herself, too, with furies and rages and sighs of her own. Her resistance to wedding the Wind faded. She threw her arms wide to embrace her bridegroom and the drama the role offered her. They became husband and wife, and she sang evermore, and not all her songs told of sorrow. The end."

"*Ah*," sighed the Wind. "*Well worth the extra work and the wait.*"

"Okay, but there's a problem," said Aaron. "I mean, I never heard the beginning, but it doesn't sound like there's anyone else in the story."

"Oh, Aaron." Geth's throat caught, breaking her words. She had to mash her lips tight and look away.

Granny Ableman said crossly, "Is this a wedding or a gab session?"

"*Yes, cease this chatter.*" The Wind blustered, swaying them all on their feet. "*I remind you by whose grace you stand here and breathe. But Gethsemane, I know something of stories myself. I wish to offer another ending.*"

"You do?" Geth nearly toppled at the unexpected suggestion. Her sense of control fluttered away. "I didn't know the Wind was a storyteller."

An angry gust rattled the bracken behind them. *"Where do you think stories come from? I blow them. But put that aside. My ending is this—The girl offered her hand and said, 'First you must teach me to sing like the breeze, that I may be a partner worthy of you. Even if my song is of sorrow.' On that we agree. But no more.*

"In fact, her trick with the veil had humbled the Wind, who rarely felt surprise before then. Plus the Wind didn't want songs filled with sorrow. So it kissed her fingers and said, 'Don't play a martyr for me. Your singing's lovely already, but I know your heart's elsewhere. With another favorite of mine, I suspect. Follow it.'"

"Aha," Aaron cried. "I heard that loud and clear. Is that me?"

"Rrrr. Hush." The Wind shoved him to all fours with a blast before easing. It continued in a gentle lilt. *"Delighted, the girl forever cast her veil aside. She never again needed to hide her true self. She replied, 'I will sing of your kindness and wisdom, dear Wind. Of your soft, cooling breezes and how you dance with the trees. My windows will always be open to you.'"*

Geth clasped her hands at her chin. "Oh, I'd be happy to—"

"Shh." A blast in the face silenced her as firmly as Aaron, still on the ground. The voice wafting around them added, *"The Wind didn't believe her. 'You say that now,' it replied. 'But I know you better. You will forget and shut those windows in winter. No matter. I slip through the cracks. Just like love. But what about that scoundrel you asked me to curse?'"*

The breeze lulled. The group exchanged glances. Aaron eased to his feet, brushing dirt off his knees, though he couldn't keep a grin off his face. Sarah nudged her, but Geth wasn't sure she should speak. The lines between her story, the Wind's alternate ending, and their troubles together all blurred.

Tentatively she said, "Would you blow healthy air to his mother, if I asked? And his brother, who sounded sick, too. Will deserves jail, and I hope he's arrested. But no one deserves to lose family." Mother's death had ripped away part of Geth's self that neither Mamie nor anyone else could repair.

The Wind circled around them to stir the dead bracken with a disapproving buzz. "*In my end for the story, the girl pondered, then said, 'Perhaps if I sing of forgiveness for him, I may feel it.'*"

Sarah dared only a whisper to Geth. "But he's not a grave robber in that story, is he?"

The Wind ignored her. "*Pleased, the Wind said, 'Your voice is what I wanted most, my lovely. Sing of love and forgiveness and kindness and me. But I don't need to hoard your voice all to myself. Raise it outdoors where I hear it well, or indoors in places when I can slip in, and we'll feel as much joy apart as together, knowing ourselves better and sharing better selves with the world.' And they did ever after. The end.*"

The breeze played without words through the grass at their ankles. Everyone's eyes turned to Geth.

Afraid to speak, to test what the Wind offered, she brushed a plum blossom down her cheek.

Granny Ableman crossed her arms and opened her mouth. Geth darted a hand up to hush her.

Sarah locked one elbow with Geth, standing

bravely beside her. Solemn again, Aaron took a reflexive step toward her, but he stopped, glancing into the air on all sides.

"I like both endings," Geth said at last. "I'm partial to the part in mine where the girl sees her own furies and rages in the Wind. But I love where she throws away the veil in yours."

The Wind didn't answer.

"Fairy tales can be like that," she added. "Different versions. Songs, too, with verses not everyone knows. And copies of the same play include different lines. Maybe there's time for them all."

They waited. The breeze lilted, warm and bearing the scent of plum blossoms. No one heard words.

"Well, that's a thing I've lived a long time to be part of," declared Granny, breaking the moment's spell. She shouted to the sky, "I'll marry you, though, if you still want a wife? I bring a different sauce to the dish."

If the Wind responded at all, it said no more than, "*Hmm.*"

Granny shrugged. "Couldn't hurt." She eyed the young people. "If I were you, I'd ask for more favors. You have a powerful friend. But if we won't have a wedding—mind you, *again*—my garden needs planting." She marched down the hill. Sarah giggled.

"Have I been left at the altar once more?" Geth wondered, not entirely joking. She let her plum branches fall to the grass.

"This time with the one you really want." Sarah nudged her toward Aaron and slipped from her side.

"Any chance of that being true?" he asked softly.

Geth dared to look into his eyes.

With two strides, he reached to embrace her.

Checking himself, he took her hands instead. She felt a twinge of disappointment, but briefly. Sarah watched with glee and a bit too much interest. Geth wanted to save the embrace for a more private moment.

Aaron dropped his head toward her to murmur, "No wedding today. But is it wrong to still ask the bride for a kiss?"

She feigned insult. "Mr. Holmes!" But she offered her cheek. His expression revealed his dashed hopes, but as he leaned to accept her offer, she whispered, "Not yet."

Then his lips brushed her skin. A plum blossom didn't compare, not at all. Not his fingertip, either. The narrow space between them, so full of longing to be pressed to nothing, made her unsteady. She tottered toward him. He held her firm, turned, and kept one of her hands as the three of them left the hill.

Sarah teased, "Should I run after Granny Ableman for vows? Third time's the charm."

"Sarah! Aaron, don't listen. She's just trying to embarrass me." And it worked. Geth watched her feet to avoid an accidental meeting of eyes. Too intense. Her wedding slippers grew grass-stained and scuffed, but with Aaron holding her hand beside her, she wouldn't want to be striding in anyone else's.

"I'd tell Sarah yes," Aaron said. "But I'm afraid I need to request a longer engagement. I can't ask for your hand until I can go to your father as a carpenter, not a gravedigger."

Geth's neck burned. Had he just proposed? And not as a solution to a desperate problem? Tossed off as they walked, it sounded improper. But reassuring, too. So matter of fact.

"I'm not sure about that," she said slowly. "The fellow I *might* want to marry digs graves."

"The girl I want to marry might be an actress."

Startled, she didn't respond. Then Granny's words echoed—*a powerful friend.*

"I wonder if the Wind would scatter notices for me," she mused. "I've been thinking. Instead of reciting alone on Beech Hill, I might try the Synder Park bandstand. That way the Wind can still hear. So you think others would enjoy Shakespeare in the park?"

"You have to ask?" Aaron squeezed her hand. "The Wind could bring powerful people there, too."

Geth gulped. Theater people. A daunting idea—but thrilling.

"What about your father?" asked Sarah.

Geth sighed. "By the time I get back from Dayton he will find I no longer need his approval."

"Dayton?" asked Aaron.

Geth's laugh hurt. "A long engagement? I didn't have time to tell you—I'm off to industrial school tomorrow. Half punishment and half training for secretarial work. If Mamie's not still asleep, they'll probably send me tonight. But it only lasts a couple of months." Less playful, she admitted, "Anyway, it'll take longer than that to…prepare my father for a son-in-law of my choice, not his."

"I'll do what I can to soften his view," Aaron said. They reached the nearest houses at the base of the hill. He added, "And I'll start by saying good-bye to you here so I can't be accused of improper courting. I'd have to plead guilty for that crime." Before Geth stopped walking, before Sarah looked up, he twisted to brush a kiss over Geth's lips. He straightened again fast, a blush tinting his cheeks.

She caught her breath. His kiss, although fleeting and slightly askew, burned all the way to her heart. It made her anticipate next time.

Gazing at her, he murmured, "You're the best gift the Wind's ever blown to me. I guess it knew my secret, too."

For an instant she wondered if the Wind had contrived all along to bring them together, unwitting actors in a much grander play. But never mind. A happy ending redeemed any deceit.

Aaron reclaimed her attention by pressing his lips to her knuckles. "Until I can come calling. Will you write me from Dayton?"

"Better—from the train station here before leaving. Even Poppa and Mamie can't stop the mail."

"If they try, I know a girl who delivers laundry and eggs—and would jump with delight to post secret notes, too."

Sarah squealed at the romance of it. Geth hushed her with anticipation she had not felt in weeks. Or longer. Maybe not since her mother's death.

Her spirits only flagged when she and Sarah arrived at her house, dark in the growing gloom. Mamie must still be napping. Sneaking inside was easier that way, but then Poppa must arrive any minute. Geth still faced her last night at home and a departure she dreaded even more than before.

Chapter Forty-Five

Geth and Sarah had time only to stir up the fire and set the table for supper before laughter from the porch drew them into the parlor. The front door burst open. Poppa tumbled in, still chortling. "GoGo, my darling. You'll never guess who I met at the club."

"I don't know," she said, "but it's clear you spent time there."

Mamie emerged from the hall, rubbing her face. "What's the commotion? One brew too many, my dear?" She spied the parlor clock. "Good heavens, that late?" She turned to Geth. "Why didn't you wake me?"

"You needed it," Geth said. "But Sarah's here, and supper is ready."

"Put on another plate," Poppa ordered. "I brought a friend home to meet you." He stepped out of the doorway to let his guest enter.

A tall, curly-haired man stepped in behind him, his hat in his hands. Though at least Poppa's age, he flashed a sheepish smile. "Forgive me. I'm afraid we've gotten on raucously. But I'm quite pleased to make your acquaintance as well."

Geth stared at the man—the same who lost his hat outside Augusta Morton's house.

She wasn't the only one to recognize him. "You!" Mamie cried. "You're the one slinking about my house yesterday."

"Guilty, madam," said the man. "I hope I didn't scare you. I was only confirming I had the right Joneses before I approached your husband."

"Mr. Cyrus Ray," announced Poppa. He shrugged off his coat. "Owner of Buckeye Nickelodeon downtown. And a number of other thriving business concerns."

Mamie took Mr. Ray's hat and coat, too. He flashed Geth a wink over Mamie's shoulder. "Careful with that hat," he said. "It may be cursed."

Geth stood frozen, too surprised to do more than gawk. Sarah whispered in her ear, "This is better than any nickelodeon show. I'll get out of the way and set another place at the table."

"This way to our meal, my friend." Poppa followed Sarah, bustling past Mamie and Geth. "I'll pour us a nip as a starter. Shall I?"

Mamie wagged a finger at him. "Easy, Bertram. You've clearly had plenty already."

As Mr. Ray followed Poppa, he tipped his head toward Geth. "It's you I wanted to meet," he murmured, smelling of cigars and money. "Mrs. Morton identified you. It seemed prudent to proceed through your father." He walked on as though he hadn't spoken, calling, "Nothing for me, Bert, Mrs. Jones. I can't stay long. But I'll sit and chat a moment longer while you start on your meal, if I may."

"Nonsense," Mamie retorted. "A few bites won't hurt. No place at my table stays empty."

Unsure what to think, Geth followed to help her stepmother serve supper. At least the visitor ensured neither of her parents noticed the stains on her slippers or the rosebud still pinned to her dress. She slipped off both on the way to the dining room.

Once they gathered at the table and Poppa tucked into his roast beef and greens, the circus atmosphere calmed. "I telephoned the industrial school today as planned," he told Geth. "I admit, I stopped by the club afterward, rather dull at the thought of you going. This gentleman made my acquaintance there, and I must say he has intriguing ideas."

Mr. Ray took charge of the conversation. "I'm making my own photoplays for my theater," he said. "And seeking fresh faces. Like yours, I believe. I…noticed you downtown recently." He smiled at Geth. "And I can only say a little bird put ideas in my ear. Would you have any interest in reading for me before an Edison camera?"

Geth shot a glance at her father, unable to believe he'd brought Mr. Ray home. "Oh, I'd love to. If my father allows? But I don't have—I've never appeared on a stage, except at my church and my school. Poppa has…discouraged my interest."

Her father took a bite without looking at her.

Mr. Ray raised his forefingers and thumbs in a frame shape, which he gazed through to Geth. "I couldn't care less about stage experience. Photoplays aren't like the theater, really. Close shots, for one thing. And no sound, of course—though that will come, I assure you, and not just in better accompaniment. I'm learning the hard way that it's easier to start fresh with new talent than to hire actors with stage habits that don't apply."

Poppa chewed around words. "I admit my view of the theater remains…dim. But a photoplay set has no murky backstage. And Mr. Ray assured me my fears

271

are old-fashioned. His impeccable manners and humor swayed me." He raised his glass in a casual toast to the man. "Not to mention his business successes. It's a new age, I suppose—the age of entertainment. I know I enjoy a show now and then." He looked at Geth. "And our talk about paints the other evening...recalled the pleasures of the arts to my mind."

Mamie scooped a second helping of greens onto Poppa's plate with a zest that implied she'd rather slop them onto his head. "Perhaps, dear, but I'd hate to instill vanity or laziness in our Geth. Seems to me a young lady too much in the public eye finds it hard to make beds and scrub pots the rest of the time."

"Oh, but acting is the very opposite of vanity, my good Mrs. Jones." Mr. Ray rose to spread both arms wide, displaying a touch of drama himself. "It shares stories much larger than any one person. The actors I know have the most generous souls. There's no better gift than wholesome entertainment to distract us from all of life's troubles. Is there?" He returned to his chair. "Plus, I assure you, my wife never finds me reluctant to chop kindling or fill scuttles with coal. I keep my actors equally humble."

Mamie cut a glance at Geth's father.

He patted her hand in a humoring way that implied the decision wasn't hers. "A trial, maybe, that's all," he told Geth. "It may be a lark on the path to industrial school, but I don't see harm in delaying your studies briefly for the attempt. With proper supervision, of course."

Sarah, squeezed in beside Geth, asked the question Geth hadn't dared. "Does this mean she doesn't have to leave in the morning?"

"I think we can postpone a departure, at least," Poppa said. "If my daughter agrees?"

Later, after first Mr. Ray and then Sarah left, Geth's father pulled her aside. "Too bad Mr. Ray has a wife," he whispered. "But at the club he assured me his partners include several promising bachelors. Never mind the camera—you might catch their eyes."

She hugged him, though poking him might have satisfied more. "I'll look forward to meeting them, Poppa."

He'd changed his mind about so much. She didn't want to press further. But it kindled hope for a second shift on the subject of whom she could marry.

Chapter Forty-Six

The day Gethsemane Jones was supposed to leave town, she rose before dawn to sneak out of the house. She shoved off her quilts, which she'd pulled to her neck not many hours before. Too excited by Mr. Ray's visit to sleep, she spent half the night reciting lines out her window, testing words for her ballad to the Wind. But lack of sleep didn't dull her enthusiasm for a jaunt in the twilight that morning. She dressed quickly and eased down the stairs while Poppa's clock in the parlor tick-ticked in the hush.

Just as she reached the front room, her stepmother's voice made her jump. "Geth? Is that you?" Mamie appeared, fully dressed, in the hall. "You're not stealing out of the house again, are you?"

Geth dropped onto a chair as if she'd never meant to take a step farther. "Mamie. I might ask the same question—what are you doing up at this hour?"

Mamie waggled a book in her hand. "After such a long nap yesterday, I woke early. I thought I might read." She dropped the book in Geth's lap. "Since you're awake, too, I suggest you practice reciting. We can sit knee to knee so we don't wake your father. If you're going to 'generously entertain' strangers, your stepmother ought to be entertained, too."

Despite the razor edge in her tone, Mamie leaned down to her with lips twitching. She whispered, "First, though, I'd like you to answer my question." She sounded conspiratorial now. "Remind me why we're sneaking this morning?"

Geth riffled the pages of the book. A lie came to her lips, but she stopped it. "I'm not sneaking, exactly—just going out early. But I hoped to return before anyone woke."

"The definition of sneaking, my dear. Because…?"

"I wanted to let someone know I won't be on the train," Geth admitted. She rose. "Someone who often hunts about now. It won't take me long. I'll come right back, I promise. I have to—Mr. Ray told me to call before noon."

"I see. I'll come with you." Mamie took her arm. "This 'someone' is obviously important. Don't you think it's time your stepmother met him?"

Geth pressed the book to her lips to hold back a whimper. "How do you know it's a him?" She was stalling for time and a way to escape. Even if she only returned to her room, she couldn't let this encounter with Mamie ruin her chance with Mr. Ray.

Mamie heaved a great sigh. "You must think me a fool. Sarah already knows, your other friends haven't visited lately to know about Dayton, and I doubt Eliza Ableman hunts. Though I wouldn't put it past a woman like her. I've always been good at maths, and you never used to keep secrets from me. Two plus two equals a new beau, my dear."

Geth sputtered and hoped the low flame of the lamp didn't reveal the blaze in her cheeks.

"Now, shall we go?" Mamie added. "I promise not to embarrass you much. Or tell your father, if you stay chaperoned. I have my suspicions about this young man, and if I'm right, your poppa might take some persuading. But I'm so delighted your heart's started to heal that I'll remind him I married for love, not because a station master is so elevated above…a groundskeeper, say? That alone should keep an actress from too much vanity."

Geth buried her face in Mamie's shoulder. "You're too good to me."

"Yes, I know. You forgot for a while. Can we put that behind us?"

Geth nodded. "Yes." She set the book down. "Now we'd better get sneaking."

They pulled on their coats and slipped out the front door. The sun already peeped, a bright ember on the horizon. "How will we find him hunting?" asked Mamie. "I wouldn't like to get shot. Do you know where he is?"

Geth towed Mamie down the porch steps before she could change her mind. "Only roughly. But the wind sometimes whispers advice in my ear. It seems friendly that way, now it's finally brought spring."

Mamie sniffed. "Friendly for you. Not for me. Not with my hay fever. Yesterday I felt nearly delirious. I swore I heard lullabies on the breeze."

"Oh, I don't doubt it." Geth hid a smile. "You might be surprised what you hear, if you listen."

****

On that day and over many to follow, the Wind whispered to Geth only rarely. Often, however, it played with her hair, tickled her neck, kissed her cheek. If a day threatened to pass without her speaking to it, she'd hear, "*Ssing my song,*" or perhaps "*Sstorytime?*"

But the Wind rarely needed to prompt her. She

started most days by stepping outside, tipping her face to the sky, and quoting a poem or lines she needed to learn to recite in the park on Sunday. Or before a camera for Cyrus. If anyone asked about this odd morning ritual, she explained she did it as a prayer—an offering of her voice and her talents in gratitude for the wonderments of her life. She did it as a plea for forbearance and love, for kindness and graveyard honesty. And she did it to honor the voices too often repressed but heard and lifted by the Wind.

A word about the author…

Joni Sensel is the author of more than a dozen nonfiction titles for adults, five award-winning novels for young readers, and a recent memoir, *Feeling Fate*. She holds an MFA in writing from Vermont College of Fine Arts and regularly teaches writing and creativity workshops. Sensel's adventures have taken her to the corners of fifteen countries, the heights of the Cascade Mountains, the length of an Irish marathon, and the depths of love. Her escapades included a stint in Springfield, Ohio, that inspired this book. She lives today at the knees of Mount Rainier in Washington State with a puppy who came into her life as a gift that reflected afterlife influence.

https://jonisensel.com

www.ingramcontent.com/pod-product-compliance
Lightning Source LLC
Chambersburg PA
CBHW051530260626
47170CB00003B/866